"You seeing anyone special?"

She looked up at him. "No."

Rio seemed concerned. "That's no way for a beautiful woman to live."

It gave her a thrill of pleasure hearing him say he found her attractive. "I'm not unhappy with my life."

He shrugged. "It's your business," he muttered. "I think I'll go outside for a while."

Jill jumped up, reaching for the crutches. "Let me help you."

"That's not . . ." His voice trailed off when Jill's hands braced on his forearms.

Jill's breath slammed out of her chest as heat flooded her body. His dark eyes, suddenly stormy, locked with hers. Then he grabbed his crutch. "I'll be outside," he said, his voice huskier than usual.

Jill stood where he'd left her, gripping the edge of the table. Rio was as foreign to her life as an exotic jungle animal. And for her, he was almost as dangerous. . . .

Dear Reader,

Welcome to Silhouette **Special Edition** . . . welcome to romance. Each month, Silhouette **Special Edition** publishes six novels with you in mind—stories of love and life, tales that you can identify with— romance with that little "something special" added in.

And this month is no exception to the rule—June 1991 brings *The Gauntlet* by Lindsay McKenna—the next thrilling WOMEN OF GLORY tale. Don't miss this story, or *Under Fire,* coming in July.

And to round out June, stories by Marie Ferrarella, Elizabeth Bevarly, Gina Ferris, Pat Warren and Sarah Temple are coming your way.

In each Silhouette **Special Edition,** we're dedicated to bringing you the romances that you dream about— the type of stories that delight as well as bring a tear to the eye. And that's what Silhouette **Special Edition** is all about—special books by special authors for special readers!

I hope that you enjoy this book and all the stories to come.

Sincerely,

Tara Gavin
Senior Editor

GINA FERRIS
In From The Rain

Silhouette Special Edition

Published by Silhouette Books New York

America's Publisher of Contemporary Romance

This one's for my agent—
Thanks, Denise, for everything.

SILHOUETTE BOOKS
300 East 42nd St., New York, N.Y. 10017

IN FROM THE RAIN

ISBN: 0-373-09677-1

First Silhouette Books printing June 1991

Books by Gina Ferris

Silhouette Special Edition

Healing Sympathy #496
Lady Beware #549
In From The Rain #677

GINA FERRIS

declares that she is Southern by birth and by choice, and she has chosen to set many of her books in the South, where she finds a rich treasury of characters and settings. She particularly loves the Ozark mountain region of northern Arkansas and southern Missouri, and the proudly unique people who reside there. She and her husband, John, live in Jacksonville, Arkansas, with their three children, Courtney, Kerry and David.

Chapter One

Rio tried to tune out the monotonous drivel of the overly friendly stranger who'd picked him up a couple of miles back. The guy'd had a few beers too many, so his monologue tended to ramble. Rio wondered absently where the old man had gotten the beer, since one couldn't buy alcohol in this state on Sunday. Must have been with his drinking buddies.

Normally Rio wouldn't have ridden with someone in this man's condition, particularly in the middle of a torrential rainstorm, but his motorcycle had broken down and he hadn't wanted to leave it. He'd been close to drowning by the time the guy had stopped and offered help. Now the bike was in the back of his pickup and he was out of the rain, even if he was already soaked to the skin.

Propping one booted foot on the battered, rusted dashboard in front of him, he slumped in the seat and stared sightlessly out the cracked window beside him, the bleak, rain-grayed north Arkansas landscape passing without catching his interest. He'd seen too many gray landscapes pass on the other side of cracked windows to note any difference in this one.

It would be dark soon and the storm seemed to be getting worse. He'd have to find a place to spend the night. He'd slept outside plenty of times in the past, but he'd never enjoyed sleeping in the rain. He had a couple of hundred dollars in his wallet—all that remained of his last paycheck from a construction job in Missouri—and that would allow him a motel room for the night. He'd better choose an inexpensive motel, though. He never knew when he'd find the next job.

A blowout on wet, steep roads was a potential disaster under any circumstances. Add to those conditions a driver who'd guzzled his dinner straight from a half-dozen aluminum cans, and disaster was a guarantee.

Rio dived for the steering wheel even as the old pickup left the road to plunge straight down the wooded hillside. He was unconscious by the time it settled down at the bottom, his last moment of awareness racked with an explosion of pain, and the hazy, half-formed thought that there really hadn't been anything to live for, anyway.

He was sore. The bed was too hard. A storm raged outside, lashing rain against the windows and rattling the walls with occasional claps of thunder. He wanted to go back to sleep, but some fool was moaning, keeping him awake. It took a few moments for him to realize the moans were coming from his own raw throat.

Forcing down another groan, he remembered the wreck. So he'd lived. He supposed he was glad. Maybe Gypsy would be, anyway.

He cracked one eyelid, then quickly opened both eyes. He didn't often wake to find someone leaning right into his face. He'd *never* woken to discover a freckle-faced, blue-eyed boy watching him as eagerly as if he were a sideshow exhibit, obviously hoping he'd do something interesting.

"Who the hell are you?" Rio croaked, his throat as dry as the New Mexico dirt he'd rolled in when he was this kid's age.

"I'm Gordie. Are you gonna die, mister? My dad says you ain't, but you sure was moaning like you was going to. Old man Baxter's dead." The words were spoken with inappropriate relish.

"Who's old man Baxter?" Rio asked without a lot of interest, experimentally moving his head against the crisp sheet beneath it, then wishing he hadn't when he was hit by a wave of dizziness. He didn't know where he was, had only brief snatches of memory since the wreck—pain, movement, murmuring voices, bright lights, more pain.

"Don't you remember? You were riding in his truck when you had the wreck. Bunch of teenage guys on their way home from a church youth social found you. They brought you here to Dad's office 'cause he's a doctor—sort of. We live in the rest of the house, but this part's his office. Anyway, he yelled at 'em for moving you and that made 'em mad, 'cause they said they were just trying to help. The police took old man Baxter away. Zipped him up in a bag, just like they do in the movies."

Rio was hardly sentimental, but he wished the kid would stop sounding quite so pleased about old man Baxter's fate. It didn't seem right, somehow, for a boy this young—couldn't be more than ten—to exhibit such an unhealthy interest in death. And what was that about his father being a doctor—*sort of?*

"Boy, are you going to be in trouble, Gordie! Daddy told you to stay out of here."

The smugly superior voice came from the direction of the door to the room in which Rio lay. He took the opportunity to look cautiously around, then winced at the movement. Where was he? It appeared to be a doctor's office, of sorts, though some of the equipment looked unfamiliar. He lay strapped to a narrow gurney, his bare body covered by a thin blanket, except for his right leg, which was splinted from hip to thigh and swathed in enough gauze to rewrap a mummy. He'd broken the damn leg again, he realized, chagrined. And where the hell were his clothes?

He turned his attention to the girl in the doorway. She wasn't much younger than Gordie and the resemblance between them was marked. Same straight, medium-brown hair, same scattering of light brown freckles over rather plain faces, same brilliant blue eyes, though the girl's were somewhat distorted by the lenses of the glasses that kept slipping down her short nose. Not pretty children, exactly, but interesting looking. Rio decided that Norman Rockwell would have chosen them for models.

"Aw, go on, squirrel face. Who cares what you say?" Gordie snarled at his sister, his face creased with a scowl.

"It's not what *I* say that matters, but what Daddy says," the girl retorted with a roll of her eyes. "And *he* said stay out of here. I bet you get grounded."

"Yeah? So who asked you, Miss Perfect Pants? I'll come in here if I want to."

"I'll tell."

"Tattletale, tattletale."

Rio moaned again and closed his eyes.

"Gordon! Sharon! Be quiet and get out of here. Both of you go to your rooms and stay there."

Rio risked opening his eyes at the sound of the new voice—soft, musical even when quietly scolding, obviously annoyed. The woman was attractive in an understated, rather wholesome way: hair a rich dark blond, worn in a soft sweep to her collar; features delicate, evenly proportioned. An especially nice mouth, he noted dispassionately, his gaze lingering on its lush curves and the dimple accenting her left cheek. She wasn't wearing a nurse's uniform, as he might have expected, given his surroundings, but jeans and a soft flannel shirt. Her eyes were the same brilliant blue as the children's, framed by long, dark lashes. Must be their mother. Too bad.

"I'm really very sorry the children disturbed you. Your poor head must be pounding. Can I get you anything?"

"Water," he answered without hesitation, then added, rustily, "Please." Something about this woman's open, friendly smile seemed to call for such niceties.

"Of course. I'll be right back."

He watched her turn to leave, idly studying the slight sway of her hips. Good body. Slim. Firm. A little on the short side. He never would have guessed she'd borne at least two children. She looked rather young to be the mother of a ten-year-old. Must have started early. Or maybe she was one of those women who was older than she looked.

Another clap of thunder reverberated inside his aching head, almost drawing another moan out of him. It took some effort to hold it back. Deciding to stop avoiding the unpleasant task, he took a quick inventory of his injuries. A large bandage covered most of his forehead beneath his still-damp, too-long black hair. His vision was clear enough, despite the lingering dizziness. He'd had concussions before. He didn't think this one was too bad. The small amount of skin not covered by the blanket bore a few interesting bruises, but the leg appeared to be the worst of the damage. His fist clenched in impotent frustration. What the hell was he supposed to do now? Where was he supposed to stay until the leg healed?

The woman walked back into the room carrying a glass of water, and he shifted restlessly under the lightweight blanket, which was all that covered him other than bandages. Had she—? Surely not. He was slim, but not light. A small woman like this one couldn't have undressed him alone. And surely her husband wouldn't have encouraged her to help. Reassuring himself on that count, and wondering when he'd suddenly turned modest, Rio reached for the water, then dropped his arm with a muttered oath when his hand shook so hard he knew he wouldn't be able to hold the glass.

"You're still weak," the woman observed gently, her smile telling him it didn't matter. "I'll help you."

She slipped a hand behind his head to lift him to the offered glass, her touch so light he hardly felt it. Having tensed at the very thought of moving, he relaxed and gratefully sipped the cool water, knowing better than to get greedy and take too much.

"That's all you want?" she asked when he indicated he'd had enough.

"Yeah. Thanks."

"You're welcome. I'm surprised you're awake, actually. Tom gave you a shot for pain. He thought it would keep you out for a while. That's why he strapped you down, so you wouldn't roll off and hurt yourself worse."

A shot. That explained the dizziness. And the grogginess. "Some guy kept moaning and woke me up."

She smiled sympathetically at the weak joke, then glanced toward his leg. "Is the pain very bad?"

"I've had it worse."

"I'd give you an aspirin for your head, but I don't know if you should take it on top of that shot. Tom's out trying to help with another emergency, or I'd ask him. Maybe he'll be home soon."

"I'm okay," he assured her again, then asked, "Tom's a doctor?"

"Sort of," she answered after only a slight hesitation.

It wasn't exactly reassuring that she'd chosen the same expression the boy had used when talking about his father. "Uh—where am I, anyway? How come I'm not in a hospital?" He hated hospitals, but at least the doctors there would be bona fide. No "sort of" doctors on a hospital staff.

The woman looked apologetic, her attractive face grave. "You should be, of course. But the storm is so bad and the ambulances are extremely busy tonight. The closest hospital is nearly twenty miles away and it services a large area. With all the car accidents and injuries from uprooted trees, Tom thought it would be better to treat you here temporarily, until things calm down a bit. You were very fortunate. Your injuries aren't serious, though I know you must be in pain."

"I understand the guy driving the truck wasn't so lucky."

She had the most amazingly expressive eyes. Blue as a summer lake, liquid with sympathy, they met his. "No. I'm sorry. Mr. Baxter died in the accident."

"Sorry to hear it myself, but I didn't know him," he told her brusquely, uncomfortable with her unwarranted concern. "I hitched a ride with him after my bike broke down a few miles back."

"Oh. I see." Her face mirrored her curiosity about the stranger in the bed, but she didn't ask any of the questions he might have expected. Instead, she smiled tentatively and offered, "By the way, my name is Jill. I'm sure Tom will be home soon and we'll be able to transfer you to the hospital. In the meantime, is there anything else you need?"

Rio thought of the hospital where he'd most likely spend the night. And wondered how the hell he was supposed to pay for it. Maybe Gypsy would have a few extra dollars. He figured it was her turn to bail him out of a tight spot. As he remembered, he'd done the bailing last time. Fighting the grogginess that was trying to take over his mind, he lifted his head.

"Is there a phone I can use?"

"Oh, I'm sorry. The phone lines are down." Again, the woman—Jill, he remembered—looked apologetic, almost as if it were her fault he couldn't make a call.

He settled back onto the hard gurney. "No problem. It'll wait."

She nodded, hovering indecisively at the foot of the bed. "I'm really surprised we still have electricity. It has flickered a time or two, but . . ." She sighed gustily as the lights blinked, then went out.

Rio chuckled. "Spoke too soon, I think," he murmured, then yawned. Damn pain medicine.

Her voice held rueful amusement. "I guess I jinxed us." She turned her head at a cry from another room, giving him a glimpse of her deeply shadowed profile. "That's Sharon. She's probably frightened—she's afraid of the dark. I'll be back with an oil lamp as soon as I take care of her."

"No hurry. I'm kind of sleepy." He closed his eyes. "That shot your husband gave me must be taking over again."

"I'll leave you to get some rest, then. Yell if you need anything. Oh, and Tom's not—"

But Rio was too tired to care about the rest. Tuning her out, he slipped into the sanctuary of sleep. He knew what she'd been going to say, anyway, he thought just as he went under. Tom wasn't really a doctor. Only sort of a doctor.

You've landed in a weird place this time, Rio, old son.

Half an hour later, while the children were more or less congenially playing a board game by candlelight in the den, Jill tiptoed down the hallway to Tom's offices to check on her patient. The man was still sleeping soundly, though his forehead was creased with a frown as if pain were making itself known even in his sleep.

Who was he? she wondered, unable to resist lingering at his side, her eyes fastened on the intriguing, candle-lit face of the wounded stranger. He was a good-looking man—so attractive, in fact, that her breath had caught in her throat the first time she'd laid eyes on him. Jet-black hair, straight, untrimmed, tousled around a lean, darkly tanned face. Beautiful dark eyes, perfect nose, sexy mouth, slightly indented chin. His age was hard to determine. He could have been anywhere from her own twenty-five to a decade older.

The only thing marring the almost-too-handsome face was the thin, three-inch scar running along the line of his high, right cheekbone. But the scar wasn't nearly as intimidating as what appeared to be his habitual expression. *Don't get near me,* it seemed to say. She'd never seen a man who looked so very much alone, even when in the company of others. She'd never seen eyes so completely devoid of expression.

Had he not been virtually incapacitated by the broken leg, she would have been nervous having a man like that in the house with her and the children, despite her unexplainable feeling that he could be trusted. But this guy wasn't going anywhere on that leg, and the medication Tom had given him would ensure that his strength wouldn't be coming back within the next few hours, anyway. So it was safe, this time, to trust her intuition that a very nice man lurked behind the intimidating expression, and to indulge her sympathy for his obvious, if unspoken, pain.

He muttered disgruntledly and shifted, the movement causing the thin blanket to reveal a bit more of his bare abdomen. He was slim to the point of thin, but strong looking. Tanned, sleekly muscled, smooth skinned. Another scar—a longer one, this time—sliced across the upper ridge of his rib cage. She thought of the nameless drifters in the old Clint Eastwood movies, the spaghetti Westerns. And then she thought fleetingly of all the heartbroken women they left behind when they rode off into the sunset alone.

She'd better put that rampant imagination of hers away and go check on the children, she told herself abruptly, dragging her gaze away from the man's sleek chest. The storm seemed to be letting up some, so maybe Tom would be home soon. She rather hoped so. Some tiny, strangely omniscient voice had just warned her that this man might be dangerous, after all. She had the eeriest feeling that her life might never be the same, now that he'd entered it. Foolish, of course, but she found herself hurrying from the room anyway, her eyes carefully averted from the man in the bed.

"Hey, buddy. Wake up. Let's see how you're doing."

"Get lost," Rio muttered grumpily, annoyed by the disgustingly cheerful male voice.

The other man laughed, apparently unperturbed. "I can't do that. You're in my house. Guess that makes me responsible for your welfare, for the moment. Now let me see those pupils."

Scowling, Rio opened his eyes, only to blink irritably at the bright light shining in them. A moment later, the light winked out and a man's smiling face replaced it. "All done. Your eyes are responding just fine. How do you feel?"

Rio told him in two succinct words.

The man laughed again. What would it take to provoke him? Rio wondered. This guy looked as if everything amused him. Pale blue eyes framed with laugh lines, a slightly crooked nose above a broad, toothy grin, long slashes of dimples down flat cheeks. His hair looked dark, but it was damp, and Rio suspected it would dry lighter. Rio guessed his age to be around forty. "You must be Tom, the guy who's sort of a doctor," he drawled.

"Tom Curtis. And I *am* a doctor," the other man assured him. "Of course, the difference between you and my other patients is that *they* usually get shot when they break a leg."

"You're a vet."

Tom nodded. "Got it in one guess."

Great. He'd busted a leg and had a lump the size of a tennis ball on his head, and he was being treated by a veterinarian. He was afraid to ask what kind of shot Dr. Doolittle had given him. "How bad's the leg?" he asked, instead.

"Well, you're not going to be running any marathons for a couple of months," Tom replied matter-of-factly. "But we're not going to have to shoot you, either."

Rio's mouth quirked upward in reluctant amusement. "I guess that's good news."

Shrugging, Tom nodded. "The best I can offer at the moment." Running a large hand through his damp hair, he glanced toward the window. "Storm's finally letting up. I'll call an ambulance to take you to the hospital."

"The phones are working now?" Rio hoped to be able to call Gypsy before being transferred.

His hopes were dampened when Tom shook his head. "I'll have to use the radio. Phones will probably be out for another couple of hours, at least. There are lines down all over the place."

For the first time, Rio noticed that the lights were on. "The power was out when I went to sleep."

"It was off for about an hour. Came back on about five minutes ago."

Which told Rio that he'd been asleep for just over an hour, making it after seven. "This hospital you're sending me to—where is it?"

"Harrison. Closest one around here," Tom explained.

Rio cleared his throat, wondering how to explain his situation. "I don't have any insurance, and the only money I have is what's in my wallet. I'm not sure they'll even admit me," he said bluntly.

Pulling at his lower lip, Tom looked thoughtful. "Your wallet?"

"Yeah." Rio frowned at a sudden unpleasant premonition. "You *did* find my wallet didn't you?"

"The—uh—young men who brought you to me said you didn't have one on you. They said they looked for ID and couldn't find any. The police didn't find anything at the scene, either."

Rio swore fluently. "Someone lifted my wallet."

"Sounds that way," Tom agreed sympathetically. "I'll report it to the sheriff."

"For all the good it will do," Rio grumbled. "What about the rest of my things? There was a duffel bag, military issue."

Tom shook his head regretfully. "No. No bag, either. We'll look around the area tomorrow, and I'll check with the police and see if they found anything."

"Hell." He was almost afraid to ask the next question. "I had a bike. It was in the back of the truck."

"It's in my barn now," Tom assured him. "The kids brought it with them, thinking it might be yours. It's in pretty good shape, considering. Looks like it took a few dents, but it was thrown clear of the wreckage."

Rio relaxed fractionally. At least he still had the bike. If nothing else, he could sell it to get some cash. It wouldn't be the first time he'd parted with his last possession in a tight spot.

"Isn't there someone you can call? Family?"

"There's one person—maybe." Rio couldn't have guaranteed that Gypsy would be in any better financial shape than he was at the moment. Like his, her fortune tended to fluctuate.

Tom sat on the edge of the stool at the side of the gurney and crossed one ankle over his knee. "Tell you what. I'm on pretty good terms with the local doctor. He'll come here if I ask him to. There's no reason for you to be hospitalized that I can see. If he agrees, you're welcome to stay here until you reach your friend. Hospitals are expensive. We've got an extra bed for free."

Startled by the offer, Rio eyed the other man suspiciously. "Why would you do that? You don't even know me."

Tom shrugged again in what seemed to be a characteristic gesture. "Call it Southern hospitality. Around here, when someone's in need, we do what we can to help out."

"Folks get their throats cut in their sleep doing stupid things like bringing strangers into their homes," Rio pointed out dryly.

Smiling, Tom shook his head. "Not by strangers in your condition. And none of the homicidal maniacs I've met warned their victims about the folly of their generosity."

Damn, but it was hard not to like the guy. Rio smiled then, for the first time since being awakened. "Met a lot of homicidal maniacs, have you?"

"If my instincts are wrong, you'll be my first," Tom replied easily.

"Your instincts are fine. I'm no Boy Scout, but I won't cause you any trouble. Won't even steal the family silver. I accept your invitation—and I'll reimburse you for your expenses as soon as I get in touch with Gypsy. Thanks."

"You're welcome. So, what do we call you? You still haven't told me your name."

"Name's Rio."

Tom cocked an eyebrow. "Just Rio?"

He nodded. "Just Rio."

Standing, Tom shoved a hand into the pocket of his jeans. "Okay, 'Just Rio,' I'll go get the doctor. We'll move you into a bedroom once he's looked you over. In the meantime, will you be okay in here? Need anything? Jill's been worried about you being hungry."

Rio shook his head, then groaned softly at the pain that unwise movement set off. His unsteady stomach rebelled at the very thought of food. "Thanks, but I'm not hungry. My mouth's dry, though. If it's not too much trouble, I could stand something to drink."

He couldn't remember the last time he'd been so polite, but something about these people brought out the latent manners his mother had taught him in those early years before he'd lost her. The rarely allowed thought of his mother brought with it the familiar hollow pain, causing his faint smile to fade.

Studying Rio's expression, Tom nodded. "I'll have Jill bring you some juice."

The sound of Jill's name gave Rio a funny feeling, deep in the pit of his stomach. Only then did he remember that he'd been dreaming about her when Tom had woken him. She'd been smoothing his brow, taking care of him, fussing over him as no one had since he was six. Strange dream. Rio wasn't even a man who *liked* having a woman fuss over him—particularly a woman who happened to be a wife and mother. Must be the concussion, he decided finally, his frown clearing. You never knew what kind of strange fancies would pop up after a nasty crack on the head.

"How is he?" Jill demanded the moment Tom walked into the kitchen.

"He's an odd puppy," Tom answered thoughtfully, using one of his favorite expressions as he headed straight for the freshly brewed pot of coffee.

Jill sighed, rolling her eyes toward the ceiling. "His condition, Tom. How is he feeling?"

Tom repeated Rio's answer to that question. "His words," he explained hastily when Jill eyed him questioningly at the uncharacteristic coarse language.

She nodded. Of course, that was what the man had said. For *him,* it seemed very much in character. "Are you going to radio for an ambulance now?"

Tom shook his head, the overhead light glinting off the blond streaks that were showing up as his hair dried. "No. He'll be staying here awhile."

Jill dropped the plate she'd been drying. Fortunately it didn't break, just clattered noisily at her feet. "He's staying *where?*"

"Here." Tom didn't quite meet Jill's eyes as he repeated the word. "I know it'll mean extra work for you, Jill, and I'm sorry, but I couldn't just throw him out. His wallet's been stolen and he doesn't have any money. No insurance, either. How could he pay a hospital bill?"

"What about his family?"

"I'm not sure he has any. He did mention a friend— Gypsy, I think he said. Said he'd call her tomorrow."

"Gypsy?" Jill repeated in disbelief. "Oh, wonderful! And did he happen to tell you *his* name?"

"Rio."

Jill cocked her head, waiting. And then, when nothing else was forthcoming, she asked quietly, "Just Rio?"

Tom chuckled into his coffee. "Yep. Just Rio."

She threw up her hands. "Great! A total stranger with one name is staying in the same home as your children, waiting for someone named Gypsy to collect him. He'll probably murder us in our sleep."

Tom shook his head. "He promised he's not a homicidal maniac. Said he wouldn't even steal the family silver."

"Oh, *that* makes me feel better."

Sobering, Tom looked straight at Jill, his eyes locking with hers. "You want me to get rid of him? I can still call an ambulance."

She hesitated, then sighed and shook her head. She was no more capable of turning her back on someone in need than Tom was. Even if that someone was a man who made strange little frissons of warning flash in the back of her mind. It wasn't exactly that she was afraid of him, she told herself. But something about him made her nervous. It was almost as if an exotic animal had wandered into her decidedly *un*exotic life. Rio was different from anyone she'd ever known before, and she found that difference as unnerving as it was fascinating.

"Of course he can stay, if you think it's all right. Should I take him a bowl of soup or something? He's probably hungry."

Tom's smile was a fond accolade, his eyes telling her he'd known all along that she'd give in. *That's us—two old softies,* Jill thought resignedly, though she returned his smile.

"He said he's not hungry, but he's thirsty. Why don't you take him a glass of juice?" Tom suggested. "I'm going to see if Doc will come check him out."

Jill filled a glass with apple juice, telling herself everything would work out fine. This Rio was just a man—a man who was hurting, alone and down on his luck. Any member of her generous, charitable, staunchly Christian family would gladly offer assistance to someone in that condition. It was their way.

So stop being a ninny and take the man his juice, she told herself sternly. And, turning on one heel, she marched bravely down the hallway, juice glass clasped in suddenly cold hands.

Chapter Two

Rio looked up when Jill entered the room. He smiled and she found herself smiling in return. Her experience might be limited, but she knew a sexy guy when she saw one. And this was one sexy man.

"Tom said you were thirsty," she said a bit breathlessly. "I brought some juice."

"Thanks." This time he made no effort to reach out with his unsteady hand. Again, Jill lifted his head to the glass, taking care to be gentle.

His hair was soft, she found herself thinking as he drank. Thick, straight, long enough to brush the base of his neck. Had it not been limp from the events of the past few hours, she imagined that it would wave enticingly around his tanned face.

He indicated that he'd had enough, and Jill pulled back. She felt a bit awkward as she stood beside him, that disconcertingly intense gaze of his trained on her face. He had the most incredibly beautiful dark eyes she'd ever seen, despite the inscrutable sharpness of his gaze. Or perhaps because of it. Clutching the juice glass tightly, she cleared her throat. "Is there anything else I can get for you?"

"No. I'm okay."

She glanced at his splinted leg. "Tom said the break wasn't too bad, though it looked to him as if you'd broken it before."

"Twice. Fell off my bike when I was a kid, and fell off a mountain in Colorado three years ago. I always smash the same leg."

"Sounds like you're the adventurous type," Jill ventured, wondering about this man who seemed so mysterious. A lot of questions occurred to her, but something told her he wouldn't appreciate prying—from her or anyone.

As if in confirmation of her thoughts, Rio only shrugged. "I hope you don't mind about me staying here tonight," he said, changing the subject. "I don't want to cause you any trouble."

"It's no trouble," Jill assured him, hoping her words would prove true. She smiled then. "Actually, you're the one who may be sorry. You'll be sharing a room with Gordie, I'm afraid."

He managed not to wince, though she noted the slight spasm that briefly narrowed his eyes. "I don't mind if *he* doesn't. He seemed disappointed that they wouldn't be carrying me away in a body bag."

Jill sighed. "Gordie's obsessed with morbid subjects right now. We're hoping it's just a stage he's going through."

"Boys his age are like that. He'll grow out of it." Rio paused, then added casually, "Your husband seems like a nice guy."

"Tom's not my husband," Jill murmured, her eyes on the juice glass. "He's my brother-in-law."

Since she wasn't looking at him, she didn't know whether Rio's expression changed at that bit of information. From what little she'd seen of him so far, she doubted that it had.

"Then the kids are—?"

"My niece and nephew. My sister's children."

Rio glanced around as if looking for the children's mother. "I hope she doesn't mind having an unexpected houseguest."

She looked at him then. "My sister's dead," she said quietly, wondering if she'd ever be able to say those words without hurting. "I've been taking care of the house and children for Tom since she died almost two years ago."

She'd moved in only a week after Ellen's death, supposedly on a temporary basis, and the time had never seemed right for her to move out. Tom and the children needed her—and there was nothing else waiting for her. Though she may once have longed for adventure—for more of a life of her own—she'd enjoyed her stay with her sister's family, telling herself that there was plenty of time for her own needs, once the children were more self-sufficient. Or until Tom remarried, which didn't seem a likely prospect any time soon. He hadn't even dated since Ellen's death. For that matter, Jill hadn't had many dates in the past two years, either. Maybe that explained her reaction to the devilishly attractive man on the gurney, lying nude beneath the very thin blanket.

Jill was rather surprised at the sympathy in Rio's expression. "I'm sorry."

The unexpected gentleness in his voice brought a lump to her throat. She swallowed it and looked toward the doorway. "I think I hear Tom. He'll have Doc with him. I'd better go check on the children."

"Thanks for the juice." His expression was shuttered again, distant.

"You're welcome."

She wondered if he had lost someone close to him. That brief moment of empathy had left her oddly shaken, almost as if she'd caught a glimpse of a tormented soul behind the carefully emotionless mask he'd seemed to have so deliberately cultivated. She suspected that very few people were allowed such glimpses.

Rio shifted uncomfortably in the narrow twin bed and tried to ignore the ugly, vicious, Hollywood killer leering at him from behind long, knife-blade "fingernails." The poster from the popular teen slasher movie was pinned to the wall directly opposite the bed so that Rio felt Freddy's eyes on him constantly. An equally grotesque poster of a cult killer in a hockey mask adorned the wall behind him, and a rack of hideous Halloween masks took up most of a third wall. Gordie was definitely a strange kid.

Staring at the ceiling—he wouldn't have been surprised had it been painted black rather than the usual white—he thought morosely of the results of the doctor's visit earlier. The gruff, dry-witted general practitioner had turned out to be Tom's father, which explained Tom's cheerful remark that he was "on good terms" with the local doctor.

Tom had assisted with X rays and helpful hands during Rio's treatment. Muttering an obviously long-rehearsed monologue expressing his dissatisfaction with his son's choice of medical practice, "Doc" had taken care of Rio's assorted injuries with kindly efficiency. He'd also predicted that Rio would spend two weeks on crutches, followed by four weeks in a walking cast, after which he'd need a couple of weeks to rebuild the strength in the much-abused limb.

Despite Doc's careful handling and Tom's gentleness in transferring him to one of the twin beds in Gordie's room, Rio was sore and bone weary. But sleep eluded him as he considered his rather grim immediate future.

What the hell was he going to do? he wondered—not for the first time since receiving the prognosis. No money, no place to stay—not even a change of underwear to his name. He'd been down-and-out before, but he wasn't sure he'd ever sunk this low. Unless one counted the three weeks he'd spent in a jail cell in Oklahoma, he reflected. But even that had been a price worth paying for the privilege of decking the most obnoxious cop Rio had ever encountered, a man who'd gotten his kicks harassing anyone whose skin tone was a shade darker than his own.

Gypsy. His one hope at the moment, he decided. He'd call their friend Amber first thing in the morning and try to locate his only potential rescuer.

A sound at the open bedroom door made him turn his head. *Oh, great! Gordie the Ghoul.*

Seeing that Rio was awake, the boy hurried into the room. "My dad says you're gonna be staying here awhile."

"That's right. This your room?"

"Yeah. Cool, huh? You like slasher flicks?"

"No."

Gordie looked disappointed, but only for a moment. Leaning both elbows on the bed in which Rio lay, he studied his guest with a child's unabashed curiosity. "You really a hitchhiker?"

"Not exactly. My motorcycle broke down and I hitched a ride with—er—"

"Old man Baxter," Gordie supplied with relish. "The stiff." He waited expectantly for Rio's reaction to the irreverence.

Rio didn't give him the satisfaction of reacting at all. "Yeah. Whatever."

Gordie's face grew abruptly more serious. He leaned closer, his voice dropping to a macabre whisper. "Did you see him die?"

Shifting uncomfortably in the bed, Rio looked toward the empty doorway and wished Jill would rescue him again, as she had earlier. "Uh—no. I was unconscious, I guess."

"You ever seen anyone die?"

"Yeah. But I don't want any questions about it." It wasn't a memory he particularly enjoyed reliving. He had no intention of going into the details with this creepy kid.

Gordie shrugged. "So you think old man Baxter knew he was gonna die? Wonder if it hurt?"

Rio scowled at the boy. "What is it with you and dying? Can't you think about football or car racing or something more interesting? Hell, dying's not something a kid your age needs to be worrying about."

"I ain't worried about dying," Gordie denied immediately, almost aggressively. "I ain't scared of nothing."

"Then maybe I'd better give you something to be scared of, young man." This no-nonsense voice came from Jill, who stood in the doorway balancing a tray containing a pitcher and a glass. Rio thought incongruously that she always seemed to be bringing him liquids. After a session with her weird nephew, he found himself hoping the pitcher held straight bourbon. He could use a stiff drink about now.

"Gordie Thomas Curtis, you were told to leave poor Rio alone, were you not?" she demanded, bringing the tray into the room and setting it on the nightstand. She then turned to face her uneasy nephew, both hands on her hips as she glared at him.

"You told me to get my stuff," Gordie argued in a near whine.

"I told you to *quietly* get your things. Now do it and go on. We'll continue this discussion in another room."

Sullenly the boy obeyed, jerking open a dresser drawer and pulling out a pair of pajamas. Giving his sternly watching aunt a last resentful glance, he slunk out of the room.

Rio found it rather amusing to watch his diminutive hostess seem to lose several intimidating inches as soon as Gordie was out of the room. She turned to him with a rueful smile, the dimple in her left cheek drawing his attention with innocent allure. "I'm really sorry. He can be a bit shocking to those who don't know him."

"Look, I don't want to butt in where it's none of my business, but has that kid ever had counseling?" Rio couldn't help asking.

Jill grimaced. "Yes. The counselor assured us that it's only a stage. Several of Gordie's friends are into this fascination with horror right now. He's forbidden to watch those awful slasher movies, but we're certain he's watching them anyway, at his friends' houses. Other than restricting him to home, we don't really know how to stop it. The counselor told us to just ignore it and keep trying to focus his interest on more cheerful subjects. Tom's tried enrolling him in every sport available in this area, bought him model airplanes, a roomful of fishing-and-camping gear, and a horse. Gordie loves the horse, but he's still obsessed with this other thing."

And then she bit her lower lip and looked embarrassed. "Oh, sorry. I didn't mean to go on like that. You just hit a touchy subject."

"I understand." But he didn't. Not really. Though he didn't know much about kids, Rio found himself disagreeing with the counselor. He thought there was more to Gordie's obsession than a normal childhood stage. Not that it was any of his business, of course, he reminded himself immediately. *Butt out, Rio.*

"I brought the water in case you get thirsty again later. Are you sure you don't want anything to eat?"

"Not tonight, but thanks." He knew he'd be ravenous in the morning, but he was just too damned tired and disgruntled to eat anything at the moment. Yet, as preoccupied as he was with his problems, he still found himself noting the way the glow from the bedside lamp brought out the golden highlights in Jill's glossy hair. Wondering if it could possibly feel as soft as it looked. She was almost close enough for him to reach out and—

He stopped abruptly. The concussion must still be affecting him, he decided. First he'd found himself interfering in her family business, and now he was fantasizing about touching her. He needed a good night's rest.

"Well, just let me know if you get hungry later. Gordie's sleeping on the hideaway in the den tonight so he won't disturb you. Tom's room is next door to this one and mine is just down the hall, so call out if you need anything during the night, okay? Tom will probably be in to check on you, anyway. He's like that."

She was chattering, Rio realized curiously. Did he make her nervous? He understood her natural caution about the unusual circumstances of his arrival, but he'd been on his best behavior. Was it just him, or was she always shy with strangers?

"You didn't need to make Gordie sleep on the couch," he told her, trying to keep his voice soft, pleasant. "This is his room, after all."

With a light smile, Jill shook her head. "Tom was concerned that you may have some pain tonight, and having Gordie in here would make you even more uncomfortable."

"It really wouldn't have bothered me. I've shared accommodations before." He glanced at the poster leering at him from the opposite wall and smiled. "Besides, I'm expecting nightmares tonight. I may need the company, even if it is just a bizarre kid."

Following Rio's gaze, Jill laughed ruefully. "I wouldn't blame you if you did have nightmares. Having that thing looking at me all night would give *me* bad dreams. Want me to take it down?"

"Uh—" What was it she'd asked? He was still reeling from the effects of her laugh. Her full smile had turned her from a wholesomely pretty woman to a staggeringly desirable one. And suddenly he wasn't at all sure his attraction to her was due to his concussion.

She looked down at him in question. "The poster," she prompted. "Would you like me to take it down?"

He cleared his throat. "No, that won't be necessary. I was only teasing."

"Oh." Her smile faded as her blue eyes softened compassionately. "You're in pain, aren't you? Isn't there anything I can do to help?"

"You've been very kind," he answered huskily, unable to look away from those deep, expressive eyes. "Thank you."

She reached out without seeming to be aware of her actions and brushed a strand of hair away from his forehead, a comforting, affectionate gesture that could just as easily have been directed at Gordie or Sharon. And then she pulled back hastily, as if realizing what she'd done. "Good night."

"Good night, Jill." It was the first time he'd said her name. Her eyes told him she was as aware of that as he was.

Long after she'd turned out the light and left the room, Rio lay awake wondering why, with his head and leg throbbing fiercely, his skin still felt sensitized from that brief touch of her cool fingers.

"So where's this mysterious stranger we've been hearing about all morning?" Mike Hammond asked loudly on

Monday morning, making Jill wince and look quickly toward the room in which Rio was still sleeping.

"Shh. You'll wake him," she scolded her brother. "Tom checked on him several times during the night and said that he was very restless, obviously in pain. He needs to sleep."

"Sorry. I thought he'd be awake by now. It's nearly eleven, after all," Mike apologized, trying without a great deal of success to lower his voice. He gave her a quick kiss, then draped his oversize frame into a kitchen chair and confiscated the cup of coffee she'd just poured for herself. "Is it true he's a hitchhiker with no ID on him?"

"He said he had a wallet," Jill replied, sliding a plate of blueberry muffins in front of her brother without asking the unnecessary question of whether or not he was hungry. "It was stolen from him sometime after the accident. Tom reported it to the police, but they said there was probably no chance of recovering it—or his duffel bag."

Mike scowled, swallowed half a muffin in one enormous bite, then demanded, "Who'd lift a wallet off a guy who'd been hurt in a car wreck?"

"Tom thinks it was someone who either saw the wreck happen or passed by soon afterward. Mr. Baxter's wallet was gone, too, along with his watch and Masonic ring. Neither Tom nor the sheriff thinks the boys who brought Rio to us had anything to do with the thefts."

Shaking his sandy head, Mike muttered a curse. "Stealing off a dead old man. What scum." And then his brow lifted in belated interest. "Rio?"

Jill nodded. "Rio. The man sleeping in Gordie's bedroom. That's the only name he's given us."

Mike frowned suspiciously. "Just who is this guy?"

"A hitchhiker," Jill answered with a little shrug. "That's all we know about him." And she decided not to add that the question "Who is he?" had been haunting her ever since she'd looked into those lost, piercing dark eyes. Despite her family's charitable generosity, if one of them suspected that "little sister" was strongly attracted to a mysterious stranger, they'd do everything short of locking her in her room to protect her heart and her virtue. In fact, she thought ruefully, she wouldn't even rule out being locked in her room. She'd had twenty-five years to discover all the drawbacks to being the baby of the family.

"Speaking of our hitchhiker," she said, keeping her voice light, "I'd better go check on him. He hasn't eaten since he's been here and I'm sure he'll be ravenous when he wakes up."

"He'll call out if he needs anything, won't he?"

"I don't think so." Thinking of the stubbornly independent cast to Rio's strong jaw, Jill suspected that he'd lie in that room and starve before calling for help. She'd seen how hard it had been for him to accept the helplessness of his situation the day before.

Mike shoved his well-cleaned plate away and pushed his chair back from the table. "I'll go with you. I want to get a look at this guy."

Knowing it would be useless to protest, Jill shrugged and led the way.

He was hungry. His leg hurt. His head hurt. His *fingernails* hurt, dammit. And he needed to go to the bathroom. Since there wasn't anything he could do about any of those problems at the moment, Rio gritted his teeth and glared at the ghoulish poster, as if the creature depicted on it had something to do with his predicament.

When the door opened slowly, he swiveled his head around, hoping Tom would be the one who'd enter. Instead, Jill came in, looking fresh and appealing in a bright yellow sweater and form-fitting jeans, her honey-colored hair tied in a loose knot at the top of her head. He'd thought maybe she wouldn't affect him as strongly today, after the confusion of the accident had cleared. He'd been wrong. She smiled a shy greeting at him and his mouth went dry. He could want this woman, he thought, somewhat dazed at the immediacy of his response to her. Want her badly.

Only then did he notice the denim- and flannel-draped mountain that loomed behind her.

Rio's gaze traveled slowly from the most massive chest he'd ever seen to a neck the size of his own thigh. Swallowing, he lifted his eyes a bit higher. The man's blue eyes were narrowed suspiciously in his broad, ruddy face, studying Rio with obvious wariness. He looked to be in his late twenties. Rio barely resisted the urge to clear his throat. Jill's boyfriend? he wondered. Had the big man sensed Rio's unwanted reactions to Jill?

"Rio, this is my brother, Mike Hammond," Jill explained, coming into the room with a glass of water cradled carefully between her hands. "How do you feel this morning? Are you hungry?"

With a short nod at her brother—knowing the man's identity didn't make him feel any safer—he then turned his attention to Jill, uncomfortably. Dammit, did she have to look so shy and nice? How was he supposed to explain his primary discomfort without embarrassing her?

"Yeah, I am kind of hungry," he answered. Maybe she'd leave him alone with Mike while she made him something to eat. Her brother was a huge, wary-looking hulk, but at least he was a guy.

"What would you like? Bacon and eggs? Oatmeal? Or I have some fresh blueberry muffins."

"The muffins sound good," he replied, then remembered he wanted her to stay away for a few minutes. "Maybe a couple of slices of bacon with them, if it's not too much trouble."

"Not at all. Is there anything else you need?"

"Well—uh—" He looked at Mike.

His suspicious frown changing to a grin, Mike took his sister's shoulders in his enormous hands and turned her toward the door. "Go fix the man something to eat," he ordered. "If he needs anything else, I'll take care of it."

"All right. I won't be long," she promised.

"So," Mike said as soon as Jill had gone. "Can you make it to the bathroom or do you need a bedpan?"

Gratefully, Rio pushed himself to one elbow. "I'd rather get up. I'll need help."

"I think I can manage."

The laconic comment made Rio smile wryly. "Yeah. There's just one problem."

"What's that?"

"I haven't got anything on under this sheet. And I'd rather not risk having your sister walk in to find me buck naked."

Mike chuckled. "I'd prefer to avoid that myself."

"I thought you might."

"I'll get you something of Tom's." He turned toward the door.

"Um—"

"Don't worry," Mike said with an over-the-shoulder grin. "I'll hurry."

"I'd appreciate it."

Jill had just lifted the last slice of crisply fried bacon onto a plate when a noise in the kitchen doorway caught her attention. Looking around, she was startled to see her brother and Rio entering slowly, Rio carefully supporting himself on a set of crutches while Mike hovered protectively behind him.

She recognized the crutches—Tom had needed them a couple of years earlier after being kicked in the shin by an angry bull. She also recognized the worn gray sweat suit Rio was wearing as belonging to Tom. The garment hung loosely on Rio's thin frame, the drawstring cinched tightly around his slender waist. One leg of the pants had been roughly cut away to accommodate the cast—Mike's work, Jill guessed. His other foot was bare.

Though she knew she should be relieved that her guest was decently covered now, she couldn't help thinking it was a shame to hide such a beautiful body beneath a layer of gray fleece. She hadn't realized quite how compactly he was built until now, seeing him standing beside her oversize brother. Dwarfed by six-foot-five-inch Mike, Rio was probably even shorter than Tom, who was five ten. What there was of him, Jill decided in approval, was prime.

Hoping her thoughts didn't show on her face, she frowned when she saw that Rio's face was pale, his upper lip beaded with perspiration, his mouth set in pain. "You shouldn't be out of bed," she scolded. "Honestly, Mike, how could you encourage him to do something so foolish?"

"He insisted," Mike answered with a futile attempt at looking innocent. "He's all right. Just needs a minute to catch his breath." He helped Rio lower himself into a chair at the kitchen table, his big, rough hands gentle in their support.

"I'm okay now," Rio said after a moment, though his voice still sounded rather strained. "Thanks."

"Hey, no problem. Give the man some food, Jilly. He's weak with hunger."

Jill noticed that Rio's hands weren't quite steady when he lifted his coffee cup to his lips. She longed to offer assistance, but prudently kept quiet. She understood his distress and frustration. Rio was a loner, a man who wasn't in the habit of depending on others; accustomed to fending for himself and preferring it that way.

Through unspoken agreement, she and Mike kept up a lively conversation so Rio wouldn't feel as if they were watching every bite he took. After a few minutes, he joined in somewhat tentatively, still a bit uncomfortable with them.

"I owe Tom for the sweats," he told Jill, motioning toward the cast-encased leg stretched out in front of him. "Your brother was ruthless with the scissors."

"Tom won't mind," Jill assured him.

"Damn straight, he won't," Mike seconded cheerfully. "Can't have a nekkid man in the house with our baby sister, now, can we?"

Though her cheeks flushed, Jill glared menacingly at her brother. "Don't be obnoxious, Mike. And why are you still hanging around? Don't you have work to do today?"

"We start framing that new house tomorrow. Guess I could go by and make sure all the materials are in," Mike answered thoughtfully, his eyes crinkled with a suppressed smile.

She smiled very sweetly at him. "Why don't you do that?"

"Hmm." Stroking his chin, Mike eyed Rio.

Rio shook his head. "If you're worried about leaving your 'baby sister' alone with me, you can relax. I'm hardly in any condition to threaten her virtue. And thanks to you and Tom's mutilated wardrobe, I'm no longer—um—nekkid."

Mike laughed and clapped Rio heartily on the shoulder. Jill winced along with Rio at the gesture, exasperated by Mike's blithe unconcern. "Darned if I don't like you, stranger," he approved rather loudly. "I'll tell the rest of the family they can quit worrying. Even though they'll probably all be over to check you out for themselves," he added.

Rio's eyes narrowed. "The rest of the family?" He directed the words to Jill.

She nodded almost apologetically. "I have three other brothers. And my parents, of course."

"Three other..." Rio's voice faded away.

She couldn't help smiling. "My parents wanted a large family," she explained. "I'm the youngest. Ellen—" She paused for a deep breath, then went on firmly, "Ellen was the eldest. She'd have been thirty-eight this year."

Rio eyed Mike. "Are all your brothers on the large side?"

"I'm the runt of the litter," Mike answered cheerily, though his eyes held an echo of Jill's pain at the mention of their dead sister.

Rio groaned.

Jill frowned repressively at her brother. "He's teasing. Mike's no smaller than Paul, Rusty or Gabe."

Not noticeably encouraged, Rio looked gravely at Mike. "Your sister is perfectly safe with me," he said emphatically.

Mike's smile was decidedly smug. "I wouldn't be leaving her with you if I doubted that." And then he turned to Jill, apparently satisfied that his point was made. "See you later, Jilly. Give someone a call if you need anything."

"I will." Embarrassed by her brother's macho teasing, she avoided looking at Rio.

"You want me to help you back to bed before I go?" Mike asked Rio.

Shaking his head, Rio shifted more comfortably in the chair, his coffee cup cradled in one hand. "I'd rather stay here for now. I get too restless in bed."

"All right. Tom'll be home for lunch before long, most likely. He can give you a hand."

"Thanks for everything, Mike."

"No prob. Bye, Jilly." He kissed her on his way out. Since their family was the demonstrative type, the embrace was automatic, habitual, but affectionate.

The house seemed unnaturally quiet after Mike left. Rio cleared his throat as Jill gathered his breakfast dishes. "Kids in school?"

She carried the dishes to the sink. "Yes. And Tom's working in the clinic. He usually comes in for lunch, when he's not busy with patients or out on a call." Still not meeting his eyes, she carried the coffeepot to the table and refilled his cup.

"Jill. Look at me, please."

Startled by the request, she complied. Their eyes met and held. She became vividly aware of how closely she was standing to him. He looked very serious when he spoke. "I know your brother was only teasing, but you're not really concerned about being alone with me, are you?"

Disturbed that he'd felt the need to ask, she hurriedly reassured him. "Of course not. And it has nothing to do with your physical condition," she added when he glanced down at his cast. "I trust you, Rio. You've given me no reason not to."

Seemingly satisfied with her answer, he nodded. "Good. I give you my word you're safe with me. Or as safe as you want to be," he added in a thoughtful murmur, studying her with speculative eyes.

Flushing, she turned away to rinse his breakfast dishes and stack them in the dishwasher. She decided not to respond to his odd comment.

"Has the phone service been restored?" Rio asked after another few minutes of silence during which Jill briskly wiped down the countertops.

"Yes, it has."

He nodded to the wall phone some six feet away from him. "You suppose that telephone cord would stretch this far?"

In answer, she reached for the phone and handed him the receiver. The extra long cord stretched easily to his seat. "Tell me the number you want to call and I'll dial it for you," she instructed. "Then I'll go and give you privacy."

He shook his head. "You don't have to leave. It's not that personal. Besides, I'll need you to hang this back up. I'm not too steady on those crutches yet."

"Oh. Of course."

He recited a series of numbers that she cooperatively punched into the phone. "I'll reimburse you for the call, of course, when I pay you back for everything else," he added, holding the receiver to his ear.

She only nodded and turned back to her work in the kitchen, giving him at least a semblance of privacy, though she couldn't help but overhear his side of the conversation.

"Amber? Hi, it's Rio. Have you heard from Gypsy lately? I really need to talk to her.... Damn. She promised to call as soon as she gets into the country.... Yeah, I'm in a little trouble. Car wreck. Busted my leg and my wallet's been stolen. I'm flat broke and stranded in Arkansas.... No, I've got a place to stay for now, but I don't want to impose for too long. Just tell Gypsy to call me the minute you hear from her, will you? Oh, yeah, the number. Jill?"

She turned her head to look at him. "Yes?"

"The number here?" he prompted, then repeated it to the person at the other end of the line as Jill gave it to him. He gave her a quick grin. "Thanks." And then he turned back to his call, concluding it rather abruptly.

Shaken by his smile, exasperated by her uncharacteristic responses to this man—this drifter, she reminded herself sternly—she ordered her traitorous senses to behave. She felt somewhat more under control when he handed her the receiver to replace in its cradle.

"I'm afraid I'm stuck here for another couple of days, if it's not too much of an inconvenience," he mumbled, looking discouraged. "Gypsy's been out of the country, but she's on her way back. She'll check in with our friend Amber as soon as she can, and Amber will give her my message."

Though she couldn't help but wonder exactly who Gypsy was, Jill didn't ask. "No problem. You're welcome to stay here."

Rio sighed and shook his head. "Damn, I hate this. I feel like an intruder. You and your family have been so nice, and there's nothing I can do to repay you until I hear from Gypsy."

"Please, Rio, don't worry about it. You're no trouble," she answered firmly. And then she smiled. "In fact, you're just about the most stubbornly independent houseguest I've ever seen."

He returned the smile somewhat ruefully. "I'm not used to depending on other people."

"Real loner, huh?" she teased gently.

He shrugged. "I suppose." *And that's not going to change,* his eyes added.

She wondered if she'd only imagined the subliminal message. Maybe her own common sense was reminding her not to let herself get too interested in this all-too-interesting man. Wherever the warning originated, it was one she'd do well to heed. He was a drifter, an adventurer. Even his name was exotic. Rio. And the women he knew had names like Gypsy and Amber. She was just plain Jill. Definitely not in the same league.

It didn't take a great deal of experience to recognize Rio as a walking heartache for any woman who wasn't very, very careful.

A door slammed somewhere at the other end of the house. Jill pulled her eyes from Rio's and smoothed her hair as she turned away. "That will be Tom, wanting his lunch. Guess I'd better get it finished."

Chapter Three

Mike hadn't been kidding when he'd said that all of Jill's family would eventually get around to checking him out, Rio thought in wry amusement. During the five days he'd been recuperating in Tom's house, he'd met Jill's parents, her other three brothers, the wives and kids of the three who were married, even her aunt and uncle. All had dropped by on one pretext or another during the week; all had looked Rio over very carefully before giving their approval of his remaining in the home.

He wasn't sure what he'd done to earn their approval, but he received it nevertheless. The Hammond clan was a warm, generous, friendly group, and they weren't shy about showing affection or sympathy in words and touches. They soon began to treat him as casually as they did each other, helping him move around the house, expressing genuine concern for his injuries and discomfort. He'd never met people quite like them. He couldn't help wondering what it would have been like to grow up among them.

"You do any fishing, Rio?" Paul, at thirty-six, the eldest of Jill's brothers grinned encouragingly at Rio as he asked the question.

"Yeah, sometimes," Rio answered, reaching for his coffee. Jill made the best damned coffee he'd ever had, he'd decided days earlier. Perhaps that was one reason her brothers tended to drop by during the morning hours when they weren't busy. Three of them surrounded him now at the kitchen table, watching as he ate the breakfast Jill had just set in front of him, their own coffee cups emptying and refilling at an amazing rate. They all looked very much alike—large, blue-eyed, sandy-haired. Rio was intensely aware of the contrast between them and his own black hair and eyes, darker skin and slender physique.

"We've got some good fishing around here," the next-eldest brother, Rusty, announced. "Maybe you could go with us one day while you're here."

"Yeah. I want to see him climb into a boat with that cast on," Mike suggested with a chuckle, reaching into a ceramic jar on the counter and pulling out a handful of Jill's oatmeal-raisin cookies.

Paul laughed. "Remember the time Gabe tried it? Fell in the lake. Doc replaced the cast and chewed us all out." At twenty-eight, Gabe was the only one who didn't work for their father's construction business. Rio had heard more than a few jokes about their brother, the banker—the closest thing to a Yuppie in the Hammond clan, he'd thought with a stifled smile upon meeting Gabe and his Junior-League-type wife, Cissy.

Rusty nodded, grinning broadly at Rio. "That was nothing compared to the time Tom and Paul and I decided to climb Ol' Bald-Top. Sheer cliff all the way up the north side. Signs everywhere warning off climbers. We made it about halfway up and got stranded on a ledge. Ground was crumbling beneath our sneakers and we were scared spitless. Couldn't go up or down, just sat there yelling our fool heads off for help.''

Paul winced. "They sent a helicopter to rescue us, and the newspaper sent a photographer. It was the talk of the area for days. We were all grounded for a month.''

"Speak for yourself," Tom complained. "I was grounded for six weeks.''

"Yeah, but you got off without the belt. Paul and I had to eat our dinner standing up that night.''

"You deserved it," Jill commented cheerfully, coming into the room with a basket of laundry in her arms. She'd obviously overheard enough to know what they were talking about. "It wasn't climbing the mountain that got you in the most trouble. It was letting Dad overhear you bragging about it to your friends after he'd already lectured you about how stupid you'd been.''

"Dad sure could swing a belt," Paul mused ruefully. "Your dad ever tan your hide for you, Rio?''

The question brought Rio's eyes quickly around from his study of Jill's face, flushed and slightly damp from her vigorous housework. Strands of hair had escaped her loose topknot to trail around her neck and temples. He thought she looked sexy as hell. Clearing his throat, he answered Paul's questions gruffly. "I never knew my old man. He took off when I was still in diapers.''

An awkward silence followed Rio's blunt remark, making him wish he'd just shrugged off the question as he usually did whenever anyone asked anything too personal. He'd been lulled by this gregarious family into being too candid about his less-than-ideal past. He could almost see them withdraw from him, though they immediately camouflaged the reaction. He wondered how they'd react if they heard some of the stories he could tell about his youth.

He could make their escapade on Ol' Bald-Top sound like a Boy Scout hike. He wouldn't, of course. People like these—trusting, sheltered, privileged to have grown up surrounded by love and acceptance—didn't need to hear about the darker, harder side of life that Rio had seen. He'd leave them their illusions, he told himself, feeling rather noble.

"Sorry, Rio," Paul said after the momentary pause. "I didn't mean to pry."

Rio only shrugged—which was what he should have done in the first place, he told himself.

"Haven't you guys got anything better to do than sit around dirtying up my kitchen all day?" Jill scolded, returning from the adjoining laundry room to stand with her hands on her hips as she eyed her brothers meaningfully.

Paul frowned. "Yeah. Actually, we do. We've just been procrastinating." He looked at Rusty and Mike. "We've got to get over to the Quattlebaum place."

His brothers groaned in noisy unison. "Aw, hell," Rusty muttered. "We haven't been able to please that old battle-ax since we started the house. We follow the plans to the T and she still gripes about it. She's had us redo the same window three times now."

"She's about to start paying dearly for some of these last-minute changes she's making," Paul added, pushing his chair back from the table. "It's not our fault she can't make up her mind about what she wants."

"She thinks it is," Mike put in.

They were still complaining about the difficult customer when they tramped out the door, leaving a noticeable silence in their wake. Mike poked his head back inside the door just as Jill seemed about to speak. "Forgot to ask, Rio. You need anything before we go? Want some help getting back to your room?"

Rio shook his head. "Thanks, but I'm okay. I'm getting better with the crutches."

"Okay. See you, then. Bye, Jilly."

"Get going already," she said fondly. "You've got work to do—and so have I."

"Nag," Mike muttered, but his parting shot was spoken as affectionately as her own words.

Shaking her head in exasperation, Jill smiled at Rio. "Do you want anything else to eat? No? Looks like there's about one cup of coffee left in the pot. Want it?"

"Yeah, thanks." He shoved his cup toward her. He and Jill spent most days alone together while Tom was at work and the kids in school. He wasn't complaining.

It was an interesting household routine. Tom had been called away twice in the middle of the night for animal emergencies—something Rio had been told was fairly common in his line of work. The children caught a school bus each morning after being roused and fed by Jill. The bus pulled away from the gate every morning at almost the same time Debbie, Tom's office manager, drove in to unlock the clinic door and get the office ready for business.

Jill had been a bit shy of Rio those first couple of days they spent alone, but had begun to relax, soon treating him much as she did Tom and her brothers. The Hammonds were a demonstrative clan, and Jill was as likely to pat Rio's head or shoulder as she was her brothers' or nephew's, seemingly unaware that he tensed every time she did so. She seemed completely at ease with him. Most of the time.

There were moments when Rio caught her looking at him as if he were an alien suddenly thrust in the midst of her small-town American family. There'd also been a time or two when he'd glimpsed something in her eyes that had made him wonder if his growing attraction to her was not entirely one-sided.

Not that he intended to do anything about it, regardless, he warned himself each time he found himself speculating. She wasn't the type to indulge in a fling with a man who was just passing through, and he was in no physical condition to initiate that fling if she were. Besides, her loving, protective and decidedly large brothers would probably put him in a full body cast if he tried anything with their "baby sister," he thought in wry amusement.

"Breakfast was good," he commented, both to make conversation and to distract himself from the nagging question of whether it would be worth risking his unbroken limbs for one chance at having Jill Hammond in bed.

She smiled at him. "I'll be right back," she said, heading for the doorway.

He picked up his freshly refilled cup. "No hurry. I'll just sit here and enjoy the coffee."

Jill was back in the kitchen in less than ten minutes, carrying a sewing box and three muslin circles. Setting the supplies on the table, she sat across from Rio and opened the sewing box. "I'll keep you company while I work on these," she said, selecting a needle and some black embroidery floss.

She'd enjoyed talking with Rio during the past few days, though she found him exasperatingly reticent about anything of a personal nature. She still didn't know his last name or where he was from. He seemed to have no home, no family, no career aspirations. And yet he was obviously intelligent, gentle natured and considerate, if distant. How could he be content with such an aimless existence? she'd wondered more than once.

And who was this person named Gypsy that he was trying to track down? A friend? A lover?

She'd tried not to wonder what it would be like to have this broodingly attractive, enigmatic, rather dangerous-looking man as a lover. She hadn't been able to stop herself from fantasizing. She told herself that her fantasies were perfectly natural, nothing to worry about. They only proved that she was a healthy, normal woman with healthy, normal urges that she'd been largely ignoring for the past two years. She could continue to do so now. At least, she hoped she could.

"What are you making?"

Rio's sudden question intruded into her illicit thoughts, making Jill jump and prick her finger with the embroidery needle. "Damn," she muttered, eyeing the bright-red drop of blood on her fingertip.

"Sorry. I didn't mean to startle you. I didn't realize you were concentrating so deeply on your work," Rio apologized.

Relieved by his misinterpretation, she shook her head and smiled ruefully at him. "You've been so quiet, I almost forgot you were there," she teased.

"I've been watching you," he replied, causing her to swallow in a sudden rush of self-consciousness. "Is that a face you're embroidering?"

"Yes." She lifted the muslin circle to show him the round eyes and half-moon nose she'd sketched out with black thread. "I'll add blue or brown pupils to the eyes and then fill in pink lips. It's the face for a doll."

Rio tilted his head in interest. "Like the one Sharon carries around all the time?"

"Yes. I made that one," she confirmed, rather surprised he'd noticed Sharon's beloved doll. She suspected that very little got by Rio; that he observed more than most people might think if they were fooled by his air of detached disinterest.

"I've noticed that hers was rather unusual. Where did you get the pattern?"

"I designed it myself," she admitted, pleased with his comments.

"Really?" He seemed unexpectedly interested. "Have you been doing this long?"

She shrugged. "I've been sewing since I was ten. I make a lot of my clothes and Sharon's, and I enjoy making quilts. I made the one on your—or rather, on Gordie's bed," she corrected herself. "But Sharon's was the first doll I'd attempted. I made it for her after Ellen died, hoping it would comfort her."

"Who are those for?" Rio asked, nodding toward the two circles still awaiting her attention. "Your nieces?"

"No. I've already made dolls for Paige, Amanda and Gail. I promised the PTA I'd donate these three to be used for a raffle at the school Halloween carnival at the end of the month."

He pushed his empty coffee cup away and leaned comfortably back in his chair. "Have you ever thought of trying to sell your design? I don't know much about dolls, of course, but it looks to me like it would sell well commercially."

Her eyes on the needle she pushed in and out of the fabric, Jill shrugged slightly. "I've thought of doing a few to sell in the local Christmas craft shows," she replied. "It would be nice to have a little extra spending money for Christmas gifts. It bothers me that I'm so dependent on Tom. He insists on paying me a salary."

"He'd have to hire someone if you weren't available," Rio pointed out logically. "And he'd never find anyone half as dedicated to his family."

Jill didn't bother to dispute that. It was true, after all.

"The two of you make a nice couple, actually. Have you ever thought about—?"

She almost choked at the unspoken question. "Tom and I?" she asked incredulously. "Of course not! He's like another big brother to me. I couldn't imagine ever thinking of him in any other way!"

He only nodded, his expression unreadable. "I see." He didn't say anything else as he watched her change floss and begin to fill in the doll's eyes with a lively, bright blue. And then he spoke again, another question. "What did you do before you took over your brother-in-law's household?"

"I worked in the alterations department of a clothing store in Little Rock. I took some business classes at U.A.L.R., thinking maybe I'd go into business for myself eventually. I've done some sewing for women who are very hard to fit—women with one hip higher than the other, for example, or who suffer from osteoporosis or have had mastectomies. There seems to be a real demand for that type of work, and I think I could make a good living at it. Now that the children are getting older and more self-sufficient, I may start looking into it again."

"You don't sound particularly excited about it," Rio observed quietly.

She was vaguely surprised by his comment. "I didn't mean to sound unenthusiastic. I enjoy sewing."

"But don't you ever want to break away and do something for yourself? You were so young when your sister died and you took on so much responsibility—you're still so young to live as quietly as you seem to do here."

His comments about her age made her wonder again how old Rio was—and squirm uncomfortably in her chair at the guilty recognition of thoughts she'd occasionally had herself. She tried to phrase her answer carefully. "I've had dreams of adventure and excitement, like everyone else does at some time in their lives," she confessed. "But I've never been very far from my home or my family. And I don't think I'd be happy drifting, without roots.

"Not that I have anything against people who *do* enjoy living that way, of course," she added quickly, in case she had offended him. "It's just that it wouldn't be quite right for me."

Rio looked unconvinced, but unwilling to argue the point. Instead he changed the subject, asking what the next step would be in her assembly of the dolls.

She explained the process to him, describing the yarn hair and cloth bodies, the thin, flexible wire she'd use in the arms and legs to make the dolls posable, the individually fashioned outfits she'd sew out of brightly colored scraps of gingham and calico. She'd never tried making a boy doll, she added, but she was working on the design for one as a gift for her baby nephew, Gabe's newborn son.

"Sharon wants one, too, as a brother for her doll. Though I can't imagine why, when she and Gordie get along like a cat and a dog," she said with a laugh.

Rio grinned. "Maybe her sister doll will win all the arguments," he suggested. "Sharon's own form of revenge against Gordie."

"Maybe that's what she has in mind," Jill agreed, smiling. "There were times when I was growing up when I wished I were bigger and stronger than my brothers." And then she laughed again. "Sometimes I still do."

Rio shifted in his chair, his eyes focused thoughtfully on her face. "It must get tiresome at times being the baby sister."

She rolled her eyes. "Does it ever. I couldn't be better protected if I were surrounded by professional body-guards. The year I lived in Little Rock, one or the other of my brothers was always calling, sometimes popping in unexpectedly just to see what I was up to."

"Could be a problem with your social life."

Fashioning a smiling, pink Cupid's bow mouth, Jill nodded. "Sometimes. My brothers think it's their responsibility to personally approve any man who wants to take me out."

"I suppose it would take a damned saint to pass their inspection."

Jill couldn't help wondering why Rio suddenly sounded so disgruntled. "I'm an adult. Despite my brothers' misconceptions, I choose my own dates."

"Are you seeing anyone special?"

She looked up at him. "No. I haven't been out with anyone lately. My choice, not my brothers'."

Meeting her eyes, Rio looked concerned. "That's no way for a beautiful, single young woman to live."

In all her life no one had ever called Jill beautiful. Probably because she wasn't, she told herself realistically. Rio was just being nice. But it still gave her an odd thrill of pleasure hearing him say that he found her attractive, whether he meant it or not. "I'm not unhappy with my life," she felt obliged to assure him.

He shrugged. "Whether you are or aren't, it's your business," he muttered, visibly withdrawing from her. He reached for the crutches on the floor beside his chair. "I think I'll go outside on the porch for a while. I need some fresh air."

Jill jumped up and rounded the table, reaching for the crutches at the same time. "Here, let me help you."

He'd already started out of the chair. "That's not . . ."

His voice trailed off when their movements brought them flush against each other, Jill's hands braced on his forearms to help him with his balance as he supported himself on one foot and one crutch.

Jill's breath slammed out of her chest even as heat flooded her body from every point where she made contact with Rio. His dark eyes, suddenly stormy, locked with hers, holding her paralyzed in place. He was so close she could feel his breath on her forehead, and she shivered, imagining the touch of his lips there, his mouth on hers. He had only to lower his head a few inches and . . .

Rio grabbed his other crutch from her and shoved it under his free arm. "I'll be outside," he said, his voice huskier than usual.

Jill stepped out of his way. "Do you need any—"

"I can make it." He swung himself awkwardly out of the room without looking back.

Heart thudding dully, Jill stood for a long time in the spot where he'd left her, her white-knuckled hands gripping the edge of the table. She told herself that Rio was as foreign to her life as an exotic jungle animal. She had to keep reminding herself that, for her, he was almost as dangerous.

Her thoughts still centered on Rio and the disturbing emotions he stirred in her, Jill nearly took off the end of her finger when the telephone startled her that afternoon as she was chopping vegetables for dinner. Setting the knife down carefully, she wiped her hands on her apron and reached for the phone. "Hello?"

"Oh, hi," said a breezy, melodious feminine voice. "This is Gypsy. I was trying to reach Rio. Is he still at this number?"

Gypsy. Jill cleared her throat and answered without inflection. "Yes, Rio's here. Can you hold on for a few minutes? It may take him a little while to get to the phone."

"How is he?"

"He's fine," Jill answered gently, touched by the genuine concern in the quiet question. "His leg is broken and he suffered a mild concussion, but he's very strong and recovering more quickly than most people would."

"That's my Rio," the woman responded, audibly relieved. "Nothing holds him down for long."

My Rio. Jill swallowed hard. "I'll get him for you."

She found him in the den, sprawled on the couch as he watched a syndicated rerun of a long-running police show with Gordie and Sharon. "Telephone, Rio," she announced from the doorway. "It's Gypsy."

As closely as she watched him when she said the name, she detected no particular emotion in his expression. Rio merely nodded and reached for his crutches, brushing off Gordie's offer of help. Jill noted that Gordie watched their injured houseguest with avid interest, and wondered what, exactly, about Rio made the boy admire him so much. Even Sharon, usually shy with strangers, treated Rio with the same fond respect that she reserved for her uncles. Jill wondered if she would be the only one affected by the void that would remain when he left their lives as abruptly as he'd entered.

She held the swinging door open for Rio, following him into the kitchen. "I'll just set this bowl in the refrigerator and then I'll leave you in privacy," she told him, hurrying toward the counter where she'd been working.

He shook his head. "There's no need for that. Go on with whatever you were doing. This won't take long, and I don't need privacy."

Uncertain, she picked up the knife and glanced at the pile of vegetables waiting to be chopped for the stir-fry dinner she'd planned. Then she shrugged and reached for a stalk of broccoli. Knowing Rio, he'd have told her if he really wanted to be alone for the call. Turning her back on him to give at least a semblance of privacy, she told herself she wouldn't listen.

She did of course.

"Gypsy? Hi, kid. How're you doing?"

The affection in Rio's voice made Jill's hand falter in her work. She hadn't expected the hot jealously that suddenly flooded her. Bending her head so that her face was hidden by her hair, she wielded the knife with more vigor, calling herself every unflattering synonym for *stupid* she could think of at the moment.

"*I'm* fine. *You're* the one in trouble, I understand," Gypsy accused Rio indulgently. "Again."

"Hey, who was the one who had to be bailed out of jail last time?" he returned, grinning.

"Okay. So I've ended up in the wrong place at the wrong time myself a few times. How bad a fix are you in?"

"About as bad as it can get," he answered glumly, hooking a kitchen chair by the back and swinging it around so that he could sink into it before he fell on his face. "I've broken that same damned leg again and my wallet's been lifted. If it weren't for a very nice family who's taken me in, I'd be in a charity ward somewhere."

"Damn. You *have* got yourself in a mess this time, haven't you? What are you going to do?"

"I was hoping you could help me out."

Dead silence greeted Rio's words. He winced. "Gyps?"

"I'm still here. I'm flat broke, but I'm still here."

"What about that writing assignment you just finished?"

"Hey, I was just doing research. The travel article hasn't been proposed yet, much less sold."

In other words, Gypsy had used all her funds to chase after an idea that had struck her impulsively, probably stopping at a party or two in the ports she'd flitted through on her free-spirited way. "I don't suppose you have a place for me to stay until my leg's out of the cast?" he asked without a great deal of optimism.

"I'm afraid not." She sighed. "I was supposed to start a really plum house-sitting assignment in Boston next week, but it's fallen through. Actually I was planning to track you down and see if you wanted company for a few weeks."

"Under normal circumstances, I'd welcome you with open arms," Rio answered, peripherally aware of the forceful chopping noises coming from behind him. "So what are you going to do?"

"I've got a little money stashed away for an emergency. Not enough to help both of us out much, but it'll get me to where you are. We'll figure something out from there. Okay?"

"Where the hell are you, anyway?"

"Oh, I'm in London. I'd called Amber to see if she'd heard from you lately and she gave me your message about being hurt. I was worried about you, Rio."

"Thanks, Gyps. So how long will it take you to get here?"

"Couple of weeks at the most, I promise. Will you be okay until then? Think the family can put you up that long? Can't you do some work for them or something?"

"Oh, sure," he answered glumly, staring at the bulky cast that ran from the toes of his right foot all the way up to his thigh. "I can break horses or climb up on the roof and mend the shingles. Take your pick."

"Rio, as much as I love you, I hate it when you get sarcastic. I was only making a suggestion."

Rio sighed. "I know you were, and I'm sorry. I didn't mean to snap."

"I understand. It's a hell of a situation."

"Yeah, it is. And as much as I love *you,* your eternal optimism gets to me sometimes. You're always so cheerfully certain that everything will turn out for the best."

"It will, you know," she replied, as cheerfully as he'd accused her of being. "Doesn't it always?"

He thought of his broken leg, of his serious lack of finances, of not even owning a change of underwear that hadn't been bought for him by his hosts, along with two inexpensive sweat suits to add to the one Tom had sacrificed for him. He contemplated the awkward position he was in with the people who'd taken him in, expecting him to be gone in just a few days. And he thought of his even more awkward attraction to the woman who, until a few moments before, had been noisily chopping vegetables behind him. She'd gone suddenly quiet. "I don't know about this one, Gypsy."

"Then we'll play it as it comes, okay?"

"Looks like that's the only choice we've got. Give me a call when you get into the area. If I'm not still here, I'll leave a message about where I'll be."

"Rio—I'm glad you're okay. And I'm sorry I can't help you more."

"Don't worry about it, kid. We're survivors, remember?"

"That's what I keep telling myself. Bye, love."

"See you." He hung up the receiver, took a deep breath and turned. "Jill—"

But he was alone in the room. Swallowing a curse, he sighed and ran his fingers dispiritedly through his overlong hair.

Chapter Four

As much as I love you. The words echoed distantly in Jill's mind as she set a huge bowl of stir-fried vegetables in the center of the dining table beside the equally large bowl of rice she'd already placed there. Automatically checking to make sure everything else was ready, she tried not to remember the conversation she'd overheard. But one fact kept nagging at her: Rio loved Gypsy, whoever the woman was.

Jill had been jealous—so jealous she'd had to leave the room rather than suffer through any more of Rio's side of the affectionately teasing conversation. And that jealousy had demonstrated just how deeply infatuated she'd become during the past week.

She'd never considered herself a particularly foolish woman. She saw now that she could be an utter fool. It was definitely time to start pulling back before she did something even more idiotic—like fall in love with him.

"Dinner's ready," she called quickly, unable to dwell any longer on her disturbing emotions.

Sharon and Gordie jammed into the door at the same time, squirming and complaining about who was actually there first. Gordie shoved through, stumbling toward the table, leaving Sharon to follow, whining. A moment later, Tom held the door open for Rio, who swung through with increasing ease on his crutches.

"Do I have to eat red peppers, Jill? I hate red peppers."

"What are those squiggly things? Yuck, they look like skinny worms."

Jill started filling plates. "You don't have to eat the red peppers, Sharon. Gordie, don't eat the bean sprouts. You both have to eat everything else—and no more comments about the appearance of the food. Got that, Gordie?"

He answered with a long-suffering sigh and a mumbled, "Yes, ma'am."

Tom slid into his chair. "Rice? Yuck, don't you know what rice looks like?"

Jill frowned sternly at him. "How would you like to wear your dinner tonight?"

The children giggled and Tom subsided, grinning as he reached for the rice bowl.

Jill turned to Rio, aware that he looked rather left out of the family banter. "Do *you* have any comments to make about the food?" she demanded, still in her mock-dictatorial mode.

He smiled. "No, ma'am."

"Good." She immediately turned away from him, scolding herself silently for her inordinate pleasure in making him smile. That was no way to draw back from him.

"I heard from Gypsy today, Tom," Rio said when everyone had settled down to eat.

Tom looked up. "Yeah? Is everything okay?"

Grimacing expressively, Rio shrugged. "Could be better. She can't get here for a couple of weeks. But I won't impose on you that long. I'll get a room at a motel close by to wait for her. I'm getting around pretty well on these crutches now, so I can—"

"And how are you planning to pay for this room?" Tom interrupted kindly, just before Jill could break in to ask the same question. Her stomach had gone hollow, appetite gone, the moment Rio mentioned leaving.

Shrugging again, Rio muttered, "I can always sell the bike."

"The hell you will."

"Look, Tom, I can't expect you to—"

"I'm fully aware that you don't expect anything from anyone. Nevertheless, you aren't leaving this house until I'm sure you have a place to go or someone to keep an eye on you until you've recovered." He grinned cockily. "Since I'm bigger than you and in better shape at the moment, I don't recommend you challenge me on that."

"Don't go, Rio. It's neat having you here." Gordie pleaded. Noticing how upset he looked at the prospect, Jill wondered if she shouldn't have a talk with the boy about not letting himself get attached to their temporary guest.

"Yes, stay, Rio. We like you," Sharon urged sweetly, pushing her glasses up on her short nose to give him a limpid look.

Jill watched through her lashes as Rio squirmed in his seat, visibly uncomfortable at being the center of such solicitous attention.

Tom laughed. "Better give it up, boy. Looks like you're outnumbered."

With a gusty exhale, Rio threw up his hands. "Looks like you're right. All right, I'll stay until she gets here. And thanks. But somehow, I'm going to repay you. Aren't there any chores I can do?"

Holding her breath, Jill waited for Tom's answer, knowing Rio's excessive pride would be wounded, should Tom laugh at the offer coming from a man in a thigh-high cast. She should have known her brother-in-law would do no such thing. Tom rubbed his chin thoughtfully and murmured, "Can't think of anything at the moment, but I'm sure there's something. We can talk about it later, okay?"

Rio nodded, dignity intact. "Yeah. Okay." He looked across the table toward Jill. "Got enough of those vegetables for seconds?"

"Of course." She passed him the bowl, wondering at the fleeting expression that had crossed his face just as their eyes met.

"Thanks. This is really good." He paused, winked at Gordie and added, "Even those skinny-worm things."

"Eeyeww—gross!" Sharon pronounced in disgust.

Gordie laughed delightedly, relaxing now that the issue of Rio's staying was settled for the moment.

Jill finished her own dinner in silence, worrying that she wouldn't be the only one hurt when Rio moved on. But she suspected that her pain would be the deepest and most lasting if she didn't start being very, very careful.

"Careful, Rio. There's a hole right in front of you."

Rio nodded in response to Gordie's solicitous warning, picking his way carefully across the ground toward the barn and paddock on Monday afternoon. The tennis shoe on his left foot, borrowed from Tom, was a size too big; two socks kept it from sliding off altogether. Rio didn't complain, since it would have been too much trouble to get into the left boot of the pair he'd been wearing in the accident.

Gordie's buckskin, Shadow Dancer, waited impatiently, head extended over the fence, obviously anticipating the sugar cube Gordie carried in one rather grubby hand. "Ain't he a beauty, Rio?"

Rio ran an experienced eye over the si :-year-old gelding, noting the glossy, well-groomed coat. "He's a beauty, all right. You take good care of him."

The boy flushed in pride, shrugging with not very believable nonchalance. "Dad said I couldn't keep him unless I take real good care of him." He extended the sugar cube and grinned as Dancer inhaled it with delicate greed. "Usually I give him carrots and stuff 'cause it's better for him, but I like to give him a special treat sometimes."

"Just as Jill allows you an occasional candy bar, right?"

Gordie nodded enthusiastically at Rio's understanding analogy. "Yeah. It don't hurt every once in a while."

"Of course not."

Glowing in Rio's approval, Gordie practically danced around him, suddenly looking even younger than his ten years. "Want to see me saddle him up and ride him around the paddock? I can show you his trick." And then Gordie caught his lower lip between his teeth, looking concerned. "Unless you need to go back and sit down, of course," he offered haltingly, glancing at Rio's cast.

Rio shook his head and leaned against the fence, his arms crossed on top, crutches resting beside him. "I'm fine. Feels good to be outside for a change. Let's see your trick."

"All right!" Gordie bolted for the barn, leaving Rio smiling at his enthusiasm.

At times like this, he could almost like the kid, he thought. When Gordie wasn't doing his imitation of an adolescent Vincent Price, he could almost be mistaken for a normal boy. Again, Rio wondered why Gordie's family wasn't aware that the child was struggling with some real problems that were more serious than a simple boyhood stage. Rio couldn't begin to guess the root of those problems, of course; nor did he want to try. It was, after all, none of his business. He was only here for a couple more weeks.

Idly watching as Gordie saddled his surprisingly patient horse, Rio found his thoughts drifting, as they so often did, to Jill. It bothered him that something had changed between them during the past three days, ever since Gypsy's call. Rio wasn't sure whether that call had initiated the change or if it was something else. Something like that awkward moment earlier the same day when he'd come so close to kissing her that she had to have seen the intention in his face before he'd made himself pull back.

Whatever had triggered her withdrawal, it was as if she'd erected an invisible barrier between them. She was still friendly, still touchingly concerned for his welfare, but now he could detect no difference between her actions and those of the rest of her warm, demonstrative family. They'd rarely been alone over the weekend, of course, but today, while Tom had been in his office and the kids at school, he and Jill had had the house to themselves. As she had before, she'd brought her sewing into the room where he was to keep him company, but he'd still been aware that there was something different about her. Something guarded, almost wary. Something that hadn't been there earlier.

And those casual touches, pats on the shoulder, had stopped altogether. He missed them.

The invisible barrier had irritated him at first. He'd been tempted to break through it, wondering what would happen if he just grabbed her and kissed her until she had to admit that the attraction couldn't just be ignored.

As the hours had passed, he'd decided that she was right to pull back, that the attraction could lead nowhere. He wouldn't want Jill to be hurt by coming to expect more from him than he could give. Even more reluctantly, he realized that it was possible that Jill wouldn't be the only one hurt when he left.

For the first time in his restless, nomadic adulthood, Rio found himself vulnerable to another person, in danger of getting too involved to walk away without a pang or a backward glance, as was his usual custom. And, since he knew there'd come a time when he had to go, it would be better all around if he followed Jill's lead and kept his distance from her.

"Look, Rio! Watch Dancer!" Gordie called, making a third horseback lap around the paddock.

"I'm watching," Rio replied, dragging his thoughts away from Jill. He watched as the boy put the horse through his paces, and then, with an ear-to-ear grin, directed the animal to take a bow by bending one foreleg.

"Hey, that's good. Did you train him?"

Riding up to the fence, Gordie shook his head. "Uncle Rusty did. He's real good with horses. He's been riding in rodeos and horse shows and stuff since he was even younger than me."

"Have you ever shown Dancer?"

Gordie's face clouded. "Nah."

"Why not?"

The boy shrugged, his expression shuttered. "Not interested. I've got better things to do with my time."

"Like what?" Rio prodded, his eyes narrowed on Gordie's suddenly older-looking face.

"Just stuff." Gordie whirled the horse around. "Guess I'd better clean up. Jill will be calling us for dinner soon."

Vaguely troubled, Rio watched the boy dismount and lead the horse into the barn. Damn, he thought grimly. He was getting too involved with everyone in this family. Gypsy couldn't get here any too soon, as far as he was concerned.

Jill nearly dropped the plastic tote of cleaning supplies the next morning when she rounded a corner in the hallway to encounter Rio struggling to hold a towel around his waist as he maneuvered his crutches awkwardly toward

Gordie's bedroom. "Umm, do you need help?" she offered tentatively.

At the sound of her voice, he jerked and swore beneath his breath, his cheeks darkening. "I forgot to take clean clothes to wear after my bath," he muttered, clinging tightly to the white towel that contrasted so dramatically with his dark skin. His damp hair clung to his head, hanging almost to his shoulders.

Though she'd seen him seminude before, Jill was struck again with the impact of this man's beautiful body—lean and strong and tanned, marred only by that scar on his abdomen. She wanted to know how he got that scar, as well as the one on his cheek. She decided she'd probably be better off not asking.

She was suddenly very aware that they were alone in the house. Trying to keep her eyes on Rio's face, she opened Gordie's door and stepped aside. "You're going to fall if you keep holding on to that towel," she told him, trying to sound lightly amused. "I'll go into the bathroom and shut the door and you can make a run for it, okay?"

He smiled weakly. "Sounds like a workable solution."

With one last sideways glance, she stepped past him and into the bathroom, pulling the door closed behind her.

"Jill?"

She paused, opening the door a few inches to peer out at him in question. "Yes?"

His grin was knee melting. "No peeking."

"I wouldn't dream of it," she assured him, holding her crossed fingers in clear view to indicate she was lying.

Rio laughed. "Yeah. That's what I thought."

She closed the door, then was unable to resist pressing her ear to it. After a moment of silence, she heard Rio's crutches thumping in the opposite direction. Imagining the discarded towel lying behind him, she gulped and closed her eyes, her entire body feeling unusually warm.

* * *

Rio found the wood-carving knives that afternoon when, bored with his own company and unwilling to disturb Jill at her housework, he looked in a family-room cupboard for the television guide. Thinking wistfully of the much simpler set lost with his duffel bag, he examined the knives admiringly. Finer than anything he'd ever owned, the set looked barely used, in mint condition. His fingers itched for a block of wood.

"Have you done any carving, Rio?"

He glanced around at Jill's question, finding her standing in the doorway behind him. "Yeah, some. This is a nice set."

"Ellen gave it to Tom for Christmas one year. He played with it a couple of times, but he really has no aptitude for carving," Jill explained with an indulgent smile. "I'm sure he wouldn't mind if you wanted to use it while you're here. It would give you something to do with your hands, anyway."

Practically salivating at the thought of using the set, Rio hid his reaction behind a shrug. "I might try them out, if you're sure Tom wouldn't mind. Looks like they need to be cleaned and sharpened to keep them in good condition."

"There's a sharpening set and some blocks of wood somewhere in that cupboard. Help yourself. You need anything else? Something to drink? A snack?"

He shook his head, his attention focused on the knives. "No, thanks. I'm still full from lunch."

"I'll get back to the laundry, then. Call me if you need anything."

"Yeah. Uh, thanks."

She smiled at him, reaching out as if to pat his shoulder. He watched her draw back immediately when she realized what she'd almost done. His shoulders tingled as if she'd actually made the contact, and his fingers tightened around the box of knives. Biting her lip, Jill turned and all but ran from the room.

Rio muttered a curse beneath his breath and opened the cupboard again to look for the carving supplies.

Jill pulled off her apron and folded it, placing it in its drawer. Dinner was ready and it was time to call the family. She quickly checked her appearance in the mirror on the wall behind the table, a habit she'd fallen into since Rio's arrival. The kitchen door burst open behind her and she turned to find Gordie skipping around her feet, holding something up for her attention.

"Jill, look. Rio did it. Isn't it awesome?"

"Be still so I can look at it," Jill admonished him, amused at his uncharacteristic enthusiasm. She took the small wooden carving from her nephew's hands, then gasped when she studied it more closely. "Gordie, this is beautiful! It looks exactly like Dancer."

"I know. He made it for me. He said I could keep it if I'd clean his wood shavings off the porch for him."

Jill smiled, still studying the beautiful carving of the horse in full gallop, with intricately detailed mane and tail flying. "And did you?"

"You bet."

Tom pushed through the swing door, Sharon at his heels. "Dinner ready?"

"Yes. Tom, did you see this?"

"Yeah, Gordie showed me. It's good, isn't it?"

"Better than good. It's brilliant."

"It's just a carving," Rio grumbled, flushing as he swung himself into the kitchen in time to hear Jill's praise.

"Rio, it's wonderful!" she enthused. "I've seen carvings like this sell for a great deal of money at craft stores and art shows. Have you ever shown your work?"

He shook his head, reminding her of Gordie when he was embarrassed. "It's just a hobby. Usually when I work with wood it's on a construction crew—like your brothers."

"Rio said he'd make a unicorn for my collection, didn't you, Rio?"

He smiled faintly at Sharon as he headed for the table. "I'll try. I haven't seen a lot of unicorns to model it after, though."

"I'll show you my collection later," she promised earnestly, pulling her chair away from the table. "I've got lots of them."

"All right. I'll look at them later."

Jill wanted to say more about his carving talent but sensed that he wanted her to stop. Sighing, she handed the palm-size horse to Gordie and hurried to pull Rio's chair out for him. He thanked her with a smile, their eyes locking for a moment. By the time that brief, silent exchange of glances ended, Jill felt shaken, her pulse racing. Moistening her lips, she turned away as soon as Rio was comfortably seated.

Noticing that Tom was watching her with a vague frown, she flushed and picked up the platter of fried chicken to begin serving dinner.

Doc Curtis folded his stethoscope and shoved it into his medical bag after looking Rio over Wednesday evening. "Healthy as a horse," he pronounced. "We should be able to change you into a walking cast by Monday."

Leaning comfortably against one wall of Gordie's bedroom, Tom grinned. "If he's healthy as a horse, maybe I should be taking care of him."

Doc scowled and shook a stubby finger at his son. "You stick to your animals and leave people to real doctors. You wanted to work on folks, you should've done what I said and gone to medical school."

Tom shook his head, unruffled by the familiar argument. "People are too much trouble. Animals don't give you any back talk and they take much better care of themselves. *You*'re stuck with the tough patients like Rio, here."

Sitting bare-chested on the edge of the twin bed he temporarily occupied, Rio only smiled. "I resent that," he said mildly. "I've been a model patient, haven't I?"

"Humph," Doc muttered skeptically. "Did you stay in bed a couple of days like I recommended? Have you been getting plenty of bed rest? No. You were up the very next morning and haven't been down for a midday nap since, according to Jill."

"There's no pleasing him, Rio. Haven't you figured that out yet?" Tom drawled, amused by having the scolding turned to his houseguest.

Rio shrugged. "Some folks are like that."

"Couple of smartasses," Doc muttered, though his blue eyes twinkled with humor when they met Rio's. "You fit right in with this family, boy."

Rio's smile faded abruptly. He didn't respond to Doc's comment, since he knew better than to allow himself to start feeling like he fit in. All too well, he knew how painful the consequences of such foolish naiveté could be when everything fell apart, when it was inevitably pointed out that he did not—could not—belong.

One hand pressed to his back, Doc stretched and looked around the repulsively decorated room, his lip curling with distaste. "Beats the hell out of me why you let that boy keep those trashy posters on his walls," he grumbled. "It's enough to give a grown man nightmares. How's he ever going to get over this stage of his if you encourage it like this?"

Tom shrugged, looking oddly helpless for all his size and maturity. "I don't know what else to do," he admitted. "Every time I try to interfere, Gordie clams up and withdraws from us completely. The only way we can stay in any contact with him is to humor him, right now. The school counselor's convinced it won't last much longer if we'll just hang in there with it.''

Rio bit his inner lip to keep from expressing his own opinion about the school counselor. *It's none of your business,* he reminded himself flatly, reiterating his conviction that he had no place in this family. *You're only passing though*.

''Yeah. Well, you remember that time I found a bunch of nudie pictures taped to the wall of your tree house? You remember what *I* did?'' Doc demanded.

Chuckling quietly, Tom nodded. ''You ripped them to shreds and threatened to put a nude photograph of me in your waiting room if you saw any more of them. I was so mortified at the very idea that I didn't look at another girlie magazine until I went away to college. Even then, I couldn't enjoy them for thinking about how close I'd come to being the laughingstock of the area.''

''I wanted you to learn a lesson in human dignity,'' Doc agreed. ''And you did. You make Gordie take these posters down and get rid of those masks, and I bet you he'll start getting a more cheerful outlook on life.''

Tom sighed and shoved his hands into his pockets. ''Let me try it the counselor's way for a little longer, Dad. After all, she has training in this sort of thing.''

''If you ask me, she's a fruitcake,'' Doc muttered. ''What do you think, Rio?''

Uncomfortable at having his opinion asked, Rio pulled his sweatshirt over his head and tried to think of a response that wouldn't really commit him to anything. ''I'm afraid I don't know much about child psychology,'' he answered honestly.

"Me, either," Doc agreed. "But I raised me a son without it just fine. Turned out to be a good man, too, even if he was damned stubborn in his career choice."

"Let's go have some of Jill's pumpkin pie," Tom suggested, changing the subject. "She made it this afternoon just because she knew you'd be here this evening."

Doc brightened humorously. "Well, why didn't you say so? Here we've been wasting time with this guy while we could've been eating Jill's pie. Better grab those crutches and come on, boy. I ain't promising to save any for you."

Rio was sitting on the porch later that evening, idly pushing the porch swing with his good foot as he listened to the sounds of crickets and frogs singing a last farewell to warm weather when the front door opened and Jill stepped out.

Seeing him, she started. "I thought you'd gone to bed," she explained, one hand at the throat of her white cotton sweater, as if his presence had caused her pulse to beat there. Rio knew his own had abruptly changed rhythm. That was no way to ignore his attraction to her, he admonished himself sternly.

"I was enjoying the peace," he managed evenly enough. "Nice out here, isn't it?"

"Very. I didn't mean to disturb you. I'll—"

"Jill," he interrupted, annoyed that she looked ready to bolt from his presence. Despite the warnings of his common sense, he patted the swing beside him. "Sit down."

Warily, she closed the front door and approached him, perching on the edge of the swing as far away from him as physically possible. "We'd better turn in soon," she said, her voice just a shade too loud. "I'll be waking the kids up early in the morning for school, as usual. I'm afraid I can't help disturbing you, since you're sharing a room with Gordie."

"I don't mind you waking me up in the mornings," Rio murmured, shifting so that he faced her more fully, his cast stuck out in front of him, his other foot starting the swing in leisurely motion again.

Though Jill was fully dressed by the time she entered the room each morning—he suspected that was on account of him, that she'd probably worn a gown and robe before he'd arrived—there was still something soft and vulnerable about her that always got to him then. It was getting progressively harder not to taste her sleep-softened lips when she gave him his first smile each morning.

Jill cleared her throat. "Doc said you're healing very quickly. He said you should be out of the cast in another four weeks or so."

"Yeah. None too soon, either," Rio agreed ruefully. "Damn leg itches like crazy."

"I'm sure you'll be glad to get rid of these crutches, too."

He nodded. "It'll feel good to be mobile again."

She looked away from him, seeming to focus on something in the front yard. "So, where will you go when you're back on your feet again?"

It was the first time she'd asked him such a personal question since that first day he'd been out of bed, when he'd told her that he was a drifter with no particular place he called home, supporting himself by doing odd jobs as he traveled cross-country. Despite his reluctance to discuss the future, he knew it was best to make his position clear from the beginning. If she was really as attracted to him as he was to her, she needed to know right off that he wouldn't be staying any longer than necessary.

"I thought I might head for the East Coast. I'm as far east now as I've ever been. I'd kind of like to see the Atlantic."

"I've never seen the Atlantic, either," she admitted, and then laughed wryly. "Or the Pacific, for that matter. I haven't traveled much at all."

"Would you like to?"

"Someday," she answered vaguely. She glanced sideways at him. "Don't you ever get tired of it? Don't you ever want to settle down to a home and a family, like most people?"

"'The mass of men lead lives of quiet desperation,'" he quoted softly, thinking wistfully of a tattered, beautifully bound old book stashed with his carving knives in his stolen duffel bag. "Why should I want to join them?"

"Thoreau," Jill sighed. "I should have known. You've probably memorized *Walden*. All that stuff about making the best time when traveling alone and marching to a different drummer."

At least she didn't seem surprised that he'd read Thoreau, as others had when he'd quoted him in the past. Some people thought that just because he chose to live on the road, it stood to reason he wasn't particularly intelligent. Nor did it surprise him that Jill was well-read, despite her admittedly sheltered background. "You sound as though you don't approve of my life-style," he murmured.

"No more than you do mine," she pointed out, obviously remembering his questions about whether she was content to take care of Tom's family by putting her own life on hold.

Rio couldn't resist reaching out to catch a lock of her collar-length hair between his fingers, fascinated by the way the moonlight gleamed in its multicolored strands. "We don't have a great deal in common, do we?"

She went very still, her eyes searching his face. "No," she whispered.

His thumb stroked her unsteady lower lip. He was about to do something really stupid—but it wouldn't be the first time, he told himself fatalistically. "I want to kiss you, Jill. I've been wanting to kiss you from the first time I saw you."

Her throat worked with her nervous swallow. "That's not a very good idea."

"No," he agreed. "But knowing so doesn't stop me from wanting." He leaned closer, watching for her reaction. If she showed any sign of resistance, he'd stop.

Her eyelids drifting downward, Jill leaned forward, meeting him halfway. Their lips were less than an inch apart when she gasped and pulled back.

Quivering with frustration, Rio bit back a groan.

"We can't do this," Jill whispered frantically. "What about Gypsy?"

Thoroughly confused, Rio stared at her. "What does my sister have to do with anything?"

Her eyes widened in a way that would have amused him at any other time. "Your *sister?*"

"Well, yeah. Who'd you think she was?"

"I—" She stopped and shrugged. "I thought she was—"

"A lover?"

Jill nodded.

Rio couldn't help smiling a little. "She'd get a kick out of that."

As if the interruption had brought her to her senses, Jill shoved herself out of the swing. "It really is getting late," she said, twisting her hands nervously in front of her. "I think I'll go to bed now."

Rio exhaled deeply and reached for his crutches. "Yeah, me, too. I might wake Gordie up, and he needs a full night's sleep for school tomorrow."

Jill held the front door open until he'd gotten through, then closed and locked it behind them. "Need any help getting to Gordie's room?"

"No, I can make it."

"All right. I'll go make sure the kitchen door's locked. Good night, Rio."

"Night." He watched as she turned and left the room. Then, with a viciously muttered expletive, he swung himself awkwardly around on the crutches and hobbled off to bed, knowing it would be a long, uncomfortable night.

Hearing Rio making his way down the hallway toward Gordie's bedroom, Jill exhaled and sank bonelessly into a kitchen chair.

His sister. Gypsy was Rio's sister.

And he'd claimed that he'd wanted to kiss Jill since that first day, despite his very clear warning that he'd soon be moving on.

Hiding her face in her hands, Jill reflected grimly on the odd whims of fate, which had brought the enigmatic stranger into her previously safe, insulated life. She'd wanted him to kiss her more than she'd ever wanted anything before. And she'd known that one kiss from him would never be enough.

What was she going to do? she wondered bleakly, her shoulders slumping.

Chapter Five

Rio wasn't sleeping. The telephone ringing in the middle of the night had awakened him, after which he'd heard Tom leave the house on one of his animal emergencies. Lying in the narrow twin bed, staring at the ceiling, Rio thought of Jill in her room just down the hall. He cursed the one-day-old walking cast that prevented him from tiptoeing down that hallway—the same cast that kept him from rolling out of bed, jumping on his bike and getting as far away from her as possible.

It was Tuesday night, almost a week since that near kiss on the porch swing. Jill had gone back to the dancing-just-out-of-reach routine, treating him much as she did Gordie. And Rio was slowly going out of his mind.

Maybe it had been too long since he'd been with a woman. Maybe it was boredom making Jill so appealing. Or maybe for the first time in his life he was in danger of falling for a woman, and falling hard.

He really had to get away from here. Soon. *Gypsy, where the hell are you?*

He'd talked to his sister again only the day before, and she'd assured him she was doing her best to hurry to him. He'd given directions to the house, then explained that he was staying with a widowed father of two and the children's aunt.

"Oh? And just how old is this aunt, anyway?" Gypsy had asked with the uncanny perception she so often displayed.

"Four years younger than you are," he told his twenty-nine-year-old sister, his tone not encouraging any more questions.

"Pretty?" she'd asked, totally ignoring the hint.

"Yeah, I guess," he'd muttered.

"So why are you in such a hurry for me to get there?"

Unable to respond appropriately to her teasing, Rio had abruptly changed the subject.

He closed his eyes, wishing he could get back to sleep.

"No, no, no! *Mom!*"

The bloodcurdling scream from the next bed brought Rio abruptly upright, struggling to swing the heavy cast over the edge of the bed so he could get to Gordie, who was sobbing loudly into his pillow. Cursing his awkwardness, Rio finally managed to sit on the side of his bed, but Jill rushed through the door and beat him to the boy.

"Sweetheart, it's all right. It was only a bad dream," she crooned, drawing the shivering, whimpering child into her arms. "Don't cry, Gordie. I'm here."

"Jill?" Gordie murmured brokenly.

"Yes, darling. It's all right. Don't be afraid."

Rio felt his throat tighten, remembering nightmares from his own youth. Maybe if there'd been someone to hold *him* then, someone who loved him . . . maybe things would be different for him now. But there'd been only him. And

Gypsy. He pushed aside memories of holding his sister's hand through long, lonely nights, both of them wondering what the next day would bring.

He watched as Gordie stiffened and shoved himself out of his aunt's arms, swiping angrily at his tear-streaked face. "I'm not afraid of anything."

Jill tossed a helpless look at Rio before turning back to her nephew. Sitting on the edge of the bed, looking soft and approachable with her hair tousled and a fluffy robe loosely belted around her, she reached out to lovingly stroke Gordie's hair. "Wouldn't you like to talk about it, sweetheart? Is there anything that's bothering you?"

"Nah. Sharon's the one who's the scaredy-cat, afraid of the dark. Not me." Gordie's voice was gruff with bravado, despite the lingering tremor. Rio felt like shaking some sense into the kid. Didn't he know that Jill only wanted to help him? Why was he so determined to hold her away?

Jill sighed, defeated. She tucked Gordie in and stood, hovering **at** the foot of the bed. "Call me if you need me."

Gordie only shrugged and turned his back to her. Jill looked at Rio and spread her hands in a gesture of utter bafflement. He mimicked the gesture to indicate that he didn't know what to do, either.

Their gazes held for a long moment. The shadowy room, the silence surrounding them, added a sense of intimacy to the exchange. Rio felt his heart start a slow, dull pounding as his mind filled with images of removing her fluffy robe and whatever was beneath it, laying her back on a soft pillow, and finally, finally, tasting that lush, unpainted mouth.

As if those images were seeping from his mind into hers, Jill moistened her lips, her breasts rising and falling with her quickening breaths. She took a step back, then turned abruptly and left the room, murmuring a quiet good-night over her shoulder.

Left aroused and frustrated, Rio clenched his fists and threw himself back on the bed, one arm over his eyes. *Damn.*

"Rio?"

The soft question distracted him from his mental cursing. "Yeah, kid?"

"Sorry I woke you up."

"Don't worry about it. You okay?" He wanted to say more, but what did he know about talking to troubled adolescents?

"Yeah, I'm okay. Just a stupid nightmare."

"You—uh—you want to tell me about it?"

"Nah. I don't even remember it, really."

Deciding Gordie needed to regain his pride, Rio tried to sound casually sympathetic. "Yeah. Happens to everybody sometimes."

"You, too?" The question was meant to be offhand, but an underlying quiver told Rio that it was important to Gordie to believe that Rio understood.

He thought again of those long-ago nightmares. Like Gordie, he'd called for his mother, only to wake up to the grim awareness that she wasn't there to answer his cries. "Yeah, kid. Me, too."

"You're not afraid of anything, either, are you, Rio?"

Rio took a deep breath, sensing that his answer could be very important in reaching this troubled boy. "Everybody's afraid sometimes, Gordie. Even me. Best thing to do is talk it out with someone. Your dad, or Jill. Someone who really cares about you."

"Could I—" Gordie hesitated a long time, then finished tentatively "—maybe I could talk to you sometime?"

Come on, kid. Give me a break. What do you think I can do for you that your family can't? "Sure, Gord-o," he said anyway. "You can talk to me." And then he felt compelled to add, "Of course, I'll be moving on soon, so..." He let the sentence trail off.

Gordie sighed. "I know. But thanks anyway, Rio. Night."

"Night, kid."

Rio lay awake long after Gordie's breath had slowed to a deep, even rhythm, wishing he could escape into sleep so easily.

Sitting in a deep rocker in the family room, Jill snuggled her tiny nephew close, then laughed when the baby immediately began to root at her breast. "Might as well give it up, Timothy," she said, shifting the baby to her shoulder. "You're destined for disappointment there."

"He couldn't possibly be hungry again," the baby's mother Cissy, exclaimed. "I just fed him not fifteen minutes ago."

"I don't think he's really hungry," Jill assured her. "He's fine now." Aware that Rio was watching her from his seat across the room, she turned to another sister-in-law, ignoring him. "I forgot to ask you, Margaret. What did Doc say about Ty's ears?"

Rusty's plump, dark-haired wife smiled in visible relief. "He said they looked much better yesterday. He doesn't think it'll be necessary to put the tubes in after all."

"That is good news," Anita, Paul's wife and the third Hammond in-law exclaimed. "It was such an ordeal when Kyle had to have them. I was really worried that Amanda would have the same problem, but so far we've been lucky with her."

Jill joined in the discussion of the health of her nine nieces and nephews, her two years' experience with Gordie and Sharon making her a qualified participant despite being the only woman in the room who wasn't a mother. Her own mother, Ruth Hammond, seated beside Cissy on the couch, listened anxiously to every word about her grandchildren, between trips outside to check on the young brood being supervised at play in the yard by the oldest cousins.

"Can't you women hold it down?" Mike complained from the floor in front of the television on which a Saturday afternoon football game played. "Us guys are trying to watch the game."

"We could always talk about why poor Mike isn't married yet," Anita suggested sweetly, bringing up a topic so familiar that Mike groaned.

"Yes, Mike. I have several young women I'd love to introduce you to," Cissy added. "They all have such nice personalities."

Mike grumbled as the others in the crowded room laughed—everyone but Jill, who'd seen the look on Mike's face when Anita had brought up marriage. Only Jill knew that Mike had proposed a few months earlier to a longtime girlfriend, whom he'd stopped seeing after she'd turned him down. He'd told her about it—everyone in the family eventually came to her with their problems—but he'd sworn her to secrecy.

"Guess they told you, Mike," Jill said cheerfully, wanting only to make him smile naturally again.

"Look who's talking," he retorted, his smile spreading. "I'm not the only single person in the room."

"Any more of that cheese dip left, Jill?" Tom interrupted, giving her a wink.

She smiled gratefully at him. "In the kitchen. And there are more chips in the pantry."

"Good." He stood and made his way carefully through the tangle of chairs and sprawled bodies in the room. "If this family grows any more there won't be room for us in here, anyway," he muttered as he left.

"Daddy, Daddy! Someone's coming!" Sharon yelled from the front porch where she was playing a game with some of her cousins. "In a fancy red car!"

Jill's hold tightened on the infant sleeping peacefully in her arms. She looked quickly across the room to Rio, who'd instantly turned away from the television at Sharon's announcement, indicating that he, too, suspected the caller was his sister. Her chest began to ache at the thought of Gypsy taking him away, perhaps that very afternoon.

He'd been with them only three weeks and already Jill couldn't imagine having him gone. She'd come to rely on his companionship, the quiet conversation during their time alone, having him seated across from her at the table. She'd become addicted to the electricity that sizzled through her veins each time he gave her one of his rare, slow smiles, and the long, shared looks of acknowledged, though resisted, mutual attraction. She wished she'd let him kiss her on the porch. At least then, she wouldn't be left wondering what it would have been like if he had.

"Rio, Rio! There's someone out here who says she's your sister!" Sharon blurted, bursting through the front door.

"Ask the lady to come in, Sharon," her grandmother admonished, standing to hurry toward the door.

Jill also stood, still holding Timothy, her heart in her throat. Her eyes were on the doorway when her mother ushered Gypsy inside.

The woman was exotically, dramatically beautiful. Jet-black hair tumbled in a riot of curls to the middle of her back. She surveyed the room with large, outrageously made-up eyes of sparkling ebony, her Marilyn Monroe mouth tilted in a brilliant smile. A couple of inches taller than Jill, she wore her trendy, brightly colored clothes with a flair that Jill couldn't help envying.

Jill noted that the men in the room, with the exception of Rio, had all come to their feet, dazzled by the woman who stood out from the rest like a tropical flower in a field of plain white daisies. Even the women appeared fascinated by the unexpected guest.

The woman looked quickly around the room, apparently unperturbed by the attention she was receiving from so many strangers. "Hi, everyone. I'm Gypsy." And then she spotted Rio. "Oh, there you are."

Making her way to him with a well-practiced sway of slender hips, she leaned over to kiss his cheek, leaving a smudge of crimson on his skin when she pulled away. "How's the leg?"

He nodded toward the cast stuck out in front of him. "See for yourself."

"Poor baby. Are you in pain?"

He shook his head. "I'm fine."

Gypsy turned back to the others. "You must be the generous people who have been so very kind to my brother during his misfortune. I want you to know that I'm grateful to you."

"We've all become quite fond of Rio," Jill's mother answered for everyone, smiling. "I'm Ruth Hammond and this is my family. My husband, Ray, our son Paul and his wife, Anita, Rusty and Margaret, Gabe and Cissy, and our son, Mike, and our daughter, Jill." Each Hammond smiled and nodded at Gypsy when introduced. Jill was well aware that her own smile was rather strained.

"Oh, and this is Tom Curtis, my son-in-law," Ruth added when Tom came back in from the kitchen, arms loaded with chips and a big bowl of dip. "Tom, this is Rio's sister Gypsy."

Jill happened to be looking at Tom when he first spotted Gypsy. She couldn't quite analyze the expression that fleetingly crossed his face, but it was one she'd never seen there before. And then it was gone and he looked the same as always, his pleasant face creased with his warm smile. "Nice to meet you, Gypsy."

Gypsy gave him a long, thoughtful look. "Hello."

"This is Tom's house," Rio explained. "Everyone else is here visiting for the afternoon."

"I wondered how many bedrooms this house had," Gypsy said with a laugh. "It didn't look quite big enough to hold this roomful of people, much less all those kids running around outside."

Tom grinned, depositing the chips and dip on the coffee table. "Only two of those kids are mine. The others will be going home soon. Thank goodness."

As soon as Tom's hands were free, Gypsy extended her right one to him. "I want to thank you for taking Rio in, Tom. Not many people would have been so kind and generous to a stranger."

Tom took her hand in his, his smile deepening. Jill noticed the handshake lingered a bit longer than was strictly necessary. "It was our pleasure," he replied politely.

Timothy woke suddenly with a startled cry. Squirming in Jill's arms, he announced lustily that he was hungry. Cissy reached for him. "We'd better be going soon, Gabe. Is the game almost over?"

Her husband glanced at the television. "It's over now," he answered, seemingly surprised. "The Raiders won."

"All right! Rusty, you owe me ten bucks," Mike exclaimed.

"I'll take it off the twenty I loaned you last week," his brother replied before turning to his wife. "You ready to go, Margaret?"

Half an hour of semichaotic leavetaking later, the house was empty except for its usual residents, in addition to Rio and Gypsy.

"Whew," Tom sighed, shaking his head wryly. "It always seems so quiet when the clan leaves. That's what I get,

I guess, for having the only house big enough to accommodate everyone.''

"You love having them here and you know it," Jill accused him, trying not to show her anxiety about what Rio would do now.

Perched on the arm of her brother's chair, Gypsy smiled. Jill thought she looked vaguely wistful. "It must be nice to be a part of such a big, close family."

"It is," Tom answered. "But it takes some adjustment. I was an only child and my mother died when I was very young, so for several years it was only my father and me. Marrying into such a big family was a bit of a shock at first, even though I'd known the Hammonds all my life."

"Except for Rio, I've been pretty much alone for so long that I'm not sure I could ever make an adjustment like that," Gypsy said with a laugh, though Jill wondered if the wistfulness didn't still linger behind the breezy words.

"Oh, I expect you could, given the right incentive," Tom murmured.

Whatever Gypsy may have said in response was lost when Gordie and Sharon dashed into the room, having put away the toys that had been strewn about during their cousins' visit. "Everything's straightened up now," Sharon announced, shoving her glasses higher on her nose as she eyed Gypsy with poorly concealed curiosity.

"Very good, Sharon," Jill told her, smiling approval.

Tom stood between the siblings, his hands on their shoulders. "Gypsy, these are my children, Gordie and Sharon. Kids, this is Rio's sister, Gypsy."

Visibly dazzled by the strikingly beautiful woman, Sharon ventured close enough to hold out her hand in what she obviously hoped was a very grown-up gesture. "It's nice to meet you, Gypsy. I like your name."

"Thank you, Sharon," Gypsy replied gravely, politely shaking the small hand. "I like yours, too."

Sharon blushed, immediately won over.

Gordie wasn't so easily charmed. "Are you here to take Rio away?" he demanded belligerently.

"I'm here to collect him," Gypsy agreed, smiling winningly.

Refusing to return the smile, Gordie glowered. "He can't travel yet. His leg's still not healed. He couldn't even get it in that little car of yours."

"Gordie—" Jill admonished, wanting nothing more than to side with him.

"We'll manage, Gord-o," Rio assured the boy. "You knew I had to leave sometime."

"Couldn't you stay until your leg is well? Who's going to take your cast off? How's Doc going to know if everything's all right? Where will you go?" Gordie looked as though he were fighting tears. Both Rio and Gypsy seemed uncomfortable with the child's distress.

"I don't mean to pry, but *do* you have anyplace to go?" Tom asked Rio, with a quick sideways glance at Gypsy.

Rio shrugged. "We'll manage," he repeated.

"Why don't you both stay here, at least until you're out of the cast?" Tom suggested. "You can't work in that thing, and Gordie's right about how uncomfortable you'd be, trying to fit into a sports car. There's plenty of room here for the both of you for the next three weeks."

Jill caught her breath, tensing as she awaited the answer.

"Oh, we couldn't do that," Gypsy said immediately, obviously startled by the generous offer. "Neither one of us is in a position to pay you for room and board and—"

"Which means you couldn't pay anyone else, either," Tom pointed out.

She grimaced. "I know. We'd have to go to our friend Amber in New Mexico. The three of us were in school together, and Rio and I keep in touch through her. She'd let us stay there awhile."

"I can sell the bike for enough to get us by until we're working again," Rio added.

"New Mexico's a long, hard car trip from here," Tom argued. "Rio, you'd be miserable. Why not wait until the cast comes off before starting on a trip that long?"

Obviously torn by the thought of her brother's discomfort, Gypsy looked from Rio to Tom, then quickly at Jill, who sat silently watching, afraid to second the invitation for fear that her voice would reveal how desperately she wanted Rio to stay.

"Would there be anything I could do to repay you if we stayed?" Gypsy asked tentatively. "Housework, maybe? Or I could do the cooking—I'm a pretty good cook."

"Of course you could help out," Tom answered heartily, making Jill turn to stare at him. Taking care of this household was *her* job! Shouldn't she have some say in this?

Seeming to understand Jill's unspoken questions, Tom smiled. "She can fill in for Debbie for the next three weeks," he told her, then looked back at Gypsy. "Debbie's my office manager. I'm a veterinarian—my office is attached to the back of the house. Debbie's leaving for a three-week Caribbean cruise Monday and Jill had planned to fill in, but that would mean a lot of extra work for her. If you'd be interested, you'd be doing us both a big favor."

"What would it entail?" Gypsy asked, obviously interested.

"Answering the phone, scheduling appointments, sending out notices for yearly checkups, accepting and logging payments—just the usual office-type stuff," Tom explained with a smile. "Think you can handle it?"

Gypsy's chin rose a full inch. "I can handle it."

"Good. I'll pay you—"

"You won't pay me anything," she interrupted flatly. "Rio and I will both still owe you even after your office manager returns."

Obviously aware that this was a point of pride and that he could not change her mind, Tom gave in. He glanced at Jill. "This will give you a chance to make those new school clothes for Sharon without sitting up nights."

Jill only nodded, uncertain what she felt at the moment. Their lives had already been disrupted by Rio's presence in the household for the past three weeks. What further changes would come about during the next three? And how quickly would the household revert to normal once these unconventional siblings were gone?

Something about the way Tom was looking at Gypsy bothered her. She hadn't seen him look at another woman—*really* look—since Ellen died. It was going to take some adjusting on everyone's part if he were ready to start dating again. But this woman was all wrong for him. Tom wasn't the type to get involved with a woman who was only passing through. He'd only be hurt if he—

Her thoughts skidded to an abrupt halt as it occurred to her that she was hardly in a position to criticize Tom for being fascinated by Gypsy. Hadn't she been fighting an equally unwise infatuation with Gypsy's equally unsuitable brother? And, judging by the dismay she'd felt at the thought of his leaving, she wasn't doing a very good job of resisting her attraction to him. Still, she hated the thought of Tom being hurt again.

Gordie, who'd been closely monitoring the adults' conversation, suddenly realized that Rio wasn't leaving immediately. His round face creased in a smile that blended his freckles together. "All right! You're staying."

"Only until the cast is off, Gordie," Rio seemed compelled to remind the boy. Jill told herself that she was glad he was so conscientious about not allowing Gordie to get too used to having him here, though the warnings so far had not prevented Gordie from becoming attached to his temporary roommate.

"You can sleep in my room, Gypsy," Sharon offered shyly. "I have twin beds, just like Gordie does in his room. Only my room's prettier," she added complacently. "I have flowers and unicorns and pretty dolls for my decorations, not ugly old posters and masks."

Though obviously a bit confused by the speech, Gypsy only smiled. "Thank you, Sharon. I'd be honored to share your room, if you don't mind."

"Hope you don't mind sleeping with a light on," Gordie said snidely, irked by Sharon's criticism. "Sharon's afraid of the dark. She's a scaredy-cat."

"I am *not* a scaredy-cat," Sharon protested, heatedly indignant.

"Gordie, Sharon," Tom warned.

Gordie pretended not to hear. "Are, too."

"Am not. Who keeps waking everybody up screaming in the middle of the night?" Sharon retorted, striking with the deadly accuracy of the average eight-year-old.

Gordie's face went deeply red. "Butt face," he muttered.

"That's enough! Another word out of either of you and you'll spend the rest of the evening in your rooms," Tom pronounced, scowling fiercely.

Both children subsided into glares that silently promised future retribution. Tom sighed and rolled his eyes in apology to his guests.

Jill thought that at least something was still normal in the Curtis household.

Chapter Six

Sunday passed in a blur of noise and confusion as various members of Jill's curious family dropped by a few at a time to subject Gypsy to the same not-so-subtle examination they'd given Rio in the beginning.

"I think you passed, kid," Rio murmured later that evening while he and Gypsy sat on the porch swing, enjoying a few moments of peace. Jill was tucking Sharon into bed, Tom helping Gordie with math homework. It was the first time Rio and Gypsy had been alone since the family had come home from church at noon.

Gypsy laughed rather wearily. "It was a test, wasn't it? All the Hammonds were making sure I wasn't going to steal the grocery money out of the cookie jar."

Rio shrugged. "I don't think it was quite that drastic. They're just a close family and very protective of each other. They're nice people, though. Once they decide they like you, they take you in like a long-lost relative."

"I've never known anyone quite like them."

"Neither have I. I like them, though."

"I think I do, too. I'll let you know after I've rested up from the friendly inquisition."

Rio draped an arm over the back of the wooden seat, his good foot gently rocking the swing. "Looking forward to going to work in the morning?"

Chuckling, Gypsy pushed a long dark curl out of her face. "I just hope I don't do irreparable damage to Tom's office. We owe him enough already."

"*I* owe him," Rio disputed flatly. "As soon as I'm on my feet, I'll get a job and pay him back. Working in his office will take care of your own room and board."

"I sent that travel article off Friday. As soon as I get paid for it, I'll loan you what I can to help you repay them."

"Gypsy—"

"Rio," she cut in firmly. "You're my brother. How many times have you come through when I needed some extra cash? Now shut up and say 'Thank you, Gypsy.'"

"I can't do both."

She smiled at him. "Then just shut up."

He couldn't help smiling back. Gypsy had always been able to make him smile.

It was a beautiful, clear evening. The air was just turning cool on this last Sunday in September, a whiff of autumn in the breeze ruffling his hair. Leaning back more comfortably in the swing, he gazed at the stars and listened to the sounds coming from inside the house, wondering what Jill was doing now.

"She's very nice."

Startled, Rio turned his head to frown at Gypsy, wondering if his sister's eclectic talents now included mind reading. "Who?"

Her expression was sly. "Jill. The woman you've been pretending not to watch all day."

"She's okay." He tried to sound convincingly casual.

"More than okay, judging from the way you were looking at her."

"Drop it, Gypsy."

"I'm not criticizing," she assured him. "From what little I've seen so far, I like her. I think you make a nice couple."

"We don't make any kind of a couple. In a few weeks, I'm out of here. Remember?"

Gypsy tilted her head inquisitively. "You don't have to leave. You seem happy here. Maybe it's time you started thinking about settling down."

"Look who's talking."

"You think I don't get tired of traveling all the time, never having anyplace to really call home? You think I don't get lonely?"

Disturbed by a vague hint of sadness in her voice, Rio turned to face her more fully. "Have you been lonely, Gypsy?"

She looked away, trying as hard as Rio to sound casual. "Sometimes."

"Gyps—"

She patted his good leg. "Don't worry about me. We're talking about you, remember? You're obviously attracted to Jill, and you like her family. Why not give it a chance?"

He shook his head, wondering at her refusal to understand that a long-term commitment between himself and Jill Hammond would be doomed from the beginning. He wasn't the type to settle down, crawl into that nine-to-five rut, drive a station wagon and join a civic club. Surely Gypsy knew that as well as he did. "It just wouldn't work."

"But, Rio—"

"I don't want to talk about this, all right?" He knew his tone was more curt than usual, but he wanted the subject dropped. Now.

Gypsy sighed. "All right. I'm sorry. I didn't mean to butt into your business."

Feeling vaguely guilty, he reached out to run his knuckles along her cheek. "I know. Forget it."

The front door opened and Jill stepped out, putting an end to the conversation. "Can I get either of you anything?" she offered.

The porch light brought out the blond streaks in her honey-colored hair, turned her bright-blue eyes almost translucent. Rio felt his mouth go dry. He wished for the hundredth time that he'd never accepted a ride with the drunk in the pickup. How long would he be haunted by images of Jill, by memories of his time with her here? By regrets about what might have been, had he been a different kind of man?

"Thanks, but we're fine. It's a beautiful night, isn't it? Why don't you sit for a while and talk with us?" Gypsy offered warmly, gesturing toward a chair drawn close to the swing.

"All right." Jill sat down, arranging her bright red skirt around her knees, drawing Rio's gaze inexorably to her shapely legs. Minutes later, Tom joined them. They spent the next hour in quiet conversation, punctuated by soft laughter.

Rio was rather quiet, aware that it would be all too easy to start imagining he belonged here if he weren't very careful.

Jill had always considered herself healthy enough, both physically and mentally. Only one phobia had haunted her from childhood, and since most people had at least one private fear, she figured she was allowed hers. She'd made no effort to conquer it, depending instead on the nearest male—or nonphobic female—to rid her of the problem whenever it happened to confront her.

She was sitting at her sewing machine, working on a school dress for Sharon, when a movement captured by the corner of her eye made her turn. She immediately lifted both her feet into the chair and screamed, effectively trapped in her seat by the creature lurking on the floor between her and the only door.

It was a very large spider, dark and ugly. Jill was quite sure it licked its lips in anticipation as it crouched there, watching her. Usually she would have called for Tom or Gordie, or even Sharon, who had saved her aunt more than once with the judicious application of a flyswatter. Now she yelled for the only other person in the house with her. "Rio! Help!"

The spider took a slow, ominous step—or was it steps?— forward, and Jill shuddered, relieved to hear Rio's cast thumping rapidly toward her. He appeared in the doorway, bracing himself with one hand on the frame as he looked at her anxiously. "Jill? What's wrong?"

Somewhat sheepishly, she pointed to the floor. "Could you please get rid of that for me? I have this phobia, you see."

He looked down and immediately paled. "That's a spider."

"Yes," she breathed, shivering again when the creature moved an inch closer. "Please get rid of it."

Rio didn't immediately leap to her rescue. "It's a—uh— big one, isn't it?"

Something in his voice sounded all too familiar. Huddling more tightly in the chair, Jill looked at him suspiciously. "Rio? Please tell me you don't happen to share my phobia?"

He cleared his throat. "I'm not afraid of it," he assured her quickly, sounding curiously like Gordie when the boy tried to sound macho. "I just don't like spiders."

"Then you'll kill it?" she asked hopefully.

He looked at her. "You want me to kill it?"

"Unless you plan to shake hands with it and make friends," she retorted, fear adding a touch of asperity to her sarcasm. "I hate to push, but would you hurry? It looks hungry and I think—oh, hell, it's moving this way!—I think I'm lunch."

He ran a finger beneath the neck of his gray sweatshirt, as if it had suddenly become too tight, and looked around for a weapon. The pattern book he snatched off the small desk in the nearest corner was big and heavy enough to flatten a small animal. It landed with a satisfying *ker-thunk* on the spider. Just to make sure, Rio stepped on the book with his borrowed, too large sneaker.

"There," he said, exhaling deeply. "That should do it."

Jill couldn't help it. She buried her face in her hands and giggled. "My hero," she managed, looking up at him, only to start laughing in earnest at his chagrined expression.

"Hey, who killed the sucker?" he demanded, hands on his slender hips as he scowled at her in mock ferocity. "You'd have just sat there and let it make a meal of you if I hadn't saved you."

"Are you kidding?" She shook her head. "If it had moved one inch closer, I'd have long-jumped from this chair to that doorway."

He grinned. "Hell, if I'd known that, I'd have just stood back and caught you."

She stood and walked toward him, carefully side-stepping the pattern book. She'd wheedle Tom into cleaning it for her later, she thought, stopping in front of Rio. "How long have you been afraid of spiders?"

Grimacing, he shrugged. "Since I was a kid. I crawled under a house once, hiding from a well-deserved paddling after breaking a lamp with a basketball, and ended up covered with spiders. They were all over me. By the time I got out from under the house and had the spiders brushed off me, I was too hysterical for the punishment my foster father had intended to give me. He took me for ice cream, instead. I have never liked spiders since then."

Jill shuddered in dramatic empathy. "I think I'd have died of a heart attack, at least."

"I nearly did," he agreed with a sexy, one-sided grin.

Intrigued by his story, she tried to sound casual with her next comment, not wanting to break the unexpected intimacy of the moment. It was the first time Rio had voluntarily brought up his past, and she wanted desperately to know more. "Your foster father doesn't sound too bad. It was nice of him to take you for ice cream because you were upset."

"Yeah, he was one of the nicer ones," Rio answered offhandedly, his eyes suddenly distant, as though he were looking back in time. "We weren't there long, though. Six months after they sent us there, he was badly injured in a work-related accident. Gypsy and I were assigned to another home—one we didn't like nearly as well—and the other two kids that had been staying there were sent somewhere else. Never heard from the guy again."

She knew better than to express the aching sympathy she felt for him then. She knew Rio well enough by now to understand his dread of pity. And his tone hadn't encouraged any further questions. Instead, she reached out to touch his arm lightly. "Thank you for saving me from the spider. It was very brave of you to kill it when you dislike them so much yourself."

His fingertips brushed her cheek, then lingered to toy with one strand of her hair. "You're welcome." His smile deepened, sending a ripple of awareness down her spine as she stood so very close to him. "So, you want to rent Spielberg's *Arachnophobia* to watch together some rainy afternoon?"

She chuckled huskily. "I think I'll pass on that treat, thank you."

"Good. It's hard to act macho when you're watching TV with your hands over your eyes," he quipped, moving almost imperceptibly closer to her.

Jill felt her own smile tremble as she wondered with nervous anticipation if he was going to kiss her. She couldn't think of anything she wanted more at the moment. She tried to remember what he'd just said. Oh, yes. He'd made a joke. "A real tough guy, aren't you?"

"Tough enough," he murmured, his mouth tantalizing inches from hers. "Do me a favor, though, will you?"

She moistened her lips, her heart pounding so heavily in her throat that she had to clear it to speak. "Um—what?"

His breath warmed her moist mouth. "Next time you're faced with a spider that size—"

"Yes?" she whispered, lifting slightly toward him in encouragement.

He brushed his lips across the tip of her nose. "Dial nine-one-one."

And then he turned and walked away, whistling cockily. Glaring after Rio in frustrated disappointment, Jill decided that if her pattern book hadn't been smeared with spider-goo, she'd have probably thrown it at him.

Rio sat at the kitchen table Tuesday afternoon, watching Jill hand-hemming a lacy, ruffled doll dress. "That's really pretty," he told her.

She looked up from the froth of pink and white to smile at him. "Thanks. Think the doll will bring in some money for the school raffle?"

He chuckled. "It should. Judging from the way Gypsy oohed and aahed over it, she'd probably bid on it herself if she were here then."

Another subtle reminder that he was leaving soon. As if she needed it. She bit her lower lip and concentrated on attaching a row of lace to the hem of the dress.

After a moment, Rio squirmed restlessly in his chair, sighed and ran a hand through his hair, pushing it away from his face. "How are you at cutting hair?"

She lifted her head. "Who, me?"

He grinned. "I wasn't talking to the doll."

"I've trimmed Gordie's hair and Sharon's bangs, but that's the extent of my expertise, I'm afraid."

"Well, Gypsy's lousy at it. Last time she got through with me, I looked like I belonged in a heavy-metal band."

Jill giggled.

"No, really, I did," he assured her. "All I needed was a pair of skintight black leather pants and a leopard-print vest."

"I think you might be exaggerating just a bit," Jill accused.

He shrugged. "So, will you?"

She frowned. "You really want me to cut your hair?" She turned her attention to his luxurious black mane, secretly thinking it looked fine as it was, framing his strongly chiseled face and falling to his collar. More than once she'd had to fight the impulse to bury her fingers in it.

"Yes, please."

"Now?"

His grin deepened. "I can wait until you've finished what you're doing."

"What if I mess it up? I could do worse than Gypsy. You could look like Don Rickles when I get through."

Laughing, Rio tossed his head. "I trust you."

"But, Rio, you have such beautiful hair. You really should have it styled," she blurted without thinking.

His smile changed at her compliment, his eyes narrowing. "Thank you. But I'd rather have you."

Oh, help! Trying to convince herself that the double en-
tendre had been an unintentional one, she cleared her
throat and said rather gruffly, "All right. If you're sure you
want to risk it. I'll see what I can do after I attach this
lace."

"Thanks."

"Maybe you'd better wait until after I've cut it before
you thank me," she suggested wryly.

Twenty minutes later, Jill took a deep breath, shears in
hand, and caught a lock of Rio's thick hair in one slightly
unsteady hand. He sat confidently in front of her, a towel
draped around his neck to protect his navy sweat suit. She'd
already dampened his hair with a misting bottle to make it
easier to handle, but she was getting cold feet again at the
thought of making that first cut.

"You're sure you don't want to change your mind?"

"Just cut it, Jill."

She bit her lip, resisted the inappropriate urge to close her
eyes, and placed shears to hair. The first snip seemed to
echo throughout the room as a dark lock fell to the floor
beside her feet. Rio looked totally unconcerned.

Oh, well, she told herself. *If he doesn't care what it looks
like, why should I?*

It took a long time. Jill concentrated fiercely on every
cut, trying to follow the lines of the easy style he wore. Already his hair was drying, its lighter weight allowing it to
curl slightly at the ends and lie softly on his nape. Moving
to the front, she bent close to him, her fingers combing
through his hair, too deeply involved with her work to be
more than subliminally aware of his proximity. She did
wonder why he'd suddenly become so squirmy and restless
when he'd been so still until now.

"I'm trying to hurry," she assured him.

"Take your time," he replied, his voice huskier than
usual.

She trimmed a few uneven hairs, checked both sides with a comb, then examined the results. It didn't look bad at all, she decided in relief. Quite good, actually. Of course, it would be very hard to make Rio look anything less than wonderful. "I guess I'm finished. I'll get you a mirror."

He reached up to catch her wrist when she would have pulled away. "I don't need a mirror."

"But—"

Suddenly aware of just how close he was, she caught her breath. She was practically leaning into his lap, the deep scoop neckline of her blue-and-gray-patterned sweater level with his face. He'd had a clear, close-up view of her cleavage for the past several minutes.

Flushing hotly, she pulled at her wrist. He didn't release her. Instead, he ripped the hair-covered towel from around his neck and tugged sharply against her efforts, causing her to tumble into his lap. Trying to regain her balance, she braced her hands against his shoulders.

"Rio!"

He didn't bother to respond to her protest. His mouth covered hers before she could say anything else.

For just over three weeks she'd watched him, wondered about him. For just over three weeks she'd fantasized about what it would be like to kiss him. He'd upset all her routines in those weeks, and yet her life would have returned to normal, eventually, had he left the day Gypsy had arrived. Now he'd kissed her, and she knew her life would never be the same again. *She* would never be the same.

His mouth was hard, as she'd known it would be. And yet, softer than she might have expected.

His kiss was demanding, which didn't surprise her. And yet, tender, which did.

Her hands left his shoulder to circle his neck, pulling herself closer to him. Rio's arms locked around her, eliminating the half inch or so that had still separated them. Her lips parted in a gasp at the odd sensation of having her breasts crushed against his chest. He took advantage of the opening to slide his tongue into her mouth. Jill closed her eyes and melted into his lap.

The kiss ended only when oxygen became a necessity for both of them. A quick, sharp breath and they met again, heads tilted to a new angle, hands tentatively exploring. The hair Jill had cut with such determined objectivity became a source of sensual pleasure as she buried her fingers in its silky depths. His back was hard and warm beneath her other hand as she flattened it against his sweatshirt.

She arched like a languorous cat when Rio ran one palm down her spine to settle at the small of her back, holding her more firmly against him. His arousal was hard and throbbing beneath her bottom; she couldn't help squirming a bit, which made him inhale sharply, his fingers clenching into her thigh. Jill reveled in his reaction, distantly amazed that she could make him want her so obviously.

His tongue flickered, tormenting her as it advanced and retreated, swirled and dipped. Shyly at first, she imitated his motions, touching her tongue to his, following it into his mouth. Eyes closed, she concentrated on every moment, every sensation, memorizing his feel, his taste, his scent. *Rio.*

"Jill," he murmured, as if he'd heard her mind caress his name. "Damn, you feel good in my arms." He lowered his head to press his passion-warmed lips to her throat.

Her head falling back, Jill took a deep, ragged breath, her breasts aching for his touch, her body quivering with needs so new she only half understood them. She wanted him, wanted him, wanted him.

Arousal jolted through her when his hand eased around her to close over one swollen, throbbing breast, lifting it. His mouth trailed lower, caressing the skin in the scoop of her sweater, easing toward the soft mound he'd partially exposed. He was breathing hard, as was she; his hands were unsteady, as were hers. Jill froze in his arms, every nerve anticipating the first touch of his lips on her breast.

She could have screamed in frustration when the telephone rang, jerking them apart as effectively as an angry hand.

Standing two feet from his chair, she struggled to regain her composure as she stared at him. The telephone rang again, but she couldn't speak clearly enough to answer it yet. Rio pulled his eyes away first, muttering a curse as he shoved a hand through his disheveled hair.

Unable to ignore the telephone any longer, Jill reached for it. "Hello?" Thank heavens her voice sounded only slightly breathless, she thought gratefully.

The caller was the school nurse. Gordie, she explained, was complaining of a sore throat and running a slight fever. Probably the virus that had been going around, she added, downplaying the seriousness of the illness.

Jill sighed quietly. "I'll come get him. Thank you for calling."

She replaced the receiver. "Gordie's sick," she said, turning. "I have to—"

But no one was there to hear her.

Rio was getting very good on that cast, she thought wearily. She hadn't even heard him leave. Catching a glimpse of herself in the mirror above the table, she knew she'd have to comb her hair and splash cold water on her face before she could face the school nurse—or her nephew.

Trying desperately to put the last few minutes out of her mind until she had time to think about them in detail, she hurried toward her bedroom.

* * *

"Gordie, stop complaining and take your medicine," Jill said firmly, holding the spoon in front of her nephew's stubbornly closed mouth.

"It tastes horrible. If you put that in my mouth again, I'm going to puke," Gordie warned belligerently, his round face flushed with the fever that made him so cross.

"And if you don't cooperate with me, I'm going to have to get your father to give this to you. Do you really want me to do that?" Jill returned evenly, knowing what an effective threat she was using. Tom would tolerate no such nonsense from his son, and Gordie knew it.

With a deep, martyred sigh, the boy reluctantly opened his mouth, then made a great show of coughing and gagging when the medicine went down. "Seems like Doc could have prescribed something that didn't taste like barf," he complained.

Jill only smiled. "You know Doc. He loves torturing children," she answered teasingly, setting the spoon down so that she could arrange Gordie's pillows more comfortably behind him. "Now why don't you try to take a nap. You'll feel better if you do."

"I don't want a nap." But his eyelids were already growing heavy even as he made the flat statement.

"All right. Then just lie here quietly awhile. I'll be back to check on you in a few minutes." Jill knew he'd be asleep before she made it to the kitchen.

"Whatever."

Carrying the medicine bottle and sticky spoon, she slipped out of the room. Passing Sharon's room, she heard the familiar chorus of a favorite children's song tape playing as the little girl finished her homework. The evening news sounded from the television in the den. She assumed

Tom, Rio and Gypsy were all in there, watching. It was time for Jill to finish dinner.

She hadn't expected to find Gypsy in the kitchen, peeking under a lid to explore the various dishes cooking on the stove. Gypsy turned when Jill entered. "Oh, there you are. Is there anything I can do to help you with dinner?"

Still a little uncomfortable with Rio's glamorous sister, Jill moistened her lips. "Well, you could set the table," she said hesitantly.

Gypsy smiled, obviously pleased at having her offer accepted. "Of course." She opened a cabinet, having already discovered where most of the dishes were kept. "Everything smells wonderful. What's in the oven?"

"Pork chops and rice in mushroom gravy."

"And that green stuff in the back pan?" Gypsy pointed to the one she meant as she headed for the table, one arm loaded with plates.

"Turnip greens. Surely you've had them before?"

"Can't say I have. I'm always open to new dishes, though."

Jill stirred a pan of peas with a wooden spoon, lifting out the ham hock she'd used for seasoning. "Next you'll try to convince me you've never had black-eyed peas."

"So that's what those are."

Jill laughed. "Just what *do* you usually eat?"

"Oh, lots of salads and vegetable pasta dishes. Lately I've had a lot of seafood and veal in rather strange sauces. It's nice to have regular home cooking for a change."

Looking curiously at the other woman, Jill slid one hand into an oven mitt. "You travel a great deal, don't you?"

"Well, you have to, to make a living at writing travel articles," Gypsy explained. "And I enjoy seeing new places."

"Just like your brother, evidently."

Gypsy hesitated. "We both move around a lot," she conceded, "though he usually stays in this country and I'm out of it a lot. I'm not sure we travel for the same reasons, though.''

Intensely curious, Jill still hesitated to pry. "Oh?'' she asked noncommittally.

Gypsy tossed her heavy black curls over one shoulder and nodded. ''Yeah. I'm always looking for something and Rio's always running away. And don't tell him I said that, or he'll be furious. He'd deny it, of course.''

Jill did everything but bite her tongue and still couldn't help blurting out the question. "What's he running away from?''

Her dark eyes sad, Gypsy sighed. "Very unhappy memories.'' Setting the last plate in its place, she opened a drawer and grabbed a handful of silverware. "You see,'' she continued conversationally, "our mother died when we were just kids and we spent the rest of our childhood in foster homes until we were old enough to get out and take care of ourselves. Neither of us fared particularly well in the homes the state selected for us.''

"You weren't...abused?'' Jill asked, horrified.

"Oh, no,'' Gypsy assured her quietly. "Just never happy. Both of us started drifting as soon as we were old enough to be out on our own. I keep hoping to find something better, Rio seems to be trying to leave the memories behind. I think I've been more successful than he has, actually.''

Jill set the steaming baking dish on a trivet and stripped the oven mitt from her hand. "I'm sorry.''

Gypsy smiled faintly. "Thanks. Maybe you can understand him a little better now.''

Understand Rio? Could anyone ever do that, with the exception, perhaps, of his sister? Automatically finishing her dinner preparations, Jill wondered if even Gypsy knew all the workings of her brother's complex mind. Did his background explain why he was so uncomfortable with the strong family ties he'd found here? Had he convinced himself as a child in foster homes that he didn't want those ties, because he hadn't ever expected to have them?

Or was he really happy drifting from one place to another? From—she swallowed hard—one woman to another?

"Should I put ice in the glasses now?" Gypsy asked, breaking into Jill's heavy thoughts.

Jill straightened her shoulders and went back to work. "Yes, thanks. I hope you like iced tea. That's all I have tonight, other than milk."

"Iced tea is fine for me. What will the children have?"

"Sharon will want milk—oh, and she always drinks out of the Snoopy glass on the second shelf. I'll take Gordie's dinner to him when we've finished eating. He's sleeping now. The medicine Doc prescribed makes him drowsy."

At Jill's summons, the rest of the family came into the room—Tom first, followed by Sharon and then Rio. Jill met Rio's eyes when he entered, then felt herself flushing as she quickly looked away. Her gaze clashed with Tom's concerned scrutiny, and again she turned away, briskly serving dinner.

"Any picante sauce, Jill?" Tom asked, convincingly casual despite the searching look he'd given her.

She pulled a jar from the refrigerator and set it down in front of him before taking her own seat. Gypsy watched with interest as Tom liberally poured the spicy tomato sauce over his greens and black-eyed peas. "Do most people eat them that way?" she asked.

Tom grinned. "Most folks around here like a little pepper sauce on their greens and peas. I like the picante sauce better. And it has to be the kind made in San Antonio," he added solemnly. "Not that stuff from New Jersey."

Gypsy smiled back at him in a way that made Jill wonder just what was brewing between them. "I believe I'll try some."

Tom passed her the jar, his eyes holding hers for a long moment before accidentally meeting Jill's. She imagined that he looked as sheepish as she probably had when he'd caught her watching Rio.

Idiots, the both of them, she decided in exasperation. Both drawn to these unconventional siblings who were so totally wrong for them.

She was constantly aware of Rio throughout the remainder of the meal, even when they weren't speaking directly to each other. She suspected that he was just as aware of her, his own thoughts lingering on the passion that had flared between them in that very same kitchen only hours earlier.

"I'm always looking for something and Rio's always running away," Gypsy had said.

Would he soon be running away from Jill? And could she quietly stand by and let him go, even though he'd be taking her heart with him?

Chapter Seven

The unicorn took shape beneath the blade of the knife as Rio sliced again and again into the block of wood. He'd chosen to depict the animal rearing on slender back legs, long tail flaring out behind, mane flying, its single horn raised defiantly skyward. He'd never thought much about unicorns, but he visualized this one as a solitary, standoffish creature, proud of its individuality, fiercely protective of its elusive mystique.

Rio could identify with the animal he was carving.

He brushed wood shavings off the knee of the black sweat suit he'd selected that morning from his wardrobe of four similar suits. As soon as he was out of this cast, he was borrowing enough money from Gypsy to buy a couple of pairs of jeans, he decided. He was really getting tired of sweat suits. He was going to have to try to find a used jacket, too. It had just turned October and there was an occasional nip in the air now, especially at night.

Faint explosions of sound from inside the house made him look up briefly from the carving. Gordie was lying on the couch in the den, watching a noisy Ninja Turtles cartoon. It was his second full day home from school and the boy was rapidly growing bored. Jill had promised he could return to school the next day, Friday, if his fever from earlier in the week didn't reappear. Scratching ineffectively at the top of his cast, Rio wished he would be back on his own feet so quickly. He could certainly understand Gordie's restlessness.

A battered brown pickup pulled into the long driveway. Rio identified the single occupant as Jill's father, Ray. He didn't mind the interruption. He rather liked the quiet, laconically humorous man. Talking to Ray would give him something to do besides sit here and think about Jill, remembering the kisses they'd shared, wondering who'd been avoiding whom ever since.

Ray climbed the three steps to the porch with the same economical use of energy with which he did everything else. "How's the leg, boy?" he inquired, tugging at his faded yellow cap that advertised a major tool manufacturer.

"Still there," Rio responded, tapping his knuckles against the top of the cast. "How's it going, Ray?"

"That Quattlebaum woman is driving us all crazy. I had to leave before I said something I shouldn't. Paul's better at soothing difficult customers than I am. I'm on my way over to Harrison to check on the house Rusty's supervising, but I thought I'd stop by and see about Gordie first. How's he feeling?"

"Better. He's watching television now. Jill says he can probably go back to school tomorrow."

"Bet that just delighted him to no end," Ray drawled with a lazy grin.

Rio chuckled. "He groaned very loudly but I think he's looking forward to it. Not that he'd ever admit it, of course."

"No, he wouldn't do that." Ray watched as Rio went back to his carving. "You've got a real talent for whittling, Rio. I saw the horse you did for Gordie. That one for Sharon?"

"Yeah. She wanted one for her collection." Rio grimaced and held up the palm-size sculpture. "Does this look like a unicorn to you?"

"Don't know if it looks like a unicorn, being as I never saw one, but it's damn good," Ray answered. "You ever do any other woodwork? Cabinets, furniture?"

"I've done some cabinetwork," Rio admitted. "I usually find jobs on construction crews when I need cash. I've seen more than a few houses go up in the past few years."

"Yeah? You like the work?"

"As work goes, it isn't bad," Rio answered tactfully, knowing the Hammonds all enjoyed the construction business—well, all but Gabe, the banker.

Ray smiled at the cautious answer. "You know, my business has been pretty good lately. Mike's taken on the bidding and ordering full-time and Paul and Rusty are both supervising crews. I've been thinking about starting a third crew. How'd you like the job of foreman?"

"You're offering me a job?" Rio asked, startled. "As foreman?"

"Yeah. I've been watching you the last couple of weeks. I think you'd work out just fine. You're levelheaded, seem to get along with people."

"Not always," Rio murmured, absently running his thumb along the scar on his right cheek.

Ray followed the gesture with his eyes. "Yeah, well, everyone gets into a ruckus sometime. Especially when we're young. You interested?"

Rio framed his answer carefully, aware of how intently the older man was watching him, wondering what lay behind the offer. Did Ray suspect that something was going on between Rio and Jill? Was this his way of indicating that he didn't disapprove of the possibility? Or was it a test to find out whether Rio was serious about the budding relationship?

"I might be interested in a temporary job, until I could repay what I owe Doc and Tom. As far as a permanent position—well, I hadn't really thought about settling down here. Or anywhere, for that matter. I've been on the road since I was sixteen. I tend to get restless when I've stayed anywhere more than a few weeks."

"You feeling restless now?"

Rio resisted the urge to clear his throat. "I'm ready to get out of this cast," he answered truthfully, evading the real question.

"Guess you are, at that. Tell you what—why don't you think about my offer until the cast comes off. We can talk more about it then."

"I'll do that. Thanks, Ray."

"Don't mention it." Nodding as if the conversation had been satisfactorily concluded, Ray shoved himself out of the chair. "Guess I'll go in and see Jill and the boy for a few minutes before I head for Harrison. You need anything?"

"No, thanks." Rio watched Ray enter the house with a comfortable familiarity that Rio couldn't feel even after living here for nearly a month.

What was it with these people? he found himself wondering. Didn't they ever stop being kind and generous? They'd taken him in—a penniless, nameless stranger— doctored him, fed him, bought him clothes, given him a bed in the same house with their children. They'd treated him like one of the family, even taking in his flighty sister. And now Ray had offered him a job. As a foreman, no less.

He was beginning to worry about the bighearted Hammonds and Curtises. A good con man could make a killing with these people.

Or were they really as naively trusting as they appeared? Could it be that they somehow knew Rio wasn't a threat to them? Maybe they'd been nice to him just because they liked him. If so, it would be the first time he'd been accepted just for himself since...

Hell, it would be the first time.

He was getting too involved here. He was going to miss these people when his own demons drove him to move on. And he would leave. As nice as it had been, Ray's offer of a permanent position didn't exactly fill Rio with enthusiasm. Unlike Jill's brothers, Rio wouldn't be content reporting to a construction job every day for long. Even if it included the possibility of having Jill to come home to every evening.

No, it wouldn't work. He'd have to go. The least he could do was to try not to hurt anyone while he was here. He thought of the way Jill had looked at him after he'd kissed her, and his chest tightened painfully.

The screen door creaked and Rio looked up, expecting to see Ray again. Instead, Gordie stepped out, still rather hollow-eyed from his illness, but looking much better than he had a day or two before. "Mind if I sit out here with you for a while?" he asked diffidently.

"Not if Jill doesn't."

"She said it wouldn't hurt me to get some fresh air." Gordie draped himself bonelessly in the chair his grandfather had occupied, studying the unicorn Rio had almost completed. "You sure are good at that. You think you could teach me how to carve?"

"I don't know if your dad would want you using these knives yet," Rio answered carefully. "They're very sharp."

You could ask him, though. If he doesn't mind, I'd be glad to show you some things before I go."

Gordie's face fell. "I keep forgetting you'll be leaving in a few weeks," he muttered.

Rio knew he was in danger of forgetting that, himself. He wondered if he kept reminding Gordie of his imminent departure for the boy's sake, or for his own.

Her father had offered Rio a job. Staring sightlessly out the window above the kitchen sink, Jill thought about what Ray had told her before he'd left for Harrison. He'd explained that Rio hadn't been able to commit to an answer. She'd wondered if Ray had been subtly warning her that Rio wasn't ready to make *any* commitments.

The admonition hadn't been necessary. Jill was well aware that Rio had no intention of staying for much longer. Too bad her heart couldn't be as practical as her mind. Knowing she'd be hurt, she still wanted him, still found herself halfway in love with him.

Her grim reverie was interrupted by the chime of the timer on the stove. Turning it off, she reached for the brown pharmacy bottle beside the sink. It was time for Gordie to take his medicine. She carefully measured the dosage into a hollow, calibrated plastic medicine spoon, then carried the spoon with her as she walked into the den. Gordie wasn't on the couch, so he must still be outside with Rio.

She took a deep breath and stepped toward the open door, spotting her nephew through the screen. She couldn't see Rio, but she could hear Gordie talking to him. "She died in a car wreck," Gordie was saying.

Jill stopped short. Gordie was talking about his mother? But he *never* talked about Ellen!

"Yeah, I know," she heard Rio reply and the gentle sympathy in his deep voice brought a lump to Jill's throat. "I'm sorry, Gordie."

"It was a long time ago," Gordie said with a brave effort to sound casual.

Shaken by the unexpected reminder of her late sister, Jill took a moment to regain her composure before going outside. She wouldn't want Gordie to know he'd upset her. She was just about to move when Gordie spoke again. "Your mom died a long time ago, too, didn't she, Rio?"

"Yeah. She did." Jill could detect no emotion at all in Rio's voice this time.

"I guess, after a while, it stops hurting so bad, huh?" What might have been desperate hope colored the boy's voice, bringing hot tears to the backs of Jill's eyes.

It took a very long time for Rio to answer. When he did, his tone was gruff. "No, Gord-o. It doesn't ever stop hurting," he replied frankly. And then he exhaled slowly. "But you learn to let go of the anger eventually. I guess that's when you start to grow up."

"Have you ever let go of the anger, Rio?"

"I think—maybe—I'm learning to. Guess it's taking me longer to grow up than most guys."

Gordie shifted in his chair. "Yeah. Me, too," he muttered almost sheepishly.

"You'll be okay, Gordie. You're a lucky kid, you know? You've got a lot of people who care about you."

Gordie looked up at the man who sat out of Jill's vision, his expression, even in profile through the screen door, entirely too revealing. "Are you one of 'em, Rio?" he asked, trying so hard to sound as if it didn't particularly matter. Failing so pathetically.

Jill tensed, praying that Rio would answer compassionately. She should have known that he would. "Yeah, Gord-o. I'm one of 'em," Rio said quietly.

Gordie's smile was radiant. "Thanks, Rio. Want me to clean up those wood shavings for you?"

"Yeah, I'd appreciate it."

Jill stood frozen in place for another long moment, then turned and silently headed back for the kitchen, swiping at tears with her free hand. Gordie could take his medicine a little later.

She couldn't face Rio yet. She had just made the utterly stupid mistake of crossing that invisible line from being halfway in love with him to completely, totally in love. She needed time to hide those feelings. She couldn't bear to have him read them in her eyes, to have him pity her for being foolish enough to love a man who was only passing through.

Jill found herself at loose ends after dinner. Tom, Gordie and Rio were in the den, watching an Arnold Schwarzenegger adventure movie Tom had rented that afternoon. The movie didn't particularly interest Jill. Gypsy had helped Jill clean the kitchen, then had taken Sharon into her room for a promised manicure.

Curling her own short, unpolished nails into her palms, Jill sighed. Sharon idolized Gypsy, was thoroughly enraptured by the beautiful, colorful woman. Jill couldn't expect to compete with anyone so glamorous. After all, she was only Jill, the woman who'd been quietly in the background for the past two years, cooking meals, sewing school clothes, attending PTA meetings, bandaging scraped knees. Nothing at all glamorous about that.

Realizing she was succumbing to a bout of self-pity, she straightened her shoulders and stepped out the kitchen door into the fragrant autumn evening. The days were getting shorter now. It was already quite dark. Following the path to the stable by instinct more than sight, she leaned her arms on the top of the wooden fence and listened to Dancer snuffling in his grain trough. Tiny unseen creatures made a valiant effort at cheering her up with their repetitive melodies. She took a deep breath and rolled her head from side to side, relaxing her taut shoulder muscles.

She was content here, she told herself firmly. She'd chosen the path her life had taken and she had no regrets. Tom's family had needed her very badly the past two years, and she'd been there for them. They didn't have to constantly shower her with affection for her to know how genuinely they loved her, how grateful they were to her for being there when they'd needed her most.

She was still young. There was time for her to start building her own life. Her own boutique, maybe, or tailoring business. Perhaps she'd look into Rio's suggestion about finding a market for her dolls. They did seem to be quite popular with the few people who'd seen them.

As for her love life—well, there were other men besides Rio. Maybe someday, when Rio had been gone long enough for her memories of him to fade, maybe then she'd find someone. Maybe.

But that thought did little to ease the ache she felt now, the deep longing to be held in his arms, to have him share this lovely night with her.

A shuffling sound behind her made her whirl around, already knowing who would be there. His face shadowed, Rio stood watching her, his dark eyes glittering in the fringe of light from the pole lamp on the other side of the barn.

"Is something wrong?" he asked, his deep voice hushed in deference to the peacefulness around them.

Jill pushed her hair away from her face self-consciously. "No. Why do you ask?"

"You looked troubled earlier. I'm a pretty good listener if you want to talk."

Touched by his offer, as well as by his obvious uncertainty in making it, she smiled and shook her head. "No, I'm fine. I just needed a few minutes alone."

"Want me to go back in?"

"Of course not. Is the movie over?"

"Yeah. Tom's putting the kids to bed."

"Oh." She leaned back against the fence, trying to think of something light and clever to say. Nothing came to her.

"I wanted to talk to you about Gordie, if you don't mind," Rio said carefully, mimicking Jill's position against the fence.

They stood side by side, not looking at each other, each aware of the other's proximity. Jill cleared her throat noiselessly. "What about Gordie?"

"He's got some real problems. I think he's having trouble getting over his mother's death. This obsession he has with morbid subjects—I believe it's his way of trying to deny his fear of death, his confusion about his mother."

Jill frowned. "What makes you think that?" she asked, unable to avoid sounding a bit belligerent. What did Rio know about troubled kids? she asked herself. What did he know about *her* nephew?

"Has anyone ever talked to him about the way your sister died? Does he know exactly what killed her?"

Shocked, Jill shook her head. "Of course not! Rio, he's just a child. He was only eight when Ellen died. We tried to protect him from the details, telling him only that she'd died in a car accident."

"That doesn't stop him from wondering. He wonders if she died in pain, if she knew what was happening. If she lived for a while or died instantly."

"He said these things to you?" Jill demanded incredulously, turning her head to stare at him.

"Not exactly, no. I've just figured it out on the basis of a couple of questions he's asked me, some of the remarks he's made. He's confused, Jill. He needs someone to be straight with him. Let him ask his questions. Give him honest answers. The truth couldn't be worse than the things he's imagined after sneaking off to watch those gruesome movies with his friends.''

''I don't know that we need to encourage him to continue to think about death,'' Jill argued, still wondering what made Rio think he knew best on this subject. ''What makes you suggest these things? Were those the questions you had after your own mother's death?''

Rio's face shut down as effectively as though he'd pulled on a plastic mask. ''I knew exactly how my mother died,'' he answered flatly. ''I'm the one who discovered the body. She'd put a gun to her head and pulled the trigger. She was still holding the gun when I found her.''

Jill's hand flew to her throat. ''My God. How old were you?''

''A little younger than Sharon. She'd been involved in a series of disastrous relationships with men and she was a very unhappy woman—only a few years older than you are now.''

''Your—your father?'' Jill asked tentatively, remembering that he'd told her brothers his father had abandoned him.

''I never heard from him. Gypsy and I were placed in foster homes after that. I got out when I was sixteen and I've been on my own ever since.''

''Rio, I'm so sorry.''

He shifted restlessly against the fence, visibly uncomfortable with her sympathy. ''We were talking about Gordie, not me. Will you tell Tom what I suggested?''

Feeling as if her family were slipping away from her a little at a time, her own grief at Ellen's death reactivated by the discussion, her heart torn by Rio's unhappy past, Jill hugged her arms to her chest and stared at her feet. ''Why don't you tell him?''

''I'm not as comfortable talking to him as I am to you. I think you should be the one to discuss this with him.''

"And if you're wrong? If talking about Ellen's death only upsets Gordie further?"

"I never claimed to be an expert," Rio muttered. "It was only a suggestion—something for you and Tom to think about."

Somehow compelled to resist him, Jill slanted him a seething, sideways glance. "I think we've been doing all right with the kids by ourselves for the past two years. Gordie has problems, but he's a good boy. His schoolwork is fine, he doesn't get into trouble, he's very close to his father—and to me."

"I wasn't trying to criticize you or Tom. You're doing a great job with the kids, from what I can tell. Look, forget it. Okay? It was just an idea. I probably don't know what I'm talking about." He started to step away, his movements jerky, as though he were controlling his temper with an effort.

She reached out impulsively to touch his arm. "I'm sorry," she whispered. "I didn't mean to... I appreciate your concern. It's just that I—"

The muscles beneath her hand tensed. Rio stood very still as her voice faded off to nothing. And then he turned, ever so slowly, and looked down at her. "Dammit, Jill," he muttered. "What are you doing to me?"

What was *she* doing to *him?* How could he ask that when she was standing in front of him, trembling like a leaf, incapable of even speaking coherently? Helplessly she stared up at him.

Muttering a curse beneath his breath, he reached out to her. She moved into his arms without hesitating, drawn by a need too overpowering to resist. Their lips met in an explosion of raw passion, made desperate by their futile attempts to repress it. Beyond caution, Jill opened her mouth to him, deepening the kiss. Her arms locked around his neck, she flattened herself against him, needing to be closer than was physically possible.

Groaning deep in his chest, Rio tightened his arms until he could draw her no nearer. One strong hand clamped against the small of her back, holding her relentlessly against the hard ridge beneath his loose sweatpants. Rather than being intimidated by such blatant desire, Jill gloried in it, her hips moving eagerly against him. Her unschooled responses seemed only to inflame him further. Rio turned to press her against the fence, balancing himself on his good leg as he kissed her until she thought she'd pass out from lack of oxygen.

She gasped for breath when he released her mouth, but didn't loosen her hold on him. Instead she tugged at his head, wanting only to kiss him again. "Rio," she murmured huskily. "Oh, Rio."

His answering mutter was unintelligible. His hands slipped beneath the hem of her sweater and lingered on the soft skin above the waistband of her jeans. And then they moved upward. Jill caught her breath, expanding her already swelling breasts. Her head falling back, eyes closed, she didn't resist when he lifted her sweater and unsnapped her bra.

A sharp intake of breath—his—made her open her eyes to look at him. He was staring at her breasts, which gleamed palely in the shadows cloaking Rio and her from view from the house. Though she couldn't quite read his expression, she knew she pleased him—and the knowledge thrilled her. Rio covered one soft breast with his hand, and the contact of bare skin against bare skin made her shudder with pleasure. He lowered his head. She almost screamed at the shock of glorious sensation when his warm, wet mouth captured her taut, straining nipple. Biting the inside of her lip, she moaned softly.

His tongue flickered, circling and teasing, then captured her against the roof of his mouth to exert a strong, suckling pleasure that made her arch as though electrified. Her fingers clenching his hair, she gasped and squirmed against him, aching as she'd never ached before, wanting him with a hunger that would have shocked her, had she been able to think clearly. A slow, heavy throbbing centered between her legs, a gnawing emptiness that only Rio could fill. She wanted him there, wanted his bare, throbbing body against her, around her, deep within her. Imagination filling the gaps inexperience left in her fantasies, she yearned to make love with him. If only they had the time—and the privacy.

Slowly brought to an awareness of their surroundings, of the proximity of the house and its occupants, Jill pushed reluctantly against Rio's shoulders with trembling hands. "Rio, stop. We can't—not here, not now."

He released a sharp, ragged breath. "I know. Dammit, I know," he grated, his body rigid with frustration. He raised his head to kiss her again, lingeringly, deeply, and then he drew back. Shoving a hand through his hair, he stepped away.

Jill straightened her clothes, her unsteady fingers clumsy with the fastenings, knowing that if the time and place had been more convenient, she wouldn't have stopped him. She'd have to think about that—later.

"You go on in," Rio urged her, staring out into the pasture, his profile turned to her. "I need a while."

She didn't have to ask why. "All right. Good night, Rio."

"G'night. Oh, and Jill—"

"Yes?"

"Talk to Tom about Gordie, okay?"

She shoved her hands into the pockets of her jeans and answered rather stiffly. "I will."

"Thanks."

Jill turned and hurried toward the house.

Rio stayed where he was for a long time. And then he brought his fist down hard against the top rail of the fence, startling the dozing horse into a snort of protest.

Chapter Eight

As she'd promised, Jill discussed Rio's suggestions with Tom. Though he seemed disturbed by Rio's comments, Tom was more receptive than she had been. Seemingly intrigued by Rio's theory, he told Jill he'd give it some thought.

Jill had shopping to do on Friday. She welcomed the excuse to get out for a few hours, worried about what would happen if she and Rio were alone all day. She'd spent most of the night asking herself if making love with him would only make it hurt worse when he left, and fantasizing about the possibility that maybe he would fall in love with her and stay. The restless night had left her tired and even more confused than before.

"Want me to help you carry those in?" Rio asked when Jill returned later that afternoon, her arms loaded with packages. He held the door open for her as she passed—the only contribution he could make at the time.

"I can get them," she assured him. "It would be too awkward for you to handle the steps with your cast and your arms full of packages. But I appreciate the thought."

"You had a couple of phone messages. I wrote them on the pad in the kitchen."

"Thank you. Excuse me, I have some more bags to bring in."

Very polite, very distant, she thought wryly. An outside observer would think there was nothing at all going on between the two of them. Unless, of course, that observer noticed the smoldering hunger in Rio's dark eyes—something Jill had spotted right away. She wasn't sure whether to be gratified or unnerved by the rather predatory look he gave her when she passed him.

The school bus stopped at the gate as Jill carried in the last of the bags. Gordie and Sharon ran up the drive with the boundless energy of childhood. Feeling washed out after her nearly sleepless night, Jill envied them that energy.

"How'd you feel at school today?" Tom asked Gordie after dinner.

Gordie shrugged. "Okay."

"You up to going fishing tomorrow?"

Gordie's eyes lit up. "You bet."

"Can I go, too? Please?" Sharon asked unexpectedly, surprising both Tom and Jill, since she didn't usually care for fishing.

"Well—uh—" Tom glanced at Jill for assistance.

Knowing he wanted the chance to talk to Gordie in private, Jill opened her mouth to suggest an alternate plan for Sharon, but Gypsy beat her to it.

"Sharon, I was hoping you'd go shopping with me tomorrow," she said with an engaging smile. "I desperately need a few things, and I'm not sure where the best places to shop are around here."

Sharon looked ecstatic. "Really? You want me to go with you?"

"I would love that," Gypsy assured her. "Maybe your aunt Jill would like to join us."

Jill murmured something noncommittal, aware that Rio was watching her.

"That would be great!" Sharon enthused. "Daddy, you won't mind if I go with Gypsy instead of fishing, would you?"

"Of course not, pumpkin," he replied with a fond smile for her and look of gratitude for Gypsy.

Suddenly losing her appetite, Jill stood and carried her plate to the sink, asking if anyone wanted seconds.

She avoided the shopping trip the next morning by remembering that she'd promised to help her mother and Anita make new curtains for Paul and Anita's living room. She spent most the day trying to evade her family's not-particularly-subtle questioning about Rio and Gypsy.

Yes, she thought Rio was attractive. Yes, she agreed that he was a rather mysterious type. No, she didn't expect him to stay for long after his cast came off. Yes, she thought Tom was attracted to Gypsy. No, she didn't know if Gypsy felt the same way.

Emotionally drained after the probing gossip fest, she stopped for pizza on her way home, not in the mood to cook that evening. She arrived only minutes before Tom and Gordie returned, both rather subdued, eyes a bit red-rimmed. They hadn't caught any fish, but she watched Gordie give his father a long, hard hug before loping off to put away their fishing gear. She started to ask how it had gone.

Gypsy stepped past her and put a hand on Tom's arm. "Is everything okay?" she asked solicitously, proving to Jill that Tom had discussed the situation with Gypsy.

"Everything's fine," he assured her. "Your brother is a pretty sharp guy. I'll tell you all about it later." He looked at Jill with a somewhat tired smile. "Do I smell pizza?"

"Yes. I thought it would make a nice change from my cooking," she answered, trying to smile naturally.

He hugged her quickly as he passed to wash up. "Nothing's better than your cooking, Jill."

She didn't answer. Catching Gypsy's quizzical look, she managed another smile and turned to walk into the kitchen.

The children tore into the pizza with typical enthusiasm, cheerfully picking off the peppers and leaving them in neat piles on their plates. "This is good, Jill," Gordie mumbled around a mouthful of food, his high spirits already reasserting themselves.

"I'm glad you're enjoying it," she answered. "But don't talk with your mouth full."

He swallowed. "Yes, ma'am." He turned to Rio. "We saw a beaver in the lake today. A big one."

"Did you?"

"Yeah. I almost caught a big fish, but it got away."

Wanting her share of the attention, Sharon chimed into the conversation, patting the neat French braid Gypsy had styled for her that morning. "Gypsy let me help her pick out some new nail polish. She's going to paint my nails with it. And she's going to show me the pictures she took when she went on a safari in Africa."

"Africa?" Gordie repeated, obviously impressed as he turned his attention to Gypsy. "You've been on safari?"

She nodded, delicately wiping tomato sauce off her mouth with a pink paper napkin. "I wrote an article about some of the different safari packages available to tourists. I had a wonderful time."

"Did you see any lions?"

"I came face-to-face with a tiger on a morning walk," she told him, her big dark eyes widening for dramatic effect. "I thought I was going to be breakfast, for sure."

Both children leaned forward in fascination. "Yeah? What'd you do?" Gordie demanded.

"I stood very still and prayed a lot. He turned around and walked away. That was the last time I went walking alone."

"I'd have been terrified," Sharon breathed, shoving at her glasses.

Gordie glanced scornfully at her sister. "What else is new? You're scared of everything."

"Am not."

"Are too. Who still sleeps with a night-light?"

"Not me," Sharon retorted proudly. "Gypsy helped me learn not to be afraid of the dark, didn't you, Gypsy?"

"Yeah, but only because she's sleeping in your room," Gordie pointed out with the superiority of his ten years.

Sharon shook her head. "No, it's not. She told me a secret that I can use even when she doesn't sleep in my room with me."

"What secret?" Gordie asked suspiciously.

"If she told you, it wouldn't be a secret anymore, would it?" Gypsy interrupted with a quick wink at Sharon.

Tom laughed. "That's telling him, Gypsy." He reached out to affectionately tweak her chin, causing Gypsy to blush prettily.

Jill's throat tightened until she thought she might choke on her pizza.

"Oh, by the way, Gordie, Aaron called while you were washing up," Tom said. "He invited you to his house after dinner."

Gordie hesitated, glanced from his father to Rio, then shook his head. "I think I'll stay here."

GET 4 BOOKS

Return this card, and we'll send you 4 brand-new Silhouette Special Edition® novels, absolutely FREE! We'll even pay the postage both ways!

We're making you this offer to introduce you to the benefits of the Silhouette Reader Service™: free home delivery of brand-new romance novels, months before they're available in stores, AND at a saving of 33¢ apiece compared to the cover price!

Accepting these 4 free books places you under no obligation to buy. You may cancel at any time, even just after receiving your free shipment. If you do not cancel, every month, we'll send 6 more Silhouette Special Edition novels and bill you just $2.92* apiece—that's all!

Yes, please send me my 4 free Silhouette Special Edition novels, as explained above.

Name

Address   Apt.

City   State   ZIP

235 CIS ACJT

DETACH ALONG DOTTED LINE AND MAIL TODAY! – DETACH ALONG DOTTED LINE AND MAIL TODAY! – DETACH ALONG DOTTED LINE AND MAIL TODAY!

Get 4 Books FREE

SEE BACK OF CARD FOR DETAILS

Surprised, Tom tilted his head. "You sure, son? You can go to your friend's house if you want."

"Nah. He'll just want to watch another slasher movie. I'm getting kinda tired of those."

Obviously pleased, Tom smiled. "Maybe we could all play a board game tonight."

Gordie brightened. "And we could make popcorn?"

"Sure, why not?"

"Let's play Trouble!" Sharon suggested.

"No, Monopoly," Gordie argued immediately.

"That takes too long. Can we play Trouble, Daddy?"

"Let's play Monopoly, Dad. You like that one, don't you?"

Tom sighed and rolled his eyes comically at the other adults.

Gypsy laughed. Rio chuckled. Jill tried very hard to smile.

For the first time, Gypsy accompanied the family to church on Sunday. From her seat in the choir loft, Jill watched her family. Gordie sat beside Tom, squirming uncomfortably in his Sunday clothes, obviously ready for the service to be over. Sharon sat at Gypsy's side, prissy and proper in her best dress, her hair curled à la Gypsy. And in the middle, Tom and Gypsy looked very much like a couple, his sandy head close to her dark one, sharing a songbook and an occasional discreet smile.

Jill could remember when Tom had sat by Ellen in church—the teenage steadies holding hands during the service, blushing when their eyes happened to meet; and later, as husband and wife, content to be together with their small children. Jill knew that Tom had been very happy with Ellen, that he'd taken her death hard. But the fascination she saw in his eyes when he looked at Gypsy had never been there with the woman he'd known from childhood.

As much as she wanted Tom to be happy, as much as she genuinely liked Gypsy, Jill still couldn't help resenting that her sister couldn't be in this church with her husband and children. She knew her feelings were only natural, that anyone who'd prematurely lost a loved one would regularly face such feelings. But she had to admit, in this place where lies should be unacceptable, that much of the resentment she'd been fighting for the past few days came strictly from her own feelings of jealousy.

She'd come to view Tom's household as hers during the past two years. Its occupants had once turned to her for advice and assistance. Now they were beginning to look elsewhere, and she couldn't help wondering if she'd failed them in some way.

For the first time, Jill realized that she had worked herself into the role of adviser/confidant so well that there was no longer anyone for her to turn to with her own problems. Her parents were so protective of their youngest child, so certain she was happy with her life. Knowing they were still grieving over the loss of their elder daughter, Jill hated to burden them with her own problems.

As for her brothers—well, they were all busy with their own families. It would be hard for them to understand Jill's vague feelings of dissatisfaction, of longing for things she couldn't even name.

Mike, of course, was single, but his idea of solving problems was to take them on full tilt. If he considered Rio a problem to his sister, he'd wade in with both fists. She loved her brother, but knew him to be hotheaded, tactless and not always discreet. Besides, he'd just broken up with a girl he'd loved for years. Though he concealed his emotions well, Jill knew he was privately battling his own difficulties.

So who did that leave?

"I'm a pretty good listener if you need to talk," Rio had said Friday night. His voice echoed now in her mind, over-riding the pastor's sermon. She smiled wryly. Was she ac-tually considering talking about her feelings with the major source of her confusion? Ridiculous, of course.

Strangely enough, she realized that it wasn't at all hard to imagine turning to Rio with her problems. It was all too easy to fantasize about having him by her side, for always. All too dangerous to allow those fantasies to continue.

Biting her lip, she focused fiercely on the minister's back, forcing herself to concentrate on the words he was speak-ing, hoping to find a message in those words that would help her through whatever was to come in the next few weeks.

More perceptive than Jill could have suspected, Rio knew exactly what was troubling her. He'd been watching her for days, recognizing her fear that she was losing control of her family, her battle against the resentment that was only nat-ural when outsiders began to play an important role in the lives of those she'd considered her own.

He didn't blame her for those feelings, didn't find them petty—he understood them all too well. Hadn't he worried all along that he would hurt her, disrupt her comfortable routine? Wasn't that why he tried not to get involved with the people he met in the places where he stayed so briefly during his travels? Just as he'd protected himself from being hurt again, so he'd tried to ensure that he didn't in-tentionally hurt anyone. And yet he suspected that he was hurting Jill. And the thought twisted his gut.

He tried to stay away from her, told himself his growing need for her could be controlled. He even suggested to Gypsy that she might pull away from Sharon a bit, before the child became too attached to her. Gypsy effectively told him to mind his own business. Surprised by her vehemence, he said nothing else on the subject, though he began to wonder whether Gypsy could be happy settling down in this quiet, pleasant household after so many years of frantic traveling.

His aloofness lasted until he hobbled into Jill's sewing room Thursday afternoon with a telephone message and found her wiping away tears as she worked on Sharon's Halloween costume. And he understood for the first time why a woman's tears could make a man promise anything. Seeing tears on Jill's soft cheeks tore him apart.

"What's wrong?" he demanded, looming over her, determined to find out what was bothering her.

Flushing in embarrassment, Jill swiped hurriedly at her tears and lowered her head so that her hair fell forward, hiding her expression. "Nothing."

He leaned over to catch her chin and lift her reluctant face to allow him to see her. "Jill. Talk to me. Why are you crying?"

"I'm not—"

"Jill," he growled, rapidly losing patience.

She sighed deeply, her eyelashes falling. "All right, I was upset."

"Why?"

She moistened her lips and he could tell by looking at her that she was going to evade the truth. "It's this costume for Sharon," she bluffed. "She just had to be a mermaid and I couldn't find a pattern for a mermaid costume so I've had to design it myself. It's really been a problem from the beginning, and I—"

Rio stopped her with a succinct obscenity. Releasing her, he shoved a stack of fabric off a straight-back chair and drew it next to her. He settled into it with the air of a man who had no intention of leaving before getting the answers he wanted.

"Is it me?" he probed. "Have I hurt you?"

"No, Rio, you haven't hurt me," she answered quietly, her shoulders sagging in surrender.

Not yet. The words hovered between them, unspoken but understood. Rio scowled. "I don't want to hurt you."

Her expression softened. "I know."

"Then why were you crying?" He pushed relentlessly.

"I suppose I was feeling sorry for myself," she admitted reluctantly. "Feeling—I don't know—useless, I guess."

He stared at her, jaw dropping. "Useless? You? Why in the world would you feel like that?"

She looked away, sheepishly toying with a strand of her hair, cheeks dark red, eyes still damp. "You wouldn't understand."

Rio's fist hit one corner of the oak cabinet with enough force to rattle the sewing machine. "Dammit, Jill! *Talk to me!*"

Her own seething emotions erupting in response to his frustrated anger, she threw the swath of sparkly green material to the floor, leaping from her chair to pace furiously behind it. "All right! You want to know why I'm upset? I'll tell you! Because in the past few days you and your sister, two total strangers, have sailed into this house and changed everything! For two years I've been trying to redirect Gordie's interests away from those slasher films and morbid thoughts. But all it took was a word of advice from you, and Tom took care of it in one afternoon.

"I've worked with Sharon for months to help her get over her fear of the dark. Gypsy comes along with French braids and nail polish and pictures of Africa, whispers some magical 'secret,' and Sharon suddenly decided she's cured. It's pretty obvious how little I've accomplished in the past two years, compared to what you and your sister have done in a matter of weeks."

He'd known, of course, that she felt that way. Hearing her saying the words, verbalizing her hurt and resentment, made him want only to take her in his arms and apologize for ever making an appearance in her life.

Ignoring the cast that made his motions so awkward and the slight pain that accompanied his abrupt movement, he shoved himself out of the chair. Balancing on his good leg, he caught her upper arms when she would have paced past him. "Be still and listen to me."

She refused to meet his eyes. "No. You're only going to tell me I'm being a self-pitying idiot, and you're right. I don't know what's wrong with me. I can't believe I'm being so petty."

"You're not being petty, Jill, you're being human. Dammit, can't you see? Those kids love you. You've been there during the hardest years of their lives, giving them love and security when their world fell apart, keeping their routines safe and normal, wiping their tears at night, making clothes and dolls and Halloween costumes. You've sacrificed two years of your life for them, and believe me, those years will always mean more to them than a few weeks with a couple of temporarily interesting strangers."

"Then why couldn't I help with the problems that were bothering them the most?" she whispered, finally lifting tear-filled blue eyes to his.

"Because you shared them," he answered gently, his fingers loosening their clench to become almost caressing. "In different ways, you were all still dealing with your grief at Ellen's death. You were too close to listen objectively, to offer suggestions that were sometimes painful—such as encouraging Gordie to find out exactly how his mother died to put a rest to his morbid speculation. Gypsy and I never knew Ellen. We could see things a little differently because our emotions weren't as involved as yours were. There's no magic or special skills there. It's always easier to be objective when you aren't personally involved in the pain."

"Maybe you weren't involved when you arrived," Jill answered quietly. "But now you are. You've become a hero and a role model for Gordie. And Gypsy—Sharon idolizes her. I think Tom is becoming involved with her, too. The way he's looked at her lately—"

"I've noticed," Rio admitted.

She lifted her chin, her moist eyes narrowing. "So, what am I supposed to do with my family when you and your sister move on? They'll be heartbroken again, and I don't know if I'll be any more effective at dealing with it than I was before."

Because I'm involved this time, too, her eyes added defiantly, locking fiercely with his. She might as well have spoken the words aloud.

"They'll get over us," Rio offered awkwardly, trying to close his own expression from her. "It's only an infatuation, in a way," he suggested, and he was no longer talking about the rest of the family. "A fascination with a different life-style than you—than *they're* accustomed to. Before long, everything will be just as it was before we came."

Her mouth quivered. "You think so?"

He bit back a groan, impulsively stroking her hair. "Gordie and Sharon are very lucky to have you, Jill. Maybe if I'd had someone like you in my life—well, maybe I would have turned out differently."

Her eyes turning warm, luminous, she lifted one soft hand to cradle her palm against his cheek. "I don't think you've turned out so badly."

He should pull back, he told himself desperately. He was only going to cause her more pain. But she was so close, her lush mouth so tempting. . . .

The kiss began as no more than a tentative brush of lips. A mere taste of what could follow, should Rio lack the willpower to draw away. He reached for that strength—and failed to find it. Her mouth softened beneath his, lips parting in artless invitation. Her fingers slid up his arm to curl into his shoulders. Her firm breasts brushed his chest as she moved closer—and he was lost.

Bracing himself on widespread legs, he hauled her closer, his hands going around her to hold her against him, his mouth slanting across hers with all traces of restraint gone, burned away. She stiffened in quick, instinctive reaction to the unexpected flare of passion, and then she responded gloriously, her mouth opening wider, head falling back, fingers clenching his hair.

It was too much, too powerful. He'd kissed other women, of course. Not as many as some might have expected; he'd been so very careful not to get involved, not to leave traces of himself behind when he moved on, not to affect the lives of those whose paths he crossed. Still, there had been those times when need had burned stronger than caution.

But never like this. He'd never held a woman in his arms and felt her emotions as deeply as his own. He'd never wanted so badly, needed so acutely that he'd trembled. He trembled now.

Tearing his mouth from Jill's with a gasp, he closed his eyes and rested his forehead against hers, but only for a moment. He hungered for more. His mouth moved over her cheeks. They tasted of tears. Shattered, he buried his face in her hair. "Dammit, Jill," he muttered, as he had once before. "What are you doing to me?"

She drew back only far enough to look at him, her face flushed, mouth moist and kiss-darkened. "What *am* I doing to you, Rio?" she asked, her voice barely audible, hardly recognizable.

"You're ripping me apart," he answered honestly.

She pressed a kiss to his throat, as though soothing a pain she didn't quite understand. "Why would you say that?"

His hand slid down her back, tracing its pliable curves. "I want you. I want you so much I'm half crazy with it. But I don't want to hurt you. I can't bear the thought of hurting you."

"Are you—" She looked up at him and moistened her lips, so open and unguarded that his throat tightened. "Are you so sure you'd hurt me?"

"I won't stay, Jill," he murmured. "I can't."

Some of her high color faded, but she didn't look away. "Is it so terrible here?"

"No. It's just not right for me."

Her nod was heartbreakingly brave. "All right. So you'll be leaving. But you'll be here until your cast comes off. We have that much time together."

He wanted so much to take her up on her innocent offer. And then his own unconscious phrasing made his eyes narrow. Innocent? Inexperience was written all over her, but just how inexperienced was she? "Have you ever been involved with a man, Jill?" he demanded gruffly, unable to be tactful. "Really involved?"

The color returned to her face in a hot wave of pink. "No. Not . . . the way you mean," she admitted softly.

"You mean, you're a—uh—"

"Yes," she supplied, smiling weakly at his obvious discomfort with the word.

His eyes closed in a spasm of self-censure. "Hell." It was as much a description of his condition as a curse.

"Why does that upset you?" she asked, so very vulnerable.

He took a deep, sharp breath, resting his cheek on the top of her head so that he didn't have to see that vulnerability. "It makes us even more wrong for each other."

"I—I want you, Rio."

He flinched. She wasn't making this any easier for him. "Do you really want to make love for the first time with a man who'll be leaving at the earliest opportunity?"

She was quiet so long that he had to look at her. What he saw made him bite back another groan. "No," she said finally. "That's not what I want."

"I can't stay, Jill," he repeated flatly. "Don't do anything foolish, like convincing yourself it might happen. It won't."

With a sigh, she lifted her face to press a lingering kiss against his cheek. While he was still frozen in surprise at her action, she murmured into his ear, "I'm afraid I've been even more foolish than that. I've started to care for you, Rio."

"Don't say that."

She drew back to look up at him, and he wondered how her eyes could suddenly have grown so much older. "Why not? It's the truth."

"Jill, I can't—"

"I know," she interrupted quickly, laying her fingers across his lips. "I know."

His fingers tightened spasmodically against her hips, and then he forced himself to loosen them. He turned too quickly away from her, cursing bitterly when he stumbled. She reached out automatically to help him, but he flinched from her touch. "No. I can do it."

She pulled away. "All right."

He didn't look back when he left the room. He couldn't. It was the only way he could make himself leave her.

Jill stood very still for a long time after he left, gathering her composure, wondering at her own audacity in admitting her feelings to Rio. And then she returned to her sewing, her thoughts surprisingly calm, her heart no longer torn by the self-pity she'd suffered earlier. Now her sympathy was all given to a man who was so terribly alone, so desperately in need of the love he vehemently rejected. So heart-wrenchingly afraid to reach out for that love.

Would he ever take the chance? Or was Jill a fool for allowing a wisp of hope to grow stronger inside her heart? For beginning to believe that she could be the one to reach him?

Chapter Nine

"Stand still, Sharon. I can't zip you up if you keep squirming around."

Sharon sighed impatiently and twisted her neck to look over her shoulder at Jill. "I want to see it. Can't I look in the mirror yet?"

"Just a minute," Jill admonished, fastening the tiny neckline hook. She walked around her niece, checking the fit of the costume. The long-sleeved top was flesh-toned to give the appearance of a strapless mermaid garment and still be warm enough for a cool October evening. Sparkly green fabric began just under Sharon's arms and fell straight to her ankles, where a mermaid's "tail" flared out to cover her sneakered feet. Jill had sewn scalloped rows of sequins down the length of the outfit to simulate fish scales and had added discreet tucks at the waistline to suggest curves in Sharon's straight, eight-year-old figure.

"All you need is your wig and makeup," she said, deciding the costume required no further alterations.

Sharon clapped her hands and bounced on the balls of her feet. "Could I put them on now? Please? Just to see how they'll look for the Halloween carnival?"

Jill smiled. "Sharon, the carnival is still two weeks away."

"I know. But I want to make sure everything looks right. Please, Jill."

Surrendering, as her niece had known she would, Jill reached for the long, inexpensive red wig and fitted it over Sharon's tawny braids.

"Makeup, too," Sharon urged, pulling off her hated glasses.

Obligingly Jill fetched her own makeup case, from which she drew eye shadow, eyeliner, blusher and lipstick. She'd bought a tube of glitter gel, which she stroked lightly across Sharon's freckled cheeks and used to highlight the dramatically applied eye makeup. Finished, she stepped back. "All right. You may look in the mirror now."

Sharon turned hesitantly toward the full-length mirror. One glance and her round face lit up brilliantly. Where Jill saw a little girl in a cheap wig and handmade costume, Sharon's wide young eyes visualized an exotic mermaid, beautiful enough to dazzle any handsome sailor who chanced upon her. Sharon struck a few dramatic poses, then whirled to throw her arms around Jill's waist.

"Oh, Jill, it's wonderful! I look just like Ariel in *The Little Mermaid*. Thank you."

Jill returned the hug warmly. "You're welcome, sweetheart. I'm glad you like it."

"I love it! It's beautiful. Can I go show everyone?"

"You want them to see it now? Wouldn't you rather wait until Halloween and surprise them?"

Sharon drew back and pulled her lower lip between her teeth, torn between showing off immediately or waiting for the big night. Youthful excitement won. "I want to show them now."

"Then go ahead," Jill encouraged, waving a hand toward the doorway of her bedroom, where they'd closed themselves away for the fitting of the costume she'd finished that afternoon.

Her steps shortened only a little by the fit of the long, straight gown, Sharon hurried out of the room. Jill followed close behind.

"Look, everyone!" Sharon almost yelled, bursting into the den where Tom, Gordie, Rio and Gypsy were watching Friday-night sitcoms. "Jill finished my mermaid costume."

"Who is this beautiful creature?" Tom demanded in exaggerated awe, making his daughter giggle delightedly.

"Oh, Daddy. You know who I am."

"You look like a geek," Gordie announced scornfully, jealous of the attention his sister was receiving.

"No more than you will in your Ninja costume," Sharon retorted, unperturbed for once by her brother's gibes as she stroked her long red synthetic locks.

Gordie subsided into mutters after Tom threw him a threatening glance.

"Sharon, you're lovely," Gypsy enthused, smiling sweetly at the child. "That costume is amazing. Isn't it, Rio?"

Rio had been staring at Jill since she'd entered the room, which Jill had been painfully aware of. At his sister's question, he turned his attention to Sharon, studying the costume intently. "Very impressive. You're lucky to have such a talented aunt, Sharon."

Sharon beamed at his rare compliment. "I know. She's the best aunt in the whole world," she assured him, turning to hug Jill again. Smiling up at her, she murmured, "I love you, Jill."

Blinking back tears, Jill kissed Sharon's soft, painted cheek. "I love you, too, darling. Now you'd better take off your costume and wash your face. It's almost time for bed."

"Can I wear this for Daddy's birthday party tomorrow night?"

"No, Sharon. You have to save it for Halloween. Everyone will see it then when you go trick-or-treating before the Halloween carnival."

Sighing her disappointment, Sharon reluctantly left the room to remove her disguise. Moments later, Gordie followed, ordered by his father to brush his teeth and get ready for bed. The adults could hear the usual exchange of insults fading down the hallway as the children departed.

"The costume really is beautiful, Jill," Gypsy said a moment later. "I could never have made anything like that."

"She didn't even have a pattern," Rio added, to Jill's embarrassed surprise. "She made it up as she went along."

Gypsy shook her head in awe.

"Jill's a treasure," Tom agreed, smiling warmly at his flushed sister-in-law. "I don't know what we'd have done without her the past couple of years. I couldn't have asked for a better sister if we'd been related by blood."

"Would you stop?" Jill begged, covering her flaming cheeks with her hands. "It's getting downright maudlin in here!"

"You're right," Tom said immediately, grinning ear to ear. "How about bringing me a cola, Jill?"

"How about getting it yourself, Tom?" she retorted quickly, grateful for the reprieve.

Since he'd only been teasing with his request for wait-ressing service, Tom laughed and stood. "Anyone else want anything?"

"There's more of that chocolate cake I made yester-day," Jill informed them.

Tom patted his stomach. "Sounds good. Want me to bring you a piece, Rio?"

"Yeah, thanks."

"Coffee?"

"Please."

"How about you, Gypsy?"

"I'll help you," she offered, walking to Tom's side.

He smiled down at her. "Thanks."

Jill waited until they'd left the room before turning to face Rio. "That really wasn't necessary."

Resting his elbows casually on the arms of the easy chair in which he sprawled, Rio watched her expressionlessly. "What wasn't necessary?"

"You were the one who urged everyone to give me all those flowery compliments. I don't need that to know my family loves me."

"I didn't have to urge anyone to do anything," he disa-greed stubbornly. "They meant everything they said. And everyone needs applause at times."

"You, too?"

He acknowledged her point with a shrug. "Well, maybe not everyone."

"I don't believe that. I think you crave approval as much as everyone else does."

"I don't intend to argue with you about it."

"Neither do I," she answered evenly.

"Fine."

"Fine."

Tom appeared in the doorway, balancing a tray loaded with dessert plates, followed by Gypsy, who carried another tray holding a coffee service. "I forgot to ask if you wanted anything, Jill, but we cut you a slice of cake, anyway."

Breaking eye contact with Rio, Jill thanked Tom, took her plate and settled in a chair to eat her cake. Despite her mild annoyance with Rio for what she considered his manipulation of her family, she still felt warmed by their praise.

Maybe she hadn't done such a bad job during the past two years, after all, she thought as she took a bite of the rich made-from-scratch cake the others seemed to be enjoying so much. Swallowing, she smiled as she realized with a faint sense of pride that it really was a good cake.

"Lordy, lordy, look who's forty!" Doc boomed, entering the house the next evening carrying a large, haphazardly wrapped present. "How can you be so old when I'm still so young, boy?"

Tom laughed, obviously enjoying his spot in the center of attention for his birthday gathering. "Hate to tell you this, Dad, but you're not that young."

"Shut your mouth, Thomas. I can still take you out behind the shed, you know," his father threatened ominously, dropping the gift on the floor beside an impressively large stack on the hearth. "Hi, everyone."

A chorus of greetings answered him from the many others milling in the room. Watching from a chair in one corner, Rio decided that these people didn't really need an occasion to justify a mass gathering; they simply enjoyed getting together. Hammonds and Curtises swarmed through the house and out in the yard, chattering, laughing, joking. Several young cousins began to squabble over a game in Gordie's bedroom; a shout from a parent put an end to the argument and the kids went back to playing amicably.

Didn't anyone ever feel at least a little overwhelmed by the chaos? he wondered, slightly dazed himself, despite his previous experience with this large, boisterous clan.

"You get used to it, eventually," a voice said from beside him, making him jump and wonder if there happened to be a mind reader in the room.

He looked up to find Gabe's pretty blond wife, Cissy, smiling at him understandingly as she patted the baby on her shoulder. "The first few times I attended these family gatherings, I probably looked a lot like you do right now. Sort of shell-shocked. But it's hard to stay on the sidelines for long with these people. They have a way of taking you in and making you one of them. Look at your sister."

Rio didn't have to look. He already knew that Gypsy was having a wonderful time, falling eagerly into the spirit of the evening. He also knew she'd used the last credit on her only charge card to buy Tom a nice birthday present. She'd signed the card "From Gypsy and Rio."

The noise level increased slightly when Jill carried in a huge, beautifully decorated cake alight with the glow of forty birthday candles. Children came running in anticipation of cake and ice cream. Tossing her long dark hair over the shoulder of her hot-pink top, Gypsy led the singing of "Happy Birthday." Everyone but Rio joined in.

"Forty," Mike said when the candles were blown out and presents piled in front of Tom. "Hope I'm still getting around as well as you are when I'm your age, Thomas."

Tom grimaced. "You're not that much younger, you know," he pointed out.

"Thirteen years, old-timer," Mike retorted smugly. "I'm the next to the youngest adult in the room. Go to the kitchen, Jilly, so I can claim to be the youngest." And then he frowned, looked at Gypsy and Rio, and doubled his fists on his hips. "Uh-oh. I *am* still in the running, aren't I? Let me see your birth certificates."

Gypsy laughed, shook her head and winked at Rio. "No need, Mike. I'm no competition for you. I'll be thirty in a few months."

Mike turned to Rio, eyebrows in question. Rio noticed Jill waiting curiously for his answer. He gave her a quick smile, returned his sister's wink, then looked back at Mike.

"Compared to me, you're a mere child," he assured him gravely. Disregarding actual years, he felt decades older than Jill's happy-go-lucky brother. Hard experience had taken his boyhood away years earlier than most.

"Since you're so proud of your youth, Michael, you may sit in the kitchen with the other children when we serve the cake and ice cream," Ruth announced, making everyone laugh as Mike looked dismayed. "Now sit quietly and let Tom open his gifts."

Properly chastened, Mike meekly folded his oversize frame onto the floor beside his mother's chair. His amusement fading, Rio watched as Ruth rested a hand affectionately on her son's head, much as she would if he were still just a boy.

Rio could almost remember his own mother sitting that way with him, if he tried hard enough. But then his memories veered sharply to another afternoon, as they always did whenever he was foolish enough to look back. To jumping off the school bus and quietly entering his house, just in case his mother had another headache and didn't want to be disturbed. Tiptoeing into the kitchen for a snack, only to find...

His fist clenching, he ruthlessly brought himself back to the present, away from memories he'd never been able to escape, no matter how long or how hard he'd run.

Presents were opened and duly admired; cake, ice cream and soft drinks distributed and devoured. One of the smaller children—Rio thought he belonged to Rusty and Margaret, but wasn't sure—spilled his drink on the den carpet. Ruth quietly cleaned up the mess before anyone but Rio noticed, shushing the child's tears with a grandmotherly hug.

The telephone rang, making everyone groan in certainty that the guest of honor was being called away on an animal emergency, then smiled in relief when the caller turned out to be a friend of Gordie's. A Disney movie was plugged into the VCR to entertain the smaller cousins who were banished from the games being played by the older ones. The nonsensical songs and squeaky voices from the movie blended in with the laughter and chatter of the adults. Rio wondered idly what the decibel level in the room would measure.

Someone—probably Mike—suggested a game of charades. Two teams were immediately formed. Rio used his leg as an excuse to beg off, though he assured everyone he would enjoy watching. Jill was chosen to go first for her team. He enjoyed watching her trying to act out the movie title *The Apprenticeship of Duddy Kravitz*. He'd never heard of it, though Anita remembered that it was an old Richard Dreyfuss film.

Sometime during the game Sharon entered the room and curled up on the couch beside Gypsy. Rio watched Gypsy almost unconsciously stroke the little girl's hair as she tried to guess the phrase Gabe was awkwardly pantomiming.

Gypsy looked happy, Rio realized at that moment. Happier than he'd seen her in years.

Sitting in his corner, he frowned as it occurred to him that his sister had suddenly become a part of a family. And Rio found himself on the sidelines again, feeling left out. Again.

Murmuring an excuse to those seated closest to him, he made his way carefully out of the crowded room, suddenly needing to get away from the noise and the people and the laughter he couldn't share just then.

Silence and darkness and solitude greeted him outside. Leaning against a tree, his back to the house, he mused in wry irony that these surroundings were much more typical for him. The heavy cast on his leg chafed him, weighed him down. He thought wistfully of shucking it and moving on, slipping away while everyone else was occupied. In a moment of uncharacteristic self-pity, he wondered if anyone would even notice.

He didn't know how much time had passed before a hand fell on his shoulder. Whirling in instinctive self-defense, he cursed when he nearly fell flat on his face. Laughing softly, Gypsy steadied him. "What are you doing out here by yourself when there's a great party going on inside?"

"You're the one who likes parties, remember?"

"You seemed to be enjoying yourself earlier," she answered mildly, leaning back against the tree, a colorful wraith in the deep shadows. "What happened? Did you suddenly remember that you're supposed to pretend to be a hard-shelled loner?"

Stung by the gibe, Rio glared at her, his hands clenching. "I don't pretend anything."

"Is that right?"

"That's right."

"Mmm."

He waited a moment, until it was obvious she wasn't going to say anything else. "What does that mean?"

"What does what mean?"

"That 'Mmm.' If you have something to say, say it."

She tossed her hair. "All right, I will. I don't think you're as much of a loner as you want everyone to believe. I think you've enjoyed your time here."

He shrugged. "I won't deny that. But it's time for me to move on. Just as soon as I get this damned cast off."

"Rio, how long are you going to keep running?"

He scowled. "I'm not running from anything."

"Of course you are. You're running from the past. But has it worked? Have you ever been able to forget?"

"No," he admitted, his voice gritty with temper. "But staying here won't make it go away, either."

"Maybe not," she agreed quietly. "But maybe you'd be able to put it behind you. Start a new life. Learn to be happy."

"You really think I'd be happy living here, working on a construction crew every day, trying to be something I'm not?" he asked grimly, staring past her. He was grateful for the darkness, relieved that his too-perceptive sister couldn't see the regret he'd managed to keep out of his voice. Didn't she know he wished things could be different? That he wished *he* could be different? Didn't she know he'd stay if he thought it would work?

"Maybe you'd like it," she tried to argue, though he heard the lack of true conviction in her voice.

"You're only saying that because you want it to be true," he accused her, his anger dissipating with the knowledge that she honestly wanted the best for him. "Maybe it will work out here for you—but it won't for me."

Gypsy stiffened. "Maybe *what* will work out for me?"

"C'mon, Gypsy. I'm not blind. I've seen the way you look at Tom. And the way he looks at you."

"Oh."

He suspected that she'd be blushing if he could see her clearly. He couldn't help smiling a little. "You really thought I didn't know you've fallen for him?"

In unconscious imitation of Rio, she shrugged. "I—uh—I guess I should have known you would. So what do you think?"

"I think he's a nice guy. And I think you're going to hurt him."

Taking offense at his automatic pessimism, Gypsy lifted her chin. "What makes you think that?"

Rio sighed and ran a hand through his hair. "You don't belong here any more than I do. This family is like something out of a television program. You and I are different. We don't belong in a rural Arkansas town where the bright lights come from fixtures attached to slow-moving ceiling fans, the excitement from a lively game of charades."

"Maybe we've never lived that way before, but it doesn't mean we can't learn," his sister argued, vulnerability evident behind the bravado of her words. "I've looked for a long time for a place where I could fit in. A place where I could belong. A family. Maybe I've found that here."

"It's someone else's family, Gypsy," Rio murmured gently, hating himself for saying it, unable to resist trying to protect her from the pain of disillusionment, disappointment. "Someone else's husband, someone else's children, someone else's parents and brothers and sister. Even Tom belongs only because he was married to Ellen."

Gypsy flinched. "I know that," she whispered tightly. "But Ellen's dead. And Tom and the children are still alive. They need someone."

"They have Jill."

"Jill deserves her own life."

Rio couldn't argue with that. Instead, he changed course. "Has Tom said anything to indicate that he feels the same way you do?"

Shifting restlessly, Gypsy crossed her arms defensively over her chest. "Not exactly. He's feeling a little guilty, I think. He didn't expect to care for anyone else after Ellen died. But I think he's learning to care for me, Rio. And I think—I hope—he's learning to accept those feelings, to let go of the past. Just as you and I have to do."

Rio sighed deeply. "You're setting yourself up for a fall, Gypsy. Don't do it."

There was a long, tense pause. Rio could almost feel the waves of temper coming from his sister as she straightened to her full height and glared up at him. When she spoke, her voice was low, clipped. "You're my brother, Rio, and I love you. I've always loved you. But I won't let you interfere with my chance for happiness. Maybe you are content with your drifting, though I don't believe it. I think you're just too scared to try to change."

"You're wrong. And I'm not trying to keep you from being happy, Gypsy. I want to keep you from being hurt."

"You only assume I'll be hurt because you've always expected it for yourself. But I'm not like you, Rio. Oh, I was, for a long time. Afraid to form attachments, afraid to stay too long in one place for fear of missing it too much when I had to leave. But I've found something here that's worth taking a chance on. Something I've looked for all my life. Something I don't want to run away from. I'm not saying it will be easy, but I'm saying I'm willing to try, to risk everything to make this work.

"And," she added, waving her hand toward the woman approaching them from the house, "if you don't recognize a good thing when you see it, then I must have been the one to get all the brains in our family!"

With a toss of her dark head, she flounced away, leaving Rio staring narrowly after her. He watched her pause when she met up with Jill and look back at her brother. "If you're looking for Rio," she said, making sure her voice carried to him, "you've found him. But I warn you, he may not make you feel welcome. He's having such a wonderful time out here by himself, feeling lonely and martyred."

With that last taunt, she hurried toward the house, leaving Rio and Jill alone.

Rio rested one hand on the tree trunk, trying to look casual, though his knuckles shone white in the shadows. He'd really blown that one, he thought in bitter self-disgust. It wasn't enough that he felt isolated from Jill's family. Now it seemed he'd pushed away the one remaining member of his own.

Chapter Ten

Having hesitated to intrude on Rio's privacy, Jill had still felt compelled to check on him when he'd slipped away from the party and hadn't returned. Now, watching as Gypsy stamped furiously away, she turned warily to the man standing so quietly in the deep shadows of the huge pine tree. Slipping her hands into the pockets of her wool slacks, she tried to speak nonchalantly. "Is what she said true? Are you really feeling lonely and martyred?"

"Gypsy was being sarcastic," Rio answered irritably. "We had a quarrel and that was her parting shot."

Still concerned about Gypsy's words, Jill persisted. "Has anyone said anything, done anything to make you feel unwelcome inside? Because, if so, I—"

"Look, Jill, it isn't that, all right?" he cut in abruptly. "Everyone has been great. I just needed to get away from the crowd for a few minutes."

"I guess I can understand that," she conceded, glancing at the house from which a muted roar of noise could still be heard. She watched the darting shadows moving past the curtained windows, bright rectangles in the darkness surrounding her. Had Rio been out here all this time, watching those silhouettes—a lonely outsider gazing in? Her heart twisted.

"I think I'll stay out here awhile longer," Rio said casually. "Why don't you go on back to the party?"

Jill moistened her lips, trying to read his expression in the darkness. She could only make out the glitter of his dark, shuttered eyes. "I don't like leaving you out here alone."

"I've gotten used to it," he answered flatly.

Impulsively, Jill reached out to him, needing to touch him, to make him feel less alone. He flinched from her touch as though she'd meant to strike him. "Don't."

Her hand fell, fingers curling into her palm with the hurt he'd inflicted. "Rio—"

"Go back inside, Jill."

Her voice was little more than a whisper. "Are you ever going to let anyone get close to you, Rio? Must you push everyone away?"

"I don't stay anywhere long enough for anyone to get that close. Don't forget that. It's no different here. As soon as Doc removes this cast, I'm history."

She closed her eyes. As many times as he'd warned her, as many times as he'd declared his impatience to move on, it still hurt. "You're not even tempted to stay?" she couldn't help asking. Maybe the pain would lessen if he'd only admit that he'd like to stay if he could.

"I haven't found anything here to tempt me," he answered callously, withdrawing both physically and emotionally from the entreaty in her voice.

Inhaling sharply, she quivered, then opened her eyes to look at him resentfully. "You really can be a bastard, can't you?'' With that, she turned, wanting only to get as far away from him as possible, as Gypsy had done just minutes before.

She'd taken only a step when she found herself whirled backward, pressed against the huge tree trunk as he leaned heavily into her. "Dammit, Jill, what do you want from me? Can't you see I'm trying not to hurt you?''

Tears she couldn't control spilled from the corners of her eyes. "You're doing a hell of a job of it,'' she whispered.

His face inches from hers, his eyes burning into hers, he looked like a menacing young warrior in the near darkness. Some people might have been intimidated by the fierceness of his expression. Jill loved him too much ever to be afraid of him.

"Only children expect happily-ever-after fairy tales to come true,'' he muttered, his fingers digging into her shoulders. "Life doesn't guarantee happy endings, Jill. People who sit around waiting for them are destined to be disappointed. Maybe it's time you grew up enough to figure that out. Time you learned to take your pleasures where you can find them, the way I have, knowing they're only fleeting moments that can't be expected to last forever.''

He kissed her roughly, almost angrily. She wondered if he expected her to push him away. Instead, she threw her arms around his neck and kissed him back with the same furious passion. It was a battle of lips, of tongues, of turbulent emotions. And neither combatant won, neither lost, because both surrendered at the same time, united by needs that were stronger than either of them.

The kiss changed, becoming slow, probing, sensually intimate. Rio's hips shifted, undulating slowly against her, taunting her with his arousal, fueling her own. His tongue stroked hers, advanced and retreated, making her moan breathlessly, almost soundlessly. She buried her fingers in his hair, melting into him.

Crushed between Rio's pulsing solid body and the rough bark of the tree, Jill could hardly breathe. But, rather than complaining, she held him even more tightly, shaken by hunger so raw it hurt. She wanted him, needed him, loved him. Ached to pull him even closer, to take him inside her, hold him until he would never want to leave her. And her heart bled because she knew that no matter how hard she tried, she'd never be able to hold him that bindingly. Not unless he chose to be held.

Knowing what she had to do, though everything inside her begged her to stay right where she was, she finally drew back, pushing gently at his shoulders until his arms loosened. His breathing was harsh as he stared down at her, silently demanding to know why she'd stopped what they'd both been enjoying so much.

"You're wrong, you know," she murmured, her voice nearly unrecognizable. "You've taken your fleeting pleasures, and all they've left behind is emptiness. Real, honest, lasting emotions are the only ones that bring true happiness."

She raised a hand to his hard cheek, cradling it as she would love to cradle him, if he would allow her to get that close to him. "I'm not as naive as you seem to think, Rio. I know life doesn't guarantee happy endings, that it isn't perfect or always fair. If it were, Ellen would be here celebrating her husband's birthday with her family. You and Gypsy wouldn't have lost your mother so early. No one would ever be unhappy. Yet it's still possible to find happiness for as long as life allows—but only if you're willing to work at making the happiness last, at taking the risks involved in anything worth striving for."

"Only a fool puts everything on the line, knowing the odds are stacked against him from the first," Rio answered flatly, not moving away from her touch, but not responding to it, either.

"No one could ever call you a fool, could they?" she asked sadly, knowing he was rejecting her. Again.

"No," he replied quietly, his voice heavy. "A coward, maybe, but not a fool."

She took a deep, unsteady breath. "Is it better to be a coward?"

His short laugh was bitterly self-deprecating. "A hell of a lot easier."

Determined not to break down in front of him, she blinked back incipient tears. "I see."

"I want you, Jill."

She moistened her lips. "And I want you. But I don't know if I can deal with the heartache when you're gone."

He nodded. "I know. All I can offer is a couple of weeks together. If that's not enough for you, then maybe we'd better just try to stay away from each other until I go."

"Maybe we'd better," she agreed, the words tearing at her throat.

He wrapped a hand around the back of her neck and rested his forehead against hers. "I'm sorry, Jill."

"So am I," she whispered, the tears threatening again.

His kiss was so tender that she nearly dissolved in his arms. She broke away abruptly, dashing at her eyes with the back of her hand. "I'll go back in now. Enjoy your martyrdom, Rio."

And she turned and fled, leaving him staring hungrily after her.

It was all Jill could do to get out of bed when her alarm went off the next morning. She could work up little enthusiasm for cooking breakfast or attending church. All she really wanted to do was curl up beneath the covers and try to hide from the heartache that awaited her when she found herself in the same room with Rio again, so close and yet so distant from him.

Wearily pulling on her robe, she ran a hand through her tangled hair and walked into the bathroom. At least she could take some pride in believing that she'd made it through the remainder of last night's party without anyone—except maybe Gypsy—knowing that she was upset. She'd plastered on a smile and thrown herself into the final festivities with every appearance of carefree enthusiasm.

Rio had come back in just as everyone was leaving, explaining that he'd had a headache and had needed to get away from the noise for a while. He hadn't spoken to Jill again for the remainder of the evening. They hadn't even looked at each other as they'd headed off to their separate beds.

Tom was already in the kitchen, pouring coffee from the pot he'd just made. "Good morning," he said, smiling at her as she walked into the room. "Want a cup?"

"Please," she answered fervently.

He laughed. "Need a jump start this morning?"

She nodded and opened the refrigerator door to pull out the ingredients for waffles. "I didn't sleep very well last night."

Tom grimaced sympathetically. "Neither did I."

Jill wondered if Tom had lain awake dealing with problems similar to the ones affecting her. She wasn't sure she wanted to ask, unwilling to discuss her own feelings for Rio just then.

Tom saved her having to say anything by commenting lightly, "It was a nice party, wasn't it?"

"Very nice. It was sweet of Doc to give you the new golf clubs you've been wanting."

"Yeah. And I love the sweater you made me. Thanks again, Jill."

"I'm glad you like it."

They lapsed into a comfortable silence as Jill finished making the batter and plugged in the waffle iron to warm up while she peeled and sliced cantaloupe. Tom was the one to speak first. "Hope Rio's feeling better this morning. He didn't look so hot last night."

"He said he had a headache," Jill responded, just missing the tip of her finger with the knife as her movements suddenly became awkward.

"Yeah, well, I guess our family gatherings can be a little much for outsiders to take in at first," Tom murmured. Almost too casually he added, "Gypsy seemed to fit in well enough, didn't she?"

"Yes, she did." Sensing that Tom wanted to talk, Jill turned to look at him. "You've grown very fond of Gypsy, haven't you, Tom?"

He shifted in his straight-back chair, his complexion turning a bit ruddy. "Yeah, I guess I have. I mean, I know she's only been here two weeks, but it feels like it's been a lot longer than that. You know?"

"Yes," Jill murmured, avoiding his eyes. "I know."

"She makes me laugh, Jill. And she makes me...feel things that I haven't felt in a long time."

Jill nodded. "I thought so."

He watched her closely. "Does that bother you? Would it upset you if Gypsy and I...?"

She quickly shook her head. "No, Tom. Of course it wouldn't upset me. I like Gypsy. So does the rest of the family. We've all known that someday you'd find someone. You're still young. None of us expected you to live like a monk forever."

"I loved Ellen, Jill. I loved her very much."

Her face softening, Jill rested a hand on his shoulder. "I know you did, Tom. But you have the rest of your life ahead of you. Ellen wouldn't want you to spend it alone."

Tom took a deep breath. "Gypsy's so very different from Ellen, from the rest of us. I don't know if I have much to offer a woman who's been accustomed to having the entire world for her playground. A man with a ready-made family may not seem like a bargain to her."

Remembering some of the expressions she'd seen on Gypsy's face when the other woman had looked at Tom, Jill smiled. "I wouldn't be so sure of that. I think Gypsy's smart enough to know a great catch when she sees one."

He patted her hand. "Maybe you're just a bit prejudiced?"

"Maybe you should ask her," she retorted.

He frowned. "You think so? I mean, it's only been two weeks."

"Sometimes it only takes a few hours for a person's life to change," Jill murmured, and this time she wasn't talking about Tom and Gypsy.

His eyes narrowed at something he saw in her face. "Jill, honey—"

She leaned over to kiss him, unable to talk about Rio just then, even with Tom, with whom she could always talk so easily. "Be happy, Tommy," she whispered, using her childhood nickname for him.

"Oh, excuse me." Gypsy spoke from the doorway, hovering hesitantly there. "Am I—interrupting something?"

Jill managed a smile for her. "I was just talking to my brother," she answered, making her relationship with Tom perfectly clear to the other woman, who'd looked stricken at chancing upon that affectionate kiss. "I'm making waffles, Gypsy," she added briskly, turning back to the counter. "I hope you're hungry this morning."

"You know me. I'm always hungry," Gypsy returned, entering the room with a touchingly shy smile for Tom. "Is there anything I can do to help?"

"You can set the table," Jill answered, pouring batter into the waffle iron. "You know where everything is, of course."

"Of course." Gypsy's eyes met Jill's for a moment, searchingly. And then she relaxed, obviously reading the acceptance and approval in Jill's smile. "I'd be happy to set the table."

"By the way, Tom," Jill said lightly, "do you still have that extra ticket for the Razorbacks game next weekend?"

"The one I bought for you before you reminded me that you still don't like football? Of course I have it."

Jill looked meaningfully over her shoulder at him. "Maybe Gypsy would enjoy going with you and the kids to the game."

He grinned at her before looking toward Gypsy. "How about it, Gypsy? I promised Gordie and Sharon we'd spend next weekend in Fayetteville to watch the Hogs play."

"The Hogs?" she repeated blankly.

He laughed. "You can't stay in Arkansas long without finding out about the statewide obsession with the University of Arkansas football team. They're playing the Longhorns this weekend, and believe me, it's the grudge match of the year."

"Sounds like fun," Gypsy said, then looked questioningly at Jill. "You're sure you don't want to go?"

She shook her head. "I'm a real oddity in these parts— I'm not a football fan. I'm sure Gordie and Sharon would enjoy having you along. Particularly Sharon."

"Then I'd love to. Thank you." And then she suddenly remembered something. "Oh, but Rio—"

Jill cleared her throat. "I'll take care of Rio."

Tom looked suddenly concerned. "It won't bother you being here alone with him overnight, will it?"

"Don't be ridiculous, Tom. Of course not," she answered, hoping she sounded more confident than she felt.

"He's hardly a stranger anymore. And besides, he and I have spent nearly every day together while the rest of you are gone. We'll get along fine."

"Rio wouldn't take advantage of being alone with Jill," Gypsy assured Tom, heatedly defending her brother.

He spread his hands conciliatory. "Sorry, I'm just in the habit of protecting little sister, here."

"Little sister can take care of herself," Jill reminded him spiritedly. "Besides," she added with a laugh, "you know very well that my brothers would slaughter Rio if he did anything I didn't want. I'm sure Rio is just as aware of that fact."

Tom's long dimples deepened mischievously, his pale blue eyes crinkling with his grin. "I'm not worried that he'll do anything you don't want—it's what you *do* want that bothers me."

Her cheeks flaming, Jill was spared having to respond when Gordie and Sharon burst into the room, both declaring themselves at the point of starvation. She turned back to her cooking, hiding her expression when Rio entered the room only minutes after the children.

By the time Jill turned to set his plate in front of him, she had herself firmly under control. She wouldn't slip again, she promised herself.

Tom, Gypsy and the children left the following Friday afternoon, as soon as Gordie and Sharon arrived home from school. The silence that followed their noisy departure made Jill extremely conscious of being alone with Rio, though she didn't know why she felt odd about it. They'd been alone most of the week, after all, and they'd hardly spoken during their hours together. Jill had spent most of the time on her housework and sewing, while Rio sat on the porch with his carving. They may as well have built an invisible wall between them.

When she could stall no longer, Jill put away her sewing and went in search of Rio, intending to ask what he'd like for dinner. It would feel strange cooking for just the two of them, she mused, pushing open the front door.

As she'd expected, Rio sat in the chair he'd adopted as his own, his full concentration on the wood and knife in his busy hands. Pushing her hands self-consciously into the pockets of her oversize pink cardigan, Jill took a deep breath of cool air, aware of the unmistakable scents of autumn. "It's getting cool out, isn't it?"

He glanced up at her innocuous opening remark. "Mmm."

She assumed that was a yes. "You never know what the weather will be like this time of year in Arkansas," she attempted again. "Sometimes it's very cold at Halloween. Other years the children nearly melt inside their costumes."

"Is that right?"

He wasn't making casual conversation any easier. Were they supposed to spend the next twenty-four hours in cool silence? Determined to do no such thing, she stepped closer to his chair. "What's that you've been working on for the past few days?"

Exhaling audibly, Rio looked up without expression and showed her the carving. "I just finished it."

Her eyes widened in awed appreciation. "A hummingbird! Oh, Rio, it's beautiful."

Its long, thin beak dipped into an incredibly lifelike flower, and tiny wings frozen in midbeat, the minutely detailed bird looked as though it could take flight at any moment. "I've seen porcelain figurines that were no more delicate than this," Jill assured him. "It's hard to believe you carved it from a hard block of wood."

Seemingly embarrassed by her praise, Rio shrugged. "I've spent so much time alone during the past few years that I took up carving as a way of entertaining myself. It's just something to do with my hands."

"You're very talented. You could make a living selling your carvings to the numerous craft shops here in the Ozarks. They're always looking for items like this to sell to tourists."

Ignoring her comment, he tossed her the bird, which she caught instinctively, half afraid she'd break it if she clutched it too tightly. "You keep it," he told her. "Call it a token of gratitude for all you've done for me."

She didn't want his gratitude, but she loved the impulsive gift, knowing how much care and patience had gone into it. The carving represented that sensitive, gentler side of Rio that he allowed so few people to see. Had he intended it for her all along?

Cradling the little bird in her hands, she tried to keep the emotion from her voice when she thanked him. "I'll always treasure it," she murmured, unable to meet his eyes. If this was all she would have to remind her of Rio, she would never let it out of her sight, she told herself with a twinge of sadness.

"Jill, I—" He bit off whatever he'd almost said, to her disappointment. After a moment, he shoved a hand through his hair and concentrated on cleaning the knife. "I'm glad you like it."

"I love it." *I love you, Rio. Will you ever let me tell you?*

After a long, tense silence, Jill pulled in a deep breath and acknowledged reluctantly that the brief moment of intimacy was over. "I came out to ask what you'd like for dinner," she said lightly.

"Whatever you want will be fine."

On a sudden impulse, she suggested, "Why don't we go out for dinner? You haven't left this house in weeks. You're probably ready for a change of scenery."

He seemed startled by the suggestion. "Go out?"

"Sure. You get along very well on your cast. We shouldn't have any problems." The more she thought about the idea, the better she liked it. She'd love to go out on a date with Rio—even if it was at her own initiative.

"I don't have anything to wear," Rio said, gesturing toward the wood-sprinkled navy sweat suit he wore.

"I washed your black sweat suit earlier today. It'll be fine, particularly since it's obvious you can't wear jeans or slacks over your cast," Jill replied persuasively. "Wouldn't you like to get out for a change?"

He thought about it a moment, then smiled faintly. "You know, I think I would," he answered at last. "As long as it's someplace casual."

She smiled back at him, pleased that he'd accepted her offer. "Of course. I'll freshen my makeup while you change."

His eyes skimmed her face. "You look fine."

From Rio, that was almost a flowery compliment. Her smile deepened. "Thanks. Need any help out here?"

"I can handle everything."

"Then I'll go get ready."

She had her hand on the door when he spoke, detaining her. "Jill."

She looked over her shoulder. "Yes?"

He was standing now, his chin lifted in a familiar gesture of arrogant defensiveness. "I'd almost forgotten—I don't have any money." The words seemed to irk him a great deal.

Conscious of his innate sense of pride, Jill answered carefully. "I know. This is my treat. It will be nice for me to get out for a change, too, you know. An excuse not to cook, for once."

Given that slim justification, he accepted it with dignity. "All right. If you're sure."

"I'm sure." She hurried inside before he could think of another reason not to go.

Some twenty minutes later, Jill stood rather nervously in the living room, waiting for Rio. She checked her appearance in a decorative wall mirror, satisfied that her makeup looked fine. She still wore the soft pink cardigan, along with a pink-and-gray plaid blouse and gray wool slacks. Not exactly a fashionable ensemble such as Gypsy might have worn, she thought resignedly, but she looked good enough. She wasn't Gypsy, after all. Just ordinary, wholesome Jill Hammond.

A sound in the doorway behind her made her turn. Her breath caught in her throat. The black sweat suit would have looked plain, innocuous on anyone else. Rio, with his thick black hair and mysterious black eyes, his dark complexion and intriguing scar, his hard, lean body, looked wonderful in it. Even the cast couldn't detract from the faint, primitively appealing air of danger that surrounded him.

Jill had never thought herself the type to be attracted to dangerous men. She'd always thought she wanted a nice, gentle, settled, dependable male. An accountant, perhaps, or a doctor. Someone like Tom or Gabe. She'd never fantasized about an unemployed, complex, aloof drifter. And yet, now that Rio had entered her life, she knew that he was exactly the man she'd always secretly hoped to find. A man who effortlessly brought out the previously hidden, daring side of herself.

And most amazing of all, this dangerous, gorgeous, mysterious man wasn't looking at her as though she were ordinary, wholesome Jill Hammond. He looked at her as though she were beautiful. Desirable. Special.

Rio was the one who broke the spell that had fallen over them when their eyes locked. Tearing his gaze away, he roughly cleared his throat. "Are you ready to go?" he demanded, more gruffly than he'd obviously intended.

"Yes." Her own voice wasn't quite steady. She hid her flushed cheeks behind a sweep of hair as she reached for her purse. "I'm ready."

She realized suddenly that her idea to go out had been a very wise move. She wasn't sure how much longer she could share an empty house with Rio without begging him to take her into his arms. She definitely needed the safety of other people around them, at least until she could get her stampeding hormones back under control.

That should only take a few hours, she thought bracingly, digging out her car keys—and knew all along she was lying to herself.

Chapter Eleven

"Hi, Jill. How's it going?"

"Fine, Sandy. How's your mother?"

"Much better, thanks."

"I'm glad. Tell her I'll be by to see her soon."

"I will."

"Jill! Gosh, it's been ages. What've you been up to?"

"Not much. Goodness, your boys are growing so fast, Angie. What're you feeding them?"

"Are you kidding? They eat everything that doesn't try to take a bite out of them first. Tell Tom I said hi, okay?"

"Of course."

"Hi, Jill."

"Hi, Steve."

Rio figured that roughly everyone in the casual mom-and-pop-styled restaurant had spoken while he and Jill made their way to an empty table. Her acquaintances eyed him with surreptitious curiosity, seemingly surprised to see him at her side. Did she know everyone in the area? And was he such a change from the usual type of man she dated?

As if sensing that he didn't particularly want her to, Jill made no attempt to introduce Rio to the people who spoke to her so easily. He was relieved, not knowing what he would have said to them had she done so. He'd never been one to make small talk with strangers. He was glad when he and Jill were finally able to sit quietly alone and look over their plastic-coated menus.

"The chicken-fried steak with cream gravy, mashed potatoes and green beans is the special tonight," Jill advised over the top of her menu. "That's what Tom always has here."

"What are you having?" he asked, glancing without a great deal of interest at the rather limited selections.

"I think I'll have the catfish plate. It comes with coleslaw, hush puppies and French fries, with a side order of green tomato chowchow."

He closed his menu and set it on the table in front of him. "Sounds good. I'll have that, too."

An overweight waitress with bleached hair and a bright smile approached the table, greeting Jill by name. "I hear Tom and the kids are in Fayetteville this weekend," she added, studying Rio with speculative interest.

"That's right," Jill agreed, apparently not surprised by the woman's knowledge of her family affairs. "How's Ed enjoying his new truck?"

The woman shook her parlor-curled head with an exaggerated roll of her eyes. "He's done everything but sleep in it since he bought it. Spends the better part of each evening polishing the fenders. I'm beginning to think I'm going to have to wear seat covers and fuzzy-dice earrings to get him to notice me again."

Jill laughed. "Men and their wheels."

"Ain't it the truth. So, what'll ya'll have tonight?"

Rio gestured for Jill to take care of the orders when she looked to him in question. She ordered two catfish plates and a pitcher of iced tea.

The waitress scribbled on her pad. "The fried okra's 'specially good tonight. Want a side order?"

Looking tempted, Jill made a rueful face. "Give me a break, Alma. Another fried dish? Think of the calories!"

"Humph. Wouldn't hurt you to gain a few pounds. A man likes curves, don't he, handsome?"

Realizing the woman was talking to him, Rio cleared his throat and shrugged. "There's nothing wrong with Jill's curves."

The waitress chuckled. "Noticed that, did you? I'll go get your tea."

Faintly amused by Jill's suspiciously pink cheeks, Rio leaned back in his seat and glanced around the busy restaurant. "Does everyone know everyone else around here?"

"Just about," she admitted. "The most popular local sport is neighbor-watching. I guess it's that way in any small, rural area."

"Does it ever bother you?"

"Sometimes. The gossip can be rather cruel at times. Yet, strangely enough, the same people who enjoy talking about you over the back fence will be the first on your doorstep to help in times of trouble."

"So you trade the right of privacy for a strong community-support network?"

She tilted her head thoughtfully. "I never really looked at it that way, but I suppose that's partially true."

Rio sighed and shook his head. "Very insulated, very safe. But there's so much out there that you're missing here."

"I know," she agreed quietly. "But I guess some of us are meant to seek adventures and some are more suited to stay on the sidelines."

He wanted to argue, to tell her that he and she weren't that different. But, truth was, he couldn't see himself content to settle into this cozy community any more than he could imagine Jill living the rootless, aimless existence he'd led for the past few years. Why was it that every time he was alone with her he had such a hard time remembering how totally wrong they were for each other?

"Here's your tea," Alma announced cheerfully, thumping a large plastic pitcher onto the center of the Formica-topped table. "Dinners will be out soon. And I added a couple orders of that okra, Jill. On the house."

Jill smiled at the woman, and Rio wondered if he were the only one to notice that her smile seemed rather strained. "Thanks, Alma. I'm sure we'll enjoy it."

Jill waited at the front door for Rio to catch up, her fingers clenched around the strap of her purse to keep them from reaching out in an offer of assistance she knew he wouldn't appreciate. As soon as he'd made it safely to the top step of the porch, she inserted her key in the lock.

Dinner had gone well enough, she supposed, even if Rio had seemed quieter than usual. He'd been visibly uncomfortable with the attention he'd received as Jill's dinner companion. It was obvious that he wasn't used to the avid, ill-concealed curiosity of residents of a small rural community. Rio had probably spent a lot of time blending into the shadows of the towns he'd visited previously.

Maybe going out hadn't been such a great idea, she thought, stepping into the house. She'd hoped being around other people would defuse some of the tension that always built up when she and Rio were alone. Instead, it seemed to have made it even more noticeable.

"Can I get you anything, Rio?" she asked, still clutching her purse as she turned to watch him enter behind her.

He shut the door behind him and shook his head. "I'm fine."

"Maybe there's something good on television, I'll find the program guide for you if you want to get comfortable on the couch."

"You don't have to entertain me, Jill. I'm perfectly capable of taking care of myself."

"Yes, I know." *All too well.* "I guess I'll go put my purse and sweater away, then."

Safe in the sanctity of her bedroom, she allowed her shoulders to relax as she hung her sweater in the closest. She hadn't realized how stiffly she'd been holding them until she felt the easing of tension at being alone.

And then she stiffened again when Rio's voice sounded from behind her. "I've never seen your room before. It's nice."

Jill turned slowly, hands clasped tightly at her waist. Rio stood in the open doorway, studying her country-French-influenced decor with interest. "It always surprises me how quietly you've learned to get around on that cast," she told him with a forced laugh. "You startled me."

"Sorry." But he didn't look particularly apologetic.

"Did you want something?"

His brows twitched at her wording, but he answered innocuously enough. "I forgot to thank you for taking me out to dinner tonight."

"It wasn't necessary, but you're welcome."

Rio took a step into the room. "You know, that was the first time I've been out on a date in longer than I can remember."

She cleared her throat, managing with some effort not to take a step backward as he slowly approached. "It—it wasn't exactly a date," she felt it necessary to point out.

"Kind of felt like one, though, didn't it?"

Her fingers tightened until the knuckles went white. "Yes, I suppose it did," she agreed, her voice sounding strained.

"Of course, if it *had* been a date, it wouldn't be officially over until I'd given you the traditional good-night kiss."

"I—" She swallowed, then tried to speak lightly, telling herself he could only be teasing her. Though he didn't look as if he were teasing. He looked deadly serious, actually. *Play it light, Jill.* "I'm sorry, I don't kiss on the first date."

He clucked scoldingly, his mouth crooking upward in what might have been a smile. "Very old-fashioned of you."

"Guess I'm just the old-fashioned type."

He reached out to touch her hair. "I'd already figured that out for myself."

Her smile was wry, self-deprecating. "The last twenty-five-year-old-virgin in America, huh?"

"Maybe not the last. Certainly a rarity," he agreed, his fingers threading through her hair to cup the back of her head.

Her heart already racing from that almost-casual touch, Jill looked up at him—and could think of nothing at all to say.

Rio's fingers tightened gently, pulling her closer. "Are you going to slap me if I kiss you? That's the proper, old-fashioned thing to do, I believe."

"No, I'm not going to slap you," she admitted, her hands untangling to creep up his chest. "I'm not feeling old-fashioned at the moment."

His mouth hovered inches above hers. "What are you feeling at the moment?"

Fear. Excitement. Hunger. Love. "Confused," she whispered, lumping all those rampant emotions together.

"That makes two of us," he murmured, and then lowered his head that short distance separating them.

She could almost have believed it was their first kiss. His mouth moved over hers slowly, persuasively, reassuringly. If his intention was to make her relax, his strategy worked. Lost in the tenderness of his clever lips, she melted against him.

The very tip of his tongue traced her lower lip, requesting rather than demanding entrance. Willingly she opened to him, inviting him deeper. Even then he kept his movements slow, unthreatening. His tongue dipped and swirled, teased and caressed. Needs building inside her until she trembled with them, Jill moaned softly, vaguely dissatisfied. Where was the frenzy, the fire he'd shown her before? The raw desire that had raged between them, telling her that he wanted her as desperately as she wanted him, letting her know she wasn't alone in her madness?

Frustration making her reckless, she crowded closer, her hands sliding into his hair to hold his head more tightly to hers, her mouth making demands he answered willingly. She felt his hoarse, suspiciously smug chuckle against her lips and realized that this was what he'd wanted all along—for her to show him she was very much a willing participant. Closing her eyes, she kissed him with all the skill he'd taught her during the past weeks, until she wasn't the only one trembling.

Caught up in her hunger, Rio locked both arms around her, holding her as tightly as she'd longed to be held, storming her mouth with the unleashed, almost savage passion she'd craved. This was what she'd needed from him, she thought in dazed satisfaction. This mindless, primitive, furious insanity she'd shared with no one before him.

One hand clenching her hair, he thrust more deeply into her mouth, bending her backward with the force of the kiss. And then nearly tumbled to the floor with her when he lost his balance, hindered by the awkward cast. Steadying him instinctively with arms braced against his chest, Jill couldn't help laughing, the sound breathless, husky.

After expressing his self-censure with a few pithy curses, Rio reluctantly laughed with her. "Real smooth, aren't I?" he growled. "I can't even kiss you without almost falling on my face—and carrying you with me."

"The cast will be off in a few days," she reminded him, wanting only to make him feel better. Instead, the words stabbed into her own heart, making her flinch as they sank in. *A few days.* She had only a few more days with him.

His crooked smile vanishing at the expression on her face, Rio's fingers tightened on her shoulders. "Jill. Don't."

"I can't help it," she whispered, making no effort to hide her emotions as she stared up at him. "I don't want you to go."

"But you know I have to, don't you?"

"Yes," she answered with a sigh, finally accepting the inevitable. "I know."

His own sigh was heavy. "I wish—" The words died away.

"I know," she murmured again. She lifted one unsteady hand to cup his cheek. So hard. So strong. So warm. Her fingertip traced the scar on his cheek. "So do I."

Rio covered her hand with his own, cradling it against his cheek, regret in his dark eyes. "I think I'd better get out of here now and leave you alone."

Jill raised her other hand, cupping his face between her palms. "No. I don't think so."

Standing on tiptoe, she kissed him. Her heart beat heavily in her chest, her pulse pounded in response to her own uncharacteristic daring, but a strange sense of calm had settled her mind. She knew now what she wanted, what she had to do. Whatever happened later, she had Rio all to herself now. She wasn't sure whether she'd be more foolish to keep him with her tonight or send him away, but she'd made her choice.

She'd been a fool already to fall in love with a drifter. At least she'd have this night to remember when he was gone.

"Stay with me tonight," she whispered, her lips moving seductively against his.

His eyes narrowed, searching her face for signs of uncertainty. "I don't want to hurt you, Jill."

"Then be gentle," she answered, nuzzling her mouth against his chin.

His breath caught. "That wasn't what I meant," he said gruffly. "I wasn't talking about hurting you physically."

She pulled her head back to look at him, her eyes steady on his. "I'm only asking for tonight, Rio. If all I can have is one night with you, then I'll take it. I won't expect anything more."

"But I—"

She used her lips to silence him. Pulling back only fractionally, she whispered his name and then, "I want you."

He groaned and buried his face in her hair. "God, Jill. I want you so much I hurt. I've never wanted anyone this much."

"Then don't hold back on my account." Her chin lifted proudly, she stepped back, emboldened by the hunger flaring in his dark eyes. Taking a deep breath, she reached for the top button of her blouse.

Rio's hands covered hers, stopping her. His gaze bored into hers. "You're absolutely sure?"

"I'm absolutely sure," she answered without hesitation.

His smile melted her knees. "Then let me."

Her arms dropped to her sides. Lowering his head to kiss her, he released that top button. And then the next, and the one below that, until her blouse was open and his hands were against the warm, bare skin of her sides. His palms slid upward, making her shiver in anticipation, and then he stopped. "Damn."

She opened her heavy-lidded eyes and frowned. "Now what?"

"I—uh—don't have any protection with me."

Jill blushed scarlet. "I do," she mumbled.

Rio tilted his head in question, as if not sure he'd heard her correctly. "You do?"

"Yes. Um—in the bedside table."

His dark eyes lit with a slow smile. "A recent purchase?"

"Very recent," she assured him, moistening her lips and trying not to think of that particular shopping trip. She'd had to drive an extra fifteen miles to find a pharmacy in which no one knew her. Her eyes met his rather shyly. "Since this was beginning to seem inevitable, I thought it best to be prepared."

"That's my Jill," he murmured against her lips. "Always taking care of the details."

She forgot her embarrassment in the depth of his kiss, a frisson of excitement skating down her spine at being called "his Jill." Even if for only one night.

The kiss changed, deepened, heated. Rio's arms tightened around her. He caught himself, this time, before his broken leg became a detriment. "Maybe we'd better sit down."

Smiling at his rueful tone, Jill helped him to the edge of her bed, carelessly shoving ruffled throw pillows to the floor. Sitting beside her, Rio grimaced at the cast stuck out in front of him. "We may encounter a few technical difficulties."

She kicked off her shoes. "We'll manage," she assured him with confidence inspired by trust.

He leaned back on his elbows, watching her in sensual challenge. "It's going to take cooperation on your part," he warned.

She slipped her blouse from her shoulders, letting it fall to the carpet. "I'm feeling very cooperative."

"So I see." His attention lingered for a moment on her flushed face before sliding downward to the scrap of pink lace covering her small, firm breasts. "Come here."

Rolling to his side, he faced her as she lay beside him, looking up at him with nervous anticipation. His fingertips stroked her shoulder, taking her bra strap down with them. Uncovering one breast, he traced a butterfly path across the upper swell, then downward over the hardening peak. His lips followed the trail mapped by his fingers. "You're so beautiful, Jill," he murmured against her flesh.

Her hands settling tentatively on his shoulders, Jill closed her eyes, beginning to tremble with the force of shattering sensations. Rio's breath, hot on her sensitive skin. His lips, firm and moist as they surrounded her aching nipple. His tongue, warm and wet, stroking her until she arched involuntarily, pushing herself more firmly against him. His hand fumbled behind her and then the bra was gone and both her breasts were bared to his thorough attentions.

The fabric of his black sweatshirt bunched beneath her kneading fingers. Impatient to touch him, she tugged at the hem. With one hand he helped her, sweeping the shirt over his head and slinging it away. Raising herself to him, twisting until he lay flat on his back, Jill draped half over him as she kissed his jaw, his throat, the smooth, warm skin of his chest. Imitating him, she swept her tongue over one flat brown nipple. Rio shuddered; Jill smiled in pleasure.

Her hair tumbled around her face as her lips moved over him. His stomach quivered when the ends tickled him. Tiny openmouthed kisses intended to soothe seemed only to arouse him more. He took her hand and eased it slowly downward. Jill caught her breath in wonder at the extent of his arousal, awed that he could want her so much. Being wanted this badly was a seduction in itself.

At his whispered urging, she removed the rest of her clothing and then eased the elastic waistband of his sweat-pants down his lean hips and over the bulky cast. His briefs followed, until he lay nude on her bed, watching for her reaction. She sat back on her heels, studying him with shy curiosity. She'd never known a man could be so beautiful. Sleek, pulsing bronze skin, work-honed muscles, uncompromising masculinity. She reached out to stroke his thigh and Rio jerked as if he'd been shocked.

"If you keep looking at me like that, this is going to be over before it starts," he warned her roughly, his voice gravelly.

She smiled at the dark stain of color on his usually impassive face. "I can't help it. You're a beautiful man, Rio."

He scowled, trying to hide his embarrassment. "Hardly," he muttered, gesturing toward the long, thin, jagged scar on his rib cage and the cast on his right leg.

"Oh, yes," she replied quietly, bending to place a kiss at the very top of that cast, on the soft inner skin of his thigh. "Beautiful."

His fingers clenched her hair. "You're making it very difficult for me to remember that I promised to be gentle," he grated.

She flowed up his body, settling onto him with renewed hunger. "Don't be gentle, Rio," she murmured against his lips, cupping his face in her hands. "Just make love to me. Now. Please."

A low moan reverberated in his chest. And then there was no further need for words.

Perhaps there were moments of awkwardness when Rio's cast interfered with his otherwise fluid movements. Lost in sensual delight, Jill never noticed them.

There may have been a brief stab of pain when he finally settled her on top of him, after preparing her so exquisitely with his talented hands. She didn't care.

Her head thrown back, eyes closed in bliss, she proved a willing and innately talented partner, needing no more than the gentle guiding of his hands to teach her how to please him. And in pleasing him, she found sheer ecstasy for herself. They moved feverishly together, and then slowly, savoringly until passion swept them again into the frenzy of near insanity. Neither knew nor cared how much time passed before Jill collapsed bonelessly into Rio's arms, the echoes of her startled, joyous cries of fulfillment hovering in the air around them, mingling with the memory of Rio's exultant groans.

Knowing Jill's sentimental, emotional nature, Rio wasn't surprised to see the tears on her cheeks when he rolled over to cradle her to his side afterward. He was astonished, however, and not particularly pleased, to feel them burning at the back of his own eyes.

Why tears? he wondered, pressing her head into the hollow of his shoulder in a weak attempt to hide his expression from her. He'd never been one to feel the need for them before. Not during sex, no matter how good—though he was uncomfortably aware that nothing had ever compared to what he'd just shared with Jill—not even during his lowest points. What was it about this woman that brought the emotions he'd always tamped so firmly down so dangerously close to the surface?

Even as her ragged breathing slowed, softened, he told himself he shouldn't spend the night with her in his arms. And then he thought of the awkwardness of climbing out of the bed and groping around for his clothes, and decided he may as well stay where he was. He reached out to snap off the bedside lamp and pulled the tangled sheet over them.

And even as Jill drifted to sleep against him, his cheek resting on her disheveled hair, his arms locked firmly around her, he knew that the excuse of his leg had been no more than that—an excuse to stay exactly where he wanted to be, doing exactly what he wanted to do.

Holding Jill.

Holding her as if he'd never have to let go of her.

Jill woke to the feel of sunshine on her face and a warm, callused palm sliding down the length of her bare side. Squirming in reaction, she smiled and opened her eyes. Braced on one elbow, Rio lay beside her, looking at her as though he'd been watching her sleep for a very long time.

Moistening her lips in a moment of self-consciousness, she brushed her tumbled hair out of her face. "This feels strange."

"What does?" he asked, his voice morning-gravelly.

"Waking up to find a man in my bed. Particularly," she added teasingly, "a man whose last name I don't even know."

He ran a fingertip over her freshly dampened lower lip. "Smith."

Jill frowned. "I beg your pardon?"

"My last name," he explained, his fingers stroking her throat. "It's Smith."

"Rio Smith?"

He nodded. "Yep."

She was having a little trouble accepting that. It seemed so—so ordinary. "Is Gypsy's last name Smith, too?"

"It's the only last name either of us has ever known," he replied with a slight shrug, tracing her collarbone.

"Smith," she repeated, amused. "Fancy that."

He dropped a kiss on the end of her nose. "Disappointed?"

Her smile felt wickedly feline. "You haven't disappointed me yet, Rio Smith."

She was delighted to see that he actually blushed a little. And then he covered her mouth with his, his hand settling firmly on her breast, and any other questions she may have wanted to ask were forgotten.

Chapter Twelve

They never did get around to eating breakfast. Finally driven from the bedroom by hunger, they bathed, dressed and headed for the kitchen, where Rio sipped a cola and watched as Jill prepared thick sandwiches for lunch. "At least none of your brothers dropped in for coffee this morning," he remarked, his gaze on her glowing face.

She rolled her eyes expressively. "Thank goodness. But they rarely do come by on Saturday mornings. They usually spend time with their families on the weekends."

"What does Mike do?"

Jill shrugged. "Sleeps late. Works on his car. Goes fishing when the weather's nice."

"How come he's the only one still single—other than you? Is he a confirmed bachelor?"

Jill shook her head, making her hastily-tied-up ponytail bob behind her appealingly.

Rio's fingers tightened on his glass against the urge to take down that ponytail and run his hands once more through her silky hair. And then he was distracted by a hint of sadness in her eyes when she set his plate in front of him. "What did I say?"

She blinked, seemingly brought out of deep, not particularly happy thoughts. "Oh, I was just thinking about Mike. He broke up with a girl he loved very much a few months ago. I think he's still hurting about it, and it bothers me. I hate it when any of my brothers are unhappy, but I suppose Mike and I have always been closest, since we're the nearest in age."

Rio picked up his sandwich. "Why'd they break up?"

A flicker of anger crossed Jill's face. "She decided he was too 'countrified' for her. She was a friend of mine. They grew up together, went to school together, seemed to have a great deal in common. Then, all of a sudden, she decided she wanted more out of life than a husband in the construction business and a home in rural Arkansas. She dropped Mike and went off to find adventure in New York."

Rio decided not to say anything. Jill was obviously furious with her former friend for hurting her brother. Rio tended to see the woman's side, being faced with similar choices himself. Couldn't Jill understand that there were so many fascinating things to see and do before settling down to grow old gracefully?

He changed the subject. "When do you think Tom and Gypsy and the kids will be home?"

She glanced up from her lunch, willingly sidetracked. "The game starts at one-thirty, I think. They'll be home by eight or nine, depending on whether they linger over dinner somewhere. Tom won't keep the kids out too late."

"Wonder how they're getting along?" Rio asked casually, curious about Jill's opinion of the budding romance between his sister and her brother-in-law.

The dimple in her left cheek flashed with her smile. "I've wondered about that myself. It's rather difficult to conduct a courtship with two kids along, I would think."

Rio chuckled wryly. "I'm not sure that would deter Gypsy much."

Jill took a bite of her sandwich, chewed slowly, swallowed and looked up at Rio, seeming to frame her words with care. "Do you think Gypsy will stay when you...when you move on?"

No more anxious to discuss their impending separation than Jill, Rio stared down at his plate. "Maybe."

"Would you mind?"

He shrugged. "She's an adult. She generally does what she wants. If she's happy here, then I think she should stay."

"Do you think she'll be happy here after drifting for so long?"

He spread his hands. "Who knows? That's something only Gypsy can decide."

"It's just that you're so certain that you couldn't adapt to life here—I wonder if it will be different for Gypsy."

He met her eyes briefly. "Gypsy's not me."

"I guess that's obvious enough," Jill muttered, frowning at her nearly eaten sandwich.

Rio sighed. "Look, I don't know what's going to happen, okay? Gypsy seems really taken with Tom. She's always been adaptable. Given the right incentive, I think she could be happy anywhere. So maybe it'll work out. I'd like to see her happy."

"And what about you?" Jill asked quietly.

He pushed away his empty plate, avoiding her eyes. "What about me?"

"Will you be happy?"

He shrugged. "I'll be fine." He knew as well as she did that he hadn't answered her question.

"Will you come back? To visit Gypsy, I mean?" she added quickly.

Rio hesitated, framing his answer. His affair with Jill would end when he rode away, if it hadn't already. She deserved to get on with her life when he was gone, not to wait around, clinging to some fantasy that he'd come back for good. The kindest thing would be to make a clean break— no matter how badly it hurt both of them.

"Yeah, I'll probably get back by. In a few years. If she's still here of course."

"A few years?" Jill repeated faintly. "You'd go that long without seeing your sister?"

He met her eyes then, knowing his own were expressionless. "It wouldn't be the first time."

"Oh." Jill sat very still for a moment, then stood and carried her plate to the sink. "I'd better put a load of jeans in the washer so Gordie and Tom will have something to wear tomorrow."

He hated the pain in her voice, hated himself for putting it there. "Jill—"

She paused in the doorway of the laundry room, her back to him. "Just—give me a few minutes, okay?"

He sighed. "Yeah."

She left the room. He sat at the table for a long time, wishing again that he'd never climbed into the late Mr. Baxter's truck. It would have been better for everyone if Rio had stayed in the rain that night.

Barely half an hour had passed before Jill was compelled to seek out Rio again, unwilling to waste any more of their precious time together. She found him in the den, sitting on the couch, looking distant and alone as he flipped desultorily through one of Tom's veterinary journals.

Pasting on a smile, she crossed the room, snatched the magazine from his hands and planted herself in his lap. Before he could react, she took his face between her hands and kissed him thoroughly.

Rio cleared his throat when Jill finally released his mouth, his eyes looking a bit dazed. "What was that for?" he asked, his arms locked around her to hold her in his lap.

"Because I wanted to," she answered, running her fingers through his hair. "Any objections?"

He smiled. "Nope."

"Good. I feel the need for another one." And she kissed him again.

Rio's arms tightened spasmodically. "How long did you say we have before your family comes home?"

She nibbled at his ear, chuckling when he squirmed restlessly beneath her. "A long time."

His hand slid beneath her fleece top to stroke her back. "And if someone comes to visit?"

"Then we'll just pretend we're not home."

Rio cupped the back of her head in his hand and rested his forehead against hers, staring gravely into her unfocused eyes. "Did I ever tell you that I like the way you think?"

She laughed. "No. Maybe you'd like to go back to my bedroom so we can discuss it."

"Good idea."

She slid from his lap—slowly. "Race you," she challenged, grinning as she looked at his cast.

He held out his hand as he stood. "Why don't we just walk together."

She liked that idea even better. She curled her fingers into his.

* * *

They were quite decorously watching television when the rest of the family returned. Carrying Sharon, who'd fallen asleep in the car, Tom smiled as he entered the house. "We're home."

"So we see," Jill answered, standing to help him with his burden. "How was the game?"

"We won," Gordie announced sleepily from beneath a red plastic helmet shaped like a hog.

"The game was televised. Didn't you watch it?" Tom asked.

"I'll put Sharon to bed," Jill murmured, avoiding the question.

"So, what exciting things happened here while we were gone?" she heard Gypsy ask Rio as she carried Sharon toward the hallway.

"Jill and I went out to eat last night," Rio answered. Confident of his discretion, Jill left the questions to him, knowing he would smoothly turn the conversation around to the football outing.

He was good at that sort of thing.

After the children were in bed, the adults sat in the den, drinking hot cocoa and talking quietly. Keeping her eyes on her cup most of the time, Jill was still aware of every move Rio made, every time he looked at her. She glanced up once to find him watching her, and their smiles were private ones. Still, she wasn't aware that her behavior was at all different until she caught Tom looking at her in obvious concern.

That was when she announced that she thought it was time to turn in. "Sunday mornings come early around here," she warned with assumed heartiness, making the others yawn and agree that it was getting late.

She tossed for long, sleepless hours in her lonely bed. Rio had spent only one night there, and already she missed sleeping with him. She wondered if she would ever lie all night in his arms again.

She wondered how she'd ever survive if she didn't.

They were sitting around the table eating dinner Sunday evening when the telephone rang. Tom groaned. "I guess it was too much to hope that I could spend an entire weekend without one emergency," he grumbled, standing to answer the call.

He returned to the table with a dazed expression in his widened eyes.

"Is something wrong?" Jill demanded immediately, thinking of her family.

Tom shook his head. "No, not really. Debbie got married."

"Married?" Jill repeated, startled. "But she hasn't even been dating anyone, that I know of. Who did she marry? When?"

"Who's Debbie?" Rio asked curiously.

"My assistant," Tom reminded him, still looking rather stunned. "She met some guy on her vacation cruise. They flew to Vegas as soon as the ship docked and were married yesterday. The call was from her mother, breaking the news."

Jill couldn't help laughing at the thought of Tom's plump, practical, forty-two-year-old office manager swept into a whirlwind romance. "I hope it works out for her."

"So do I," Tom agreed. "But now I'm left in the lurch at the clinic." He looked at Gypsy. "Could I talk you into staying another week or two until I can find a replacement for her?"

Gypsy returned the look with a bright smile. "As a matter of fact, I'd like to apply for the job, myself. Interested?"

Jill watched as Tom's eyes narrowed. "Full-time? Permanently?"

"Permanently," Gypsy repeated, and there was something in her voice that Tom must have understood from previous conversations. Jill wondered what it was.

Tom broke into a grin that creased his face with his long, deep dimples. "You're hired."

"Yea!" Sharon cheered, understanding only that Gypsy wouldn't be leaving. Gordie looked pleased, as well.

Glancing from beneath her lashes at Rio, Jill noticed that his face showed no expression whatever. He continued to eat his dinner as though nothing particularly momentous had just happened.

Would she ever understand him?

"Saw Doc yesterday, Rio. He said he's taking your cast off tonight," Mike said heartily, sitting at the kitchen table with his massive hands wrapped around an incongruously delicate coffee cup. "I bet you're pleased."

Jill whirled around from the counter where she'd been slicing a coffee cake. "Tonight?" she repeated, her eyes going to Rio. So soon?

He returned the look evenly. "It's been four weeks since Doc put the walking cast on, Jill."

Mike seemed surprised by Jill's reaction. "What's the matter, Jilly? Don't you want the poor guy out of that thing?"

Annoyed with her overreaction in front of her all-too-perceptive-at-times brother, Jill managed to smile. "Of course I do. I'd just lost track of the time. I was concerned that he might be rushing things...that his leg might not be properly healed."

"Doc wouldn't take the cast off if there were any question of that," Mike pointed out logically. And then, seemingly satisfied with Jill's explanation, he looked back across the table at Rio. "Guess you're looking forward to having your leg back."

"Yeah," Rio agreed. "I am." And he winked at Jill when Mike turned his attention to the cake she set in front of him.

Trying to hold on to her smile, Jill knew the wink was intended to amuse her, that it carried meanings Mike wouldn't understand. Though she looked forward to making love with Rio without the impediment of the bulky cast, she still selfishly dreaded the removal of that cast and, with it, the reason for Rio to stay.

"I hear Gypsy started working permanently for Tom this morning," Mike commented, oblivious to the undercurrents in the air around him. "Funny about Debbie getting married, wasn't it?"

"It was certainly a surprise," Jill agreed, turning back to clean the counter.

"So what do ya'll think? Will Tom and Gypsy make a match of it?"

Jill let Rio field that one. "It looks that way," he agreed evenly. "Do you mind?"

"Are you kidding?" Mike grinned. "Your sister's terrific, Rio. It'll be great having her around. In fact, if Tom hadn't staked a claim so early, I might have made a move on her myself."

Rio frowned and shook his head. "No, I'd have to draw the line there. I have standards for my sister, you know."

Mike laughed loudly and slapped Rio's shoulder hard enough to almost knock him out of his chair. "Thanks a lot, old man."

Smiling, Jill glanced around, amused at the way Rio rubbed surreptitiously at his shoulder. It pleased her that Rio and Mike had always gotten along so well. "Guess he put you in your place, Michael."

"Guess so," Mike agreed good-naturedly, always receptive to a humorous insult. "So what about you, Rio? Doc says it'll be a few days before your leg's back to full strength, but what will you do after that? Going to take Dad up on his job offer?"

Rio shrugged, avoiding Jill's questioning eyes. "I may work for him long enough to pay off the debts I owe around here, but I'm turning down the foreman's job. It's just not for me, I'm afraid."

Mike nodded, apparently not surprised. "That's what I thought you'd say. You'll be moving on soon, I suppose?"

"Most likely."

Mike stood, carrying his empty plate to the sink. "Gotta get to work. We're pretty busy this week." He turned to look back at Rio, not smiling for once. "We've kind of gotten used to having you around, you know. We'll miss you."

Blue eyes warm with sympathy, he patted Jill's cheek. "Some of us more than others, I imagine."

And then he was gone, leaving Jill flushed and ruefully aware that her brother knew her even better than she'd suspected.

"Are you finished with that plate?" she asked Rio, determined that her feelings wouldn't show in her face or voice to make him uncomfortable.

"Yeah." He waited until she'd reached for it and then grabbed her wrist, smoothly tugging her into his lap. "The dishes can wait. I can't. Do you know how many hours have passed since you kissed me?"

Linking her hands behind his head, Jill smiled weakly. "Too many," she agreed, leaning toward him.

He held her a few inches away. "Don't look like that, Jill. I'm not leaving tonight, you know."

"I know." *When, Rio? How long will you stay?*

He pressed his lips to the lightly scented curve of her throat. "In fact," he murmured, his fingers toying with the top button of her blouse. "There's no real hurry. It's not as though I have any deadlines to meet."

Foolishly taking hope from his words, Jill sought his lips and kissed him. If this was what it would take to tempt him to stay longer, she thought wistfully, then she would gladly cooperate. She couldn't think of anything she'd rather do.

Lying on his back, one arm behind his head, Rio watched as Jill dressed and brushed her hair, too lazily content to move himself at the moment. "You look beautiful, you know."

She smiled over her shoulder at him, her flirtatious dimple flashing coyly, and he wished they had more time before the kids would be getting home from school.

He tried to concentrate on something else, anything to dampen the heat her smile had ignited in him. "I'll—uh—be glad to get rid of this cast tonight. And I'm looking forward to being alone with you tomorrow," he added meaningfully, already imagining some of the things he'd like to do with her, once the cast was out of his way.

He immediately regretted those erotic mental images as his body responded vigorously. Shifting uncomfortably in the bed, he was sorry again that the day had passed so quickly.

Jill looked mildly distressed. "I won't be here tomorrow."

He frowned. "Where will you be?"

"The school," she answered apologetically. "There's a planning meeting for the Halloween carnival. I promised to be there and to bring the dolls I made."

Rio sighed, disgruntled, revising his mental plans for the next day to include long hours of sitting alone, missing Jill. Oh, well, he thought, watching with interest as she bent to tie her sneakers, her shirt gaping provocatively with the movement. There was always the day after that. As he'd told Jill, there was no real hurry for him to leave. He'd have to eventually, of course, but he wasn't ready to go just now.

He wasn't ready to leave Jill.

Jill tried hard to concentrate on the conversation she was having with Gypsy and Sharon in the den that evening, but her thoughts kept straying to Tom's clinic where, even now, Doc and Tom were removing Rio's cast. Was everything all right? she fretted. Had his leg healed properly?

And then a sound in the doorway made her look up— and catch her breath. Rio stood there, looking lean and fit in a new flannel shirt and a pair of new jeans that hugged his slim body like a second skin. She'd gotten used to seeing him in a cast and one sneaker. Now he wore the battered boots he'd arrived in. "New clothes?" she asked inanely, unable to think of anything else to say.

He nodded. "Gypsy got them for me today. I told her I couldn't wait to get back into a pair of jeans."

She could certainly understand why. Rio looked as though jeans had been invented with him in mind. "How's your leg?"

He stepped into the room, somewhat tentatively, she noticed. "Tender," he admitted. "But it feels great having that cast off."

"Wouldn't hurt him to wear a brace for a couple weeks," Doc grumbled, following Rio into the room. "Wouldn't do it, though."

"Why not, Rio?" Gypsy demanded scoldingly.

He shrugged and lowered himself into an armchair. "I'm ready to get back to normal. Babying the leg won't do any good. Remember, I've been through this before."

"You break that leg again, and you'll be lucky to maintain any use of it," Doc warned, as he and Tom both found chairs.

"I'll be careful," Rio promised.

Jill finally tore her eyes off Rio, wondering why jeans and boots should suddenly make him look so different. So much more—more dangerous than he'd looked in the sweats and cast and borrowed sneaker, all traces of vulnerability gone. And even more excitingly attractive than he'd been before.

"Want some pie, Doc?" she asked, wishing her voice hadn't shown such an annoying tendency to squeak.

He grinned at her, not seeming to notice anything unusual in her behavior. "Have I ever turned down your pie?"

Gypsy stood quickly. "I'll help you bring things in, Jill."

Jill managed a smile. "Thanks."

Knowing that Rio was watching her curiously, she avoided his eyes as she left the room, followed closely by his sister.

Rio wasn't on the porch when Jill returned from the school meeting the next day, nor was he in the house. Curious, she wandered out to the barn, wondering if he were visiting Dancer. Instead, she found him in one corner of the barn, kneeling beside his motorcycle, doing something to it with a wrench.

A bolt of pain went straight through her heart. Was he already preparing to leave? "Rio?" she managed, a quiver underlying her voice.

He glanced around and smiled. "Oh, hi. How was the meeting?"

She shoved her hands into the pockets of her navy slacks, shivering in her red-and-navy-print sweater as if from a sudden chill in the drafty building. "Fine. What are you doing?"

He stood, dropping the wrench. "Just checking out my bike. Looks like it made it through the wreck in better shape than I did."

Jill looked at the motorcycle, feeling as though she were glaring at a sworn enemy. It was this machine that would take Rio away from her, she thought illogically, needing a scapegoat. "How's your leg feeling today?" she asked, tearing her gaze away from the motorcycle.

He shrugged. "Okay. I think I'll wait a couple of days before I try kick-starting the bike, but I'm getting around pretty well."

"That's good." She moistened her lips. "It's kind of cool out here. I think I'll go make some coffee."

"Jill."

"Yes?"

He smiled enticingly. "How about a kiss first?"

She couldn't resist, of course. Nor did she try. Stepping into his outstretched arms, she lifted her face for a kiss that left her warm and trembly.

Satisfied with the pleasantly dazed expression that had replaced the frown she'd worn since she'd found him working on his bike, Rio smiled down at her. "Now you can go make coffee."

She blinked as though she'd forgotten ever mentioning the beverage. And then her expression slowly cleared. She stepped away, automatically raising her hands to smooth her hair. "Yes. The kids will be home in a few minutes. They'll want cocoa. Will you be in soon?"

"Yeah, as soon as I put away these tools."

"All right." Casting one last, resentful look at the motorcycle, Jill turned and left the barn.

Rio watched her go, pulling thoughtfully at his lower lip. Her expressions hadn't been hard to read. She hadn't liked finding him working on the bike, had resented the reminder that he'd be leaving soon. Funny thing was, just before she'd arrived he'd been fantasizing about having her on the bike behind him when he drove away.

Stupid idea, of course, he reminded himself, turning back to the tools with a snort of self-disgust. Prim, thoroughly domestic Jill leaving on the back of a motorcycle headed for who knew where, living on the road, never quite sure where her next meal was coming from, where she'd be sleeping each night? He couldn't ask it of her, nor would he want that for her. He'd tired of that life himself a long time ago, stayed with it only because he hadn't found anything more interesting yet.

No, Jill deserved a home of her own, a normal routine, the security of her close, loving family. Everything Rio couldn't provide for her. Not now. Probably not ever.

He wished it could be different. He wished he believed he could stay, give her what she needed, follow the routines without slowly dying inside, making himself and everyone around him miserable. He wished . . . he wished . . .

Growling a curse, Rio shook his head, refusing to waste any more time on futile fantasies. He knew what he was. It was something he'd accepted years earlier. And now it was time for Jill to acknowledge the truth.

There was no future for them. Once he left, their affair would be over.

Still, he thought, wiping grease from his hands on a worn shop rag, there was no real hurry. He could stay awhile longer.

The house was very quiet as Jill walked through it the next afternoon, wondering where Rio had gotten off to. Tom and Gypsy had just gone back to the clinic after having lunch with Jill and Rio, and the children wouldn't be home for another couple of hours. Jill had rather hoped that she and Rio could spend the remainder of the afternoon together. Close together.

She stepped into the den, then gasped when two arms closed around her from behind. "You startled me again," she accused Rio, turning within the circle of his arms to face him.

He grinned. "I've been waiting for you."

Delighted, she looped her arms around his neck. "Oh, yeah? How come?" she teased.

"This is why," he answered, reaching down suddenly to swing her into his arms, high against his chest.

Clutching his shoulders, Jill scolded him as he turned toward the hallway. "Rio, put me down! You shouldn't be carrying me with your leg just out of the cast."

His dark eyes swept her flushed face with wicked intent. "I've been wanting to do this since the first time I saw you."

"You have?" she asked, intrigued.

"Yep. Any objections?"

She sighed deliciously. "I can't think of a one."

"Good." He kicked her bedroom door shut behind them. Laying her on the bed, he leaned over her. "You know, that's not all I wanted to do to you that first day."

Her breathing already growing ragged, she smoothed a hand down his chest, lingering at the waist of his jeans to toy suggestively with the button there. "No?"

He reached for the top button of her blouse. "No."

"Are you going to tell me what else you wanted to do?"

He kissed her as he continued to unbutton her blouse, then asked, "How about if I show you instead?"

"I think I'd like that," she breathed, pulling him closer. "Oh, Rio."

As they'd both expected, it was much nicer making love without the inconvenience of the cast he'd worn before. Rio demonstrated quite thoroughly how much more agile he could be without it. Swept into delirious cooperation, Jill wordlessly expressed her admiration of his skill.

Her head spinning, she arched feverishly beneath him as he painstakingly caressed every throbbing inch of her. Her hands clenched his bare, sweat-glazed shoulders. "Rio," she moaned, her voice reedy. "Please. Oh, please. Now."

He raised his head only long enough to kiss her soothingly. "There's no hurry, is there, Jill? We have plenty of time." And then he slid back down her body to nibble enticingly at her inner thigh.

Jerking in helpless reaction, she could only tangle her fingers in his hair as his mouth moved inward, her voice lost in the sensations he roused in her. The tip of his tongue darted out to caress her, causing her breath to catch in broken sobs as he drove her higher than she'd ever been before, carried her into a madness that defied all coherent thought.

Much later, she lay bonelessly in his arms, as both of them tried to recover sufficiently to crawl out of the bed before the children returned home from school. Rio's breathing was hot and ragged against her forehead, stirring the damp strands of hair beneath his cheek. His chest rose and fell sharply beneath her limp hand, his heart still racing against her palm.

She'd pleased him, she thought in lazy satisfaction, even as he'd given her so very much pleasure.

Only then did his earlier words replay themselves in her mind, making her suddenly yearn for them to be true. *We have plenty of time.*

If only they did, she thought longingly. If only they did.

Murmuring incoherently in protest of grave reality's return, she buried her face in his damp shoulder, needing to hide from the truth for just a few moments longer.

Chapter Thirteen

Tom had invited his father to lunch that Sunday, so Jill made all of Doc's favorite dishes and two pumpkin pies—one for him to take home. She loved Tom's father as deeply as if he'd been another blood relative, and enjoyed cooking special dishes for him. She wasn't particularly surprised, though, when Gypsy hovered around her during lunch preparations, wanting to know how to cook for the family, where Jill kept her recipes, who preferred what dishes.

With a slight pang, Jill realized that Gypsy was subtly preparing herself to take Jill's place in running the household. She'd always known, of course, that the time would come when she'd no longer be needed here. She just hadn't expected it to come so soon. Nor had she realized her own life would be in chaos when it happened.

Tom waited until everyone was finishing dessert to make the announcement.

Standing, he cleared his throat, his face suspiciously flushed. "We wanted you all to be the first to know," he said, reaching for Gypsy's hand. "Gypsy and I are going to be married."

The children, of course, were delighted. They expressed their approval noisily as the adults dealt with the announcement in their individual ways.

"Kind of sudden, isn't it?" Doc demanded gruffly, though he didn't look displeased—or particularly surprised—by the news. "You've known each other, what, a couple of weeks?"

"A month yesterday," Tom corrected. He smiled at his future bride in a way that made Jill's throat tighten in what could almost be envy. "It only took a few days for me to know that I'd be a fool to let her get away."

Doc turned to Gypsy, his gray eyes piercing, making her blush, though she met the look bravely. "Well, girl? You going to make my boy and his kids happy? Going to quit gallivanting around and settle down to a normal life?"

"When I travel in the future, it will be with my family," Gypsy answered quietly, her fingers tightening in Tom's. "Tom thinks I should write short stories based on my experiences around the world. I think it would be fun to try. And I'm going to continue to work with him in the clinic."

"D'you suppose we could have a baby sister?" Sharon asked ingenuously, looking blissful at the prospect.

Gordie snorted. "I'd rather have a brother."

"We'll talk about that later," Tom interceded hastily, when Sharon looked inclined to argue. He glanced questioningly at Jill and Rio. "Well? Don't the two of you want to say anything?"

"Congratulations," Jill said warmly. "I hope you'll be very happy." She suspected that they would be. Tom wouldn't have it any other way.

Gypsy smiled rather tentatively at Jill before looking at her brother. "Rio?"

He met the look evenly. "You've always seemed to know what you were doing before. Is this really what you want?"

"It's what I want," she assured him.

He stood and walked to her end of the table, leaning over to drop a kiss on her cheek. "Then you have my approval. Be happy, kid."

Jill realized that she'd never seen Rio kiss his sister before. Though the siblings seemed close, they were not as demonstrative as the Hammond clan, who exchanged hugs and kisses so easily. She suspected there had been little effort made in their upbringing to encourage them to show their own emotions. For Gypsy, at least, that was about to change. There'd be no lack of affection from her new family, immediate or extended.

Gypsy would probably adapt very well. Eagerly, in fact.

Jill suspected Rio was just as hungry for love and acceptance, though that stiff-necked macho pride of his would never let him admit it. She only wished that she'd been the woman to make him acknowledge those needs. Though she still had hope that their relationship would work out, it was fading as his leg gained strength. During the past few days, she'd detected an occasional look of restlessness on his dark, beautiful face. Only during those stolen daytime hours when she and Rio were making love did he seem totally content.

And still she knew that he was quietly making plans to leave. If not immediately, at least soon.

The knowledge was slowly tearing her apart.

Rio didn't sit down again after kissing his sister and shaking Tom's hand. Instead, he pushed his hands into the back pockets of his jeans and glanced toward the back door, that faint restlessness evident in his unconsciously graceful posture. "I think I'll go work on my bike for a while. Want to come with me, Gordie?"

Gordie hastily wiped pumpkin and whipped cream from the corners of his mouth and threw down his napkin. "You bet!"

"Gordie," Tom murmured chidingly.

Gordie sighed impatiently and gathered his dirty dishes to carry them to the sink. "Just a minute, Rio."

Looking a bit sheepish, Rio walked back around to his place to collect his own dishes. "Oops," he murmured to Jill, winking as he passed her.

She smiled and cursed that damned motorcycle to oblivion.

Working side by side in the kitchen while Tom and Doc watched a football game in the den, Jill and Gypsy said little at first about the momentous announcement at lunch. Jill could hear the faint roar of Rio's motorcycle and knew he was testing it in the pasture. Fighting off incipient depression, she decided to break the ice with Gypsy. "You'll have to make Tom and the kids help you with cleaning up after you're married," she advised lightly. "This family's been spoiled too long."

Gypsy's smile was somewhat uncertain. "You really don't mind about the wedding, Jill?"

"Of course I don't mind. I'm very happy for you both."

Twirling a long black curl around one red-tipped finger, Gypsy cleared her throat. "It's just that I know it must be difficult for you. After all, this was your sister's family and it's been yours for the past two years."

"And now they're yours," Jill finished with a smile. "And I'm delighted. Really."

Knowing what must be on the other woman's mind, Jill framed her words carefully. "My sister was a wonderful woman, Gypsy. She was bright and funny and sweet, and so kind. Everyone who knew her loved her. But she's gone, and though we'll always miss her and always wish she could have stayed with us longer, we've accepted that loss. None of us wants Tom to spend the rest of his life alone. I've already told him that, and I meant it. I know the rest of the family feels the same way.''

Gypsy looked encouraged. ''I want you to know that I don't intend to take your sister's place. I want Tom and the children to always remember her with love. I'd just like to make my own place in their lives. I have so much love to give them.''

Pausing, Gypsy reached out tentatively and placed a hand on Jill's arm, still rather uncertain with the new-found demonstrativeness. ''I don't want to take your place, either, Jill. Please don't feel that you have to leave because of me. This is your home for as long as you want to stay.''

Knowing that some newlywed women would have been threatened by the presence of a sister-in-law who'd been accustomed to running the household, Jill was touched by Gypsy's words, as well as her obvious sincerity. ''Thank you, Gypsy, but I think it's time I find a place of my own soon. Time to get on with my own life.''

''Do you have any plans?'' Gypsy asked curiously.

Her chest feeling hollow, Jill unconsciously imitated Rio's habitual shrug. ''I have some ideas. I'm thinking of starting my own business.''

''Oh? Doing what?''

Before Jill could answer, there was a faint, ominous sound of a crash and then Gordie's terrified yell. ''Daddy! Doc! Come quick! Rio's hurt!''

Throwing her dish towel to the floor, Jill bolted for the door, followed closely by Gypsy. Her heart in her throat, she grabbed Gordie's shoulder as he ran toward the house. ''What happened? Where is he?''

"In the pasture. His back tire blew and he lost control and he went through the fence. His head's bleeding bad. Doc, hurry!" Gordie finished with a yell, looking near tears.

Jill was already running toward the pasture, praying silently, brokenly. *Rio! Oh, Rio! Please let him be all right.*

She could have cried in relief when she found him sitting beside the broken fence and fallen motorcycle. Instead, she hurried to kneel beside him, tugging at the hand he held to his forehead, from beneath which blood streamed down his dirt-caked cheek. "Let me see. How bad is it?"

Pale and thin-lipped in self-annoyance, Rio winced when she touched the cut bleeding copiously on his forehead. Knowing head injuries tended to bleed more than others, Jill checked the cut carefully, finally deciding it wasn't serious. "Are you hurt anywhere else?"

"Just a few bruises. I'm all right. I hope my bike's not messed up."

"Forget the damned bike, would you?" Jill snapped, furious that he'd be concerned about the motorcycle when he'd just scared her half to death.

Doc knelt beside Jill, pushing her gently out of the way as the rest of the family hovered anxiously by. "Let me look at you, boy," he muttered in his gruff-gentle manner. "I swear, you've got buzzard luck. Don't know how you shave in the morning without cuttin' off an ear or somethin'."

Still scolding, he efficiently examined the cut. "Looks worse than it is," he pronounced, glancing reassuringly at Jill. "I'll put a bandage on it so it'll heal cleanly, but it doesn't need stitches and I don't see any signs of concussion."

Rio shook his head, then bit back a groan at the movement. "It's just a cut. I went over the handlebars when the bike veered into the fence after the blowout."

"And how come you weren't wearing a helmet?" Doc demanded, grabbing one of Rio's arms as Tom took the other. They hauled him to his feet.

Rio braced his legs to prevent any sign of weakness. "I usually do. But my helmet was in the duffel bag some low-life stole from me."

Her hands smeared with his blood, Jill followed closely as Tom and Doc urged Rio toward the house. She swallowed an uncharacteristic curse when she noticed that Rio looked anxiously back at his motorcycle, obviously still concerned that it may have been damaged in the crash.

Was there ever a man who needed looking after worse than this one? she asked herself despairingly. How she wished she'd always be around to take care of him.

Jill and Gypsy finished cleaning the kitchen while Doc and Tom tended Rio's cut in the clinic. The routine was getting all too familiar, Jill thought, still inwardly shaken at the fright he'd given her.

"He always has been accident-prone," Gypsy commented, shaking her head in exasperation at her brother's mishap. "Even as a kid, he was always cutting or breaking something. The social workers got so irritated with him for being so much trouble. I remember one woman threw up her hands after one of his many trips to the emergency room and said he'd never live long enough to vote. He would've been about twelve then. I think he'd gotten into a fight."

"Sounds typical," Jill commented dryly, placing a clean bowl in a cabinet. "And he's been taking care of himself since he was sixteen? How did he ever manage?"

Gypsy chuckled. "Oh, Rio has a knack for always landing on his feet, one way or another. Even when he was in that truck wreck, he managed to find a nice family to take him in, a place to stay—he even found a home for me in the process."

Jill sighed. "Will he ever find a home for himself?"

"I don't know," Gypsy admitted, her lovely face creased with concern. She shot a searching look at Jill from beneath long, thick dark lashes. "You've fallen for him, haven't you?"

Startled by the blunt question, Jill answered automatically. "Yes. I have."

Looking pleased and worried all at the same time, Gypsy leaned back against a counter. "I thought so. You're so perfect for him. I wish—"

It was a phrase she'd heard a lot lately. Her lips twitching sardonically, Jill nodded. "Yeah. So do I."

Gypsy sighed deeply. "There's a lot you don't know about Rio, Jill. Things that explain why he's so wary about commitments."

"Then tell me," Jill pleaded, wanting so desperately to understand.

Looking torn between loyalty to her brother and her wish for his happiness, Gypsy thought a moment, then nodded briskly. "Sit down."

Jill sat at the table, leaning tensely against it, shaking her head when Gypsy asked if she wanted a cup of coffee. Pouring herself a cup, Gypsy took her time joining Jill at the table, probably trying to decide where to start. "Rio and I lost our mother when we were very young," she began.

"I know," Jill replied gently, sympathetically. "He told me she committed suicide. That he found her when he was just a little younger than Sharon."

Gypsy's eyes widened dramatically. "He told you that?"

Jill nodded. "Yes. Several weeks ago. Why does that surprise you so much?"

"He never talks about Mom's death," Gypsy answered simply. "Never. Not even to me. He must be closer to you than I thought."

"We were talking about Gordie at the time," Jill remembered. "He was comparing his feelings at the time to Gordie's now."

"Then you already know part of the problem."

Jill frowned. "He's afraid of losing people he loves? I can understand that, but—"

Gypsy shook her head. "That's not all of it. It was what happened before Mom died."

She took a deep breath, clinging to her coffee cup as she fought her own unpleasant memories. "My mother was a very insecure woman, Jill. Her own mother was an American Indian who'd been seduced and abandoned as a teenager, and was always very bitter afterward. My mother didn't have a very happy childhood, I'm afraid. She was so hungry for love and affection that she went from one destructive relationship to another, finally turning to drugs and alcohol for solace. Rio and I have never even been sure that we had the same father, though our mother said we did."

"I'm sorry, Gypsy."

Gypsy smiled sadly. "Thanks. It took me a long time to work out my feelings about my mother. Rio's still trying. He was always the serious one, you see. Even as a very little boy, he thought it was his responsibility to take care of Mom, to make her happy. He could never quite understand why she couldn't be content with the love of her children, why we couldn't seem to give enough to satisfy her. I think he took it personally when she killed herself. He thought there must be something lacking in himself, that he wasn't capable of giving enough, or perhaps not worthy enough for love."

"That's ridiculous! Rio's such a warm, giving person, though he does his best to hide those qualities," Jill defended him heatedly. "He's been so good to Gordie, so caring."

Gypsy nodded. "You and I know what he's capable of. He's the one with doubts."

"I wish—" Jill began, then stopped herself with an impatient grimace at the ineffective repetition.

"I guess I understand him so well because I've had many of the same doubts myself," Gypsy explained. "I've been afraid that I was too much like my mother. That I'd never fall in love, never find anyone who could love me enough in return, never stop looking for something that remained just out of reach. But finding Tom and the children has shown me differently."

And Rio had found Jill, who hadn't been able to reach him no matter how hard she'd tried, Jill thought dispiritedly, looking down at her tightly clasped hands.

"There's still hope," Gypsy offered with tenuous optimism. "He seems happy here. And he's obviously crazy about you. If he could just work out these old problems, the way I have. Maybe it's harder for him because he was so young when Mom died. Being older, I was able—"

"Being older?" Jill repeated, her head coming up abruptly. "You're older than he is?"

Gypsy looked surprised that she hadn't known. "Yes, of course."

"But you're only twenty-nine."

"Yes."

Jill's eyes narrowed as she thought of the times Rio had rather condescendingly mentioned her age, even telling her once that she needed to grow up; leading her to believe that he was so much older and wiser. "Just how old *is* he?" she demanded.

"He was twenty-five in August."

"August! Why that—" Rio was three months *younger* than herself! "That hypocrite!"

Gypsy laughed. "You mean you didn't know? I knew Mike was fooled at Tom's birthday party, but I thought you probably knew the truth."

"No. I'll certainly talk to him about it later," Jill promised, grasping this one thing she could be angry about. This at least would be one confrontation she had a chance of winning.

"Talk to who about what?" Tom asked, standing in the doorway with his father and Rio, who sported a neat white bandage on his freshly washed forehead.

"Never mind," Jill grumbled, glaring at Rio. "Where are you going?"

"Doc's leaving. Rio and I are going out to the pasture to get his bike and take it back to the barn. He wants to see how much damage was done."

"Of course he does," Jill remarked, unable to keep a trace of sarcasm from her voice. "I'd just hate it if anything happened to that precious motorcycle."

Rio's eyes narrowed at her tone. A muscle twitching in his jaw, he turned to Tom. "I don't think she's in a very good mood. Maybe we'd better go on out and get the bike."

"Good idea," Tom agreed, warily eyeing the familiar signs of Jill's rare but formidable temper.

Gypsy chuckled when the men were gone. "You know, Jill, if anyone has a chance of whipping my brother into shape, I'd bet it would be you."

Jill mentally crossed her fingers and hoped Gypsy was right.

Trying to ignore the dull throbbing in his forehead, Rio was still tinkering with his motorcycle in the barn when Jill found him later that evening. He didn't know she was behind him until she spoke. "Will it survive?"

Looking around rather cautiously, trying to gauge her mood, he shrugged. "Yeah. There was a sharp piece of metal shaved off the inside of the back fender, probably when it was thrown from Baxter's truck. That's what punctured the tire and caused the blowout. All I need's a new tire."

She crossed her arms tightly in front of her. "That's all you need, is it?"

"At the moment." What was with her anyway? he wondered.

"Why didn't you tell me that you're younger than I am?" she asked belligerently, making him blink at the abrupt transition to a totally unrelated subject.

"Am I?"

"Three months, according to Gypsy."

"I guess I didn't think it was important."

She scowled. "You deliberately led me to believe that you were a lot older than I am."

"In many ways, I am."

"Oh, shut up."

Lifting one eyebrow in mild question at her uncharacteristic curtness, Rio dropped the wrench he'd been using and straightened, resting his fists on his hips. "All right, Jill. Let's have it. Why are you so angry with me?"

She stared at him with glittering eyes, then seemed to sag as the brittle temper faded from her face. Dragging one hand through her hair, she dropped her gaze. "I'm not angry with you, Rio," she murmured, her voice sounding suddenly weary. "Not really."

"Then what's wrong?" he asked quietly, stepping closer to take her slender shoulders in his hands. "What's bothering you, honey?" It was the first time he'd called her by anything other than her name, having resisted endearments previously by reminding himself that they shouldn't become too serious.

Her eyes lifted slowly to his and he almost groaned at the tortured expression in their clear blue depths. He'd spent the past couple of hours trying to forget the look on her face when she'd rushed to his side after the minor accident, the near terror that made him feel so guilty. He'd tried to deny the feelings her expressions had revealed to him. But it was hard to deny what he was seeing now. "Jill, don't. Don't look at me that way."

"I can't help it," she whispered, lifting one hand to touch his face. "You frightened me so badly this afternoon. I was terrified for you."

"I'm fine, really. It's just a cut. If Doc hadn't been here, I probably would've just stuck a Band-Aid on it."

The scowl returned to her face. "You mean you would have handled it in your usual macho, martyred way. The brave, tough loner who doesn't accept anything from anyone."

Genuinely confused about her rapidly changing attitudes, Rio tried to think of something to say to change the subject. He was deliberating the possible success of kissing her into cooperative silence, when she turned away. "I'm sorry. Maybe I'd better go back in. I don't seem to be quite rational tonight."

As men so often do when dealing with a woman's emotions, Rio opened his mouth and stuck his foot quite neatly into it. "That time of the month?"

The look she gave him made him gulp, his face warming as he wished he'd had the sense to keep his big mouth closed. "Uh—sorry," he muttered.

"No," she said crisply. "It is *not* that time of the month. Excuse me for disturbing you."

His patience at an end, Rio grabbed her arm and whirled her back around when she would have stomped away. "All right, dammit, let's have it. What's really bothering you tonight? All this couldn't be about that little mishap this afternoon."

"You could have been killed in 'that little mishap,'" she retorted heatedly, tugging futilely at the arm he held in an unyielding grip. "And you act as if I shouldn't have even been alarmed."

He frowned and shook his head. It was only a cut. What was the big deal, anyway? He'd never seen her overreact like this before. "I just don't understand why you're so all-fired upset."

"I'm upset because I love you, dammit!" she cried out, tears pooling in her emotion-darkened blue eyes. "I'm upset because you've only been out of a cast a few days and you were hurt again testing that stupid motorcycle, getting ready to leave me. And I'm upset because you couldn't even figure out why I'm upset. Now let me *go!*"

Numbly holding on to her arm despite her attempts to free it from his shock-tightened fingers, Rio stared at her. She loved him? Oh, hell. "Jill—"

With tears escaping her efforts to hold them back, she struggled harder to pull away from him. "I want to go into the house."

"Not like this," he muttered, pulling her closer, wrapping both arms around her. "You don't want to go in like this."

Her breath caught in a broken sob. "Damn you, Rio." The words were muffled into his shirt.

He cupped the back of her head with one hand, his chest aching where her head rested against it, somewhere in the vicinity of his heart. "I know," he muttered in response to her dispirited curse. "I never meant to hurt you like this, Jill. I'm sorry."

Tears drying on her cheeks, she let her shoulders sag within his embrace. She couldn't bring herself to look at him, but she'd gone too far to exercise discretion now. "You didn't make me fall in love with you. I did that all by myself."

"You knew I wouldn't stay."

"Yes," she acknowledged sadly. "I've always known."

As many times as she'd fantasized that Rio would stay, that he'd take the job her father had offered and build a life with her, she'd always accepted her fantasies for what they were. Rio could no more fit himself into that mold than Jill could emulate the solitary, whim-driven, party-seeking existence Gypsy had led before finding her anchor in Tom.

Rio was too much the rebel, too unaccustomed to compromise, to suppress the unconventional individuality that made him so very special. He would find his place in life, but it would be his own place, a niche in which few people would—or could—be comfortable. She could easily imagine him supporting himself with his carving, making beautiful things from wood, living on his own terms, in his own way. She could even picture herself sharing that life with him—but it could only be by invitation. And she was all-too-painfully aware that no such invitation had been extended.

Even now, she felt the near panic in him at her admission of love for him, sensed his concern that she'd expect more than he could give, demand what he couldn't offer. "You needn't be so alarmed," she murmured, the words edged with vague resentment. "I'm not going to ask you to stay. Just don't expect me to smile and wave when you ride away."

Rio sighed heavily. "I knew this would happen. I never should have gotten mixed up in your life. I should have—"

She stiffened and pulled herself out of his arms, her chin held proudly. "Would you give me some credit for my own actions? I told you, I knew what I was doing, what risks I was taking. I don't need you taking responsibility for my happiness. I'll survive this." *Somehow. She hoped.*

He pushed his hands into his jeans pockets that barely stretched enough to hold them. "I wasn't trying to imply that you can't take care of yourself."

"Good. Because I can."

She'd survive, she reminded herself, mentally repeating the words she'd spoken with such bravado. She'd go on with her life. She just wasn't sure she would ever be the same as she'd been before. Her heart and her dreams would leave with Rio.

Catching her off guard, Rio pulled his hands from his pockets to cup her face between his callused palms. "I can't help worrying about you," he admitted, his face inches away as he looked at her with such tenderness she could almost believe he returned her love. "You take such good care of everyone else, give so much to others," he continued. "I'm concerned that there won't be anything left for Jill."

"I'm not like your mother, Rio," she whispered bravely. "I know how to be content with what I have. I know that I'm responsible for my own happiness."

His eyes narrowed at the painful comparison, but she didn't regret the words. It was past time that Rio stopped blaming himself for long-ago events over which he'd had no control.

She knew by his expression that the conversation was over. He wouldn't talk about his past, wouldn't allow himself to share his feelings with her. He couldn't afford to let her get that close to him, not without strengthening the bonds he'd resisted from the beginning. But whatever he might have said to change the subject was interrupted when Gypsy spoke apologetically from the open barn door.

"Jill? I'm sorry to intrude, but Sharon can't find the doll you made her. She says she can't go to sleep without it. Have you seen it?"

Her gaze still locked with Rio's, Jill answered slowly. "No, but I'll come help you look for it. I was just about to come in, anyway. There's nothing left to say here."

The faintest flicker of emotion crossed Rio's dark face—gone before she could even begin to analyze it. He said nothing. After a moment, Jill took a deep breath and turned away. Unable to face the sympathy in Gypsy's eyes, she kept her gaze downturned as she passed the other woman and all but ran to the house.

The doll had been recovered and over half an hour had passed when Gypsy returned from the barn, alone. Her expression was so stormy that Jill knew instinctively Gypsy and Rio had quarreled. Suspecting she may have been the cause of the argument, Jill lay awake for hours that night feeling guilty for coming between Rio and the one person to whom he'd maintained ties, of sorts. Wondering if life would ever be the same for any of them, now that their divergent paths had collided.

Chapter Fourteen

Jill attended a luncheon on Monday, sponsored by a local women's club her mother had belonged to for many years. Trying to hide her pain, she smiled and chatted and exchanged airy pleasantries with people she'd known most of her life—women who'd lived in the area for years, raised their children there, buried their loved ones there, would probably be buried there themselves. They looked happy, these women. Content, for the most part. Jill wondered if their bright, cheery smiles hid emotions as turbulent as her own. Disappointments, heartaches, shattered dreams, unnamed longings.

"Jill? Are you all right? You look kind of peaked," Ruth's longtime friend, Betty Lou Holloway, asked at one point, peering at Jill through concerned, myopic eyes.

Catching her mother watching her with a worried expression, Jill smiled reassuringly at both women. "I'm fine, really. Just a bit of a headache. But thank you for asking, Betty Lou."

"Do you want me to take you home now, dear?" Ruth offered.

"No, of course not. We haven't even seen the style show yet. I'm looking forward to seeing some of the new merchandise Bonnie has for her boutique." Besides, she was in no hurry to return home for more of the withdrawn, silent treatment Rio had given her all morning. It hurt worse to be in the same room with him and feel an invisible wall between them than to be away from him.

"Humph." Betty Lou nodded at Jill's cream knit dress. "Bet there won't be anything nicer than what you have on. Don't tell me you made this one yourself?"

"Why, yes, I did."

The older woman shook her head admiringly. "You sure have a talent for sewing, Jill. You ought to consider doing it professionally."

"I have considered that," Jill admitted, feigning enthusiasm. "Now that Tom's getting married, I may start my own business."

Her brown eyes lighting up, Betty Lou turned to Ruth. "Tom's getting married? Why didn't you tell me?"

"I just found out myself last night," Ruth replied, giving her daughter a look that indicated she knew Jill had deliberately turned the discussion away from herself.

The ploy had been an effective one. The conversation centered around Gypsy and Tom until it was interrupted by the beginning of the style show. Jill kept her eyes on the makeshift stage, but she fervently hoped no one would expect her to describe any of the outfits later. For once, she had no interest in the latest local fashions.

Rio's moodiness lasted through the remainder of the day, as well as most of the next. Jill was the only member of the family who didn't ask if he was feeling ill. She knew exactly why he'd retreated into himself.

He waited until everyone had finished eating dinner Tuesday evening to break the self-imposed silence. "I guess the only way to say this is just to say it. I'll be leaving tomorrow."

"Tomorrow?" several voices said in unison, Gordie's the loudest and most protesting. Jill didn't speak, her voice lost in the shock of his unexpected statement.

"But, Rio, why do you have to go now? Where will you go?" Gordie demanded.

Rio's answer was gentle, but resolute. "Back on the road, kid. It's time for me to be moving on." He glanced across the table at Tom, who was watching him with a frown. "I'm not forgetting everything I owe you, Tom. As soon as I find work, I'll start sending you part of my pay. I want to reimburse Doc for his services and you for room and board and everything else you did for me."

"That's not necessary. You're family now," Tom answered with a shake of his sandy head. "Besides, bringing Gypsy into our lives more than repaid us for anything we may have done for you."

"I'll send the money. I pay my debts," Rio returned flatly, leaving no question in anyone's mind that he would do just that.

"Don't go, Rio," Sharon piped in tremulously, giving him an entreating look through her glasses. "You're going to be our uncle now."

His face softened fractionally. "You've got plenty of uncles, Sharon. You don't need another one hanging around."

"I wanted you to be here for my wedding," Gypsy told him softly, her disappointment apparent. "You're the only family I have, Rio. I want you with me on my wedding day."

He shifted uncomfortably in his chair, looking vaguely guilty. "You haven't even set a date, Gyps," he reminded her gruffly. "I can't hang around indefinitely until you decide you're ready."

"Could we talk you into staying the remainder of the week?" Tom asked quietly, his eyes on his distressed fiancée. "Gypsy and I planned to hold a small ceremony soon, attended only by family. We can arrange to be married this Saturday, if you'll stay that long. It would mean a lot to your sister to have you at our wedding."

Jill saw the flare of hope in Gypsy's face, the indecisiveness of Rio's. He glanced at Jill, obviously seeking her reaction, but she kept her face carefully blank. It wasn't hard. She'd been numb with shock ever since he'd made his announcement.

"Please, Rio," Gypsy said softly, too proud to beg, but not above exerting a little sisterly pressure.

He exhaled gustily. "All right. If you want me here badly enough to rush the wedding date, I guess the least I can do is stay for the ceremony. But I'll be leaving Sunday."

Gypsy smiled. "Thank you."

He only nodded.

Jill sat mutely for another moment, until her hands began to tremble in her lap. And then she stood and, still without a word, left the room, never looking back at Rio.

Closed within the sanctity of her bedroom, she lay staring at the wall, grateful for the lingering numbness that made her anguish bearable. She didn't leave her room again that night, nor did anyone disturb her, sensing her need to be alone.

Tonight it was up to the others to clean the kitchen and lay out school clothes, tuck in children and turn out the lights.

Tonight she needed time to deal with her own pain.

* * *

Jill was sitting at her sewing machine Thursday morning, halfheartedly trying to concentrate on her work, when a sound from the doorway made her look up quickly. Her sharply accelerated heart rate slowed considerably when she found her brother Mike standing there rather than Rio, as she'd hoped and feared. "Oh. Hi."

Mike grinned one-sidedly, sauntering into the room. "Gee, this enthusiastic welcome is liable to go to my head."

Grimacing, Jill waved toward the empty chair beside the sewing cabinet, encouraging him to sit down. "Sorry. What's up? I don't usually see you this late in the morning."

With a shrug, Mike dropped into the chair. "I had some free time and decided to come and see how you're doing. Where's Rio?" he asked with a clumsy attempt at sounding casually curious.

Jill mimicked her brother's shrug. "Who knows? He's been leaving right after breakfast on his motorcycle and doesn't show up again until dinner. Gypsy asked him last night what he's been doing the past couple of days."

"And he said—?"

"'Sight-seeing.'"

Mike looked as skeptical as Jill had felt when Rio had given the succinct, unsatisfactory answer to his sister's inquisitive probing. "Sight-seeing?"

Spreading her hands to convey her own bafflement, Jill left the question hanging. She really didn't know where Rio had been the past two days. She only knew he hadn't been with her. And she strongly suspected he'd been going out just to avoid her. It hurt.

One elbow resting on a corner of the sewing cabinet, Mike watched her intently when he said "I hear he's leaving on Sunday."

Jill nodded, eyes on the fabric in front of her. "So he says. He's only staying that long because he promised Gypsy he wouldn't miss her wedding."

"I kind of thought he'd hang around awhile longer."

"Whatever made you think that?"

"He seemed happy enough."

"I guess he's just getting restless. Feeling confined here."

Mike winced, his eyes turning suddenly bitter. "Seems like that's been going around lately."

Jill knew he was thinking of Cara, the woman who'd left him in search of excitement and adventure. Only now did she understand what he must have felt—what he must be feeling now. "Are you okay?"

Mike nodded slowly. "Yeah. Are you?"

She sighed. "I will be. I guess."

"Hurts to be left behind, doesn't it?"

Obviously, Mike knew more than Jill had suspected about her feelings for Rio. Was it only because he and she had always been so close? Because he'd so recently been through a similar experience?

Or had she been so transparent that everyone knew? Would she have to contend with the family's well-meant pity in addition to her own heartbreak after Rio left? Dread of that possibility made her answer more curtly than she'd intended. "Yeah. It hurts."

"Want me to beat him up for you?"

His absurdedly hopeful expression made her smile despite her pain. "No. Thanks for offering, though."

"You sure? It would be no trouble at all." He tapped one oversize fist lightly, significantly, into his other palm.

"I'll let you know if I change my mind."

"You do that." He cleared his voice. "Did the kids have fun trick-or-treating last night?"

She appreciated the change of subject. "Yes, of course. And they enjoyed the school carnival afterward. My dolls did very well in the raffle."

"The kids looked really cute in their costumes. I hope they liked the treats I'd bought them."

"They and their dentist sincerely thank you," she answered dryly. "Gordie wanted candy for breakfast this morning. I had to talk him into a bowl of healthy, unsweetened cereal first."

Mike grinned, then cut his eyes to the dress Jill had been sewing when he'd interrupted her. "You making that for Sharon?"

Her fingertips stroking the soft swatch of dusty-rose fabric, Jill nodded. "It's the dress she's wearing for the wedding. She wanted something new."

"What's Gypsy going to wear?"

"I don't know. She hasn't said."

"It's a shame Tom couldn't arrange time off for a honeymoon."

"He didn't have enough notice to work it out. They're going to try to take a few days off next month."

"Think it will work out?"

Jill glanced at him with one lifted eyebrow. "The honeymoon?"

He made a face. "No, dummy. The marriage. Think it will last?"

She shrugged. "I think it has as good a chance as any."

"And what are you going to do?"

The question was one she'd heard a lot lately; one she'd asked herself more than once. She opened her mouth to give Mike the answer she'd given the others, the one she'd given herself. But instead she found herself speaking with total honesty. "I don't know, Mike. Nothing sounds very interesting right now."

She simply couldn't work up any enthusiasm for a life without Rio in it.

Mike looked at her a long time, without the pity she'd dreaded from the others. In his eyes she saw only sympathetic understanding. Finally, he nodded. "I know how you feel, Jilly."

Did that mean he was no longer content in his job working for their father, the career he'd always thought he wanted? Or did he still miss Cara so much that his job wasn't enough to make him happy?

Before she could ask, Mike startled her by speaking with uncharacteristic intensity. "Jill, if Rio really means so much to you, don't give up without a fight. Don't be left wondering if you should have tried harder to hold on to him."

"I've tried, Mike," she whispered, her heart aching for her brother, as well as herself. "I really have. It's up to him now."

Exhaling gustily, Mike patted her cheek. "If you need to talk, you know where to find me. Okay?"

"That goes for you, too," she answered gratefully, pressing his big, gentle hand to her face for a brief moment. "Thanks, Mike."

He stood, cleared his throat and shoved his hands into his pockets, awkward with the serious tone the conversation had taken. "I'd better get back to work. See you later, Jilly."

"See you later, Mike."

She went back to work on Sharon's dress, no more cheerful than she'd been before, but warmed by the love and support that was always available to her from her family. And she felt so sorry for Rio that he'd never known that sort of security; that he didn't know how to accept it now.

* * *

Mike's words lingered in Jill's mind that evening and again the next day, when she found herself drifting through the empty house. Knowing she had a dozen things to do to prepare for the wedding the following day, she was still unable to concentrate on anything but her own problems.

"Don't be left wondering if you should have tried harder to hold on to him."

She honestly believed she'd done all she could, reluctantly accepting that Rio couldn't stay and be happy. But something nagged at her, making her feel that there was still unfinished business between her and Rio.

Just after noon she heard the muffled roar of his motorcycle pulling into the driveway, headed for the barn. She stared at the back door, wavering in indecision for what seemed like hours. This would be her last day alone with Rio, the last chance she'd have to talk to him in private. She couldn't let the opportunity pass.

Somewhat nervously, she checked her appearance, using the excuse to stall for courage. She wore a navy sweater with floral embroidery circling the round neckline, a long, full khaki skirt, turned-down navy crew socks and scuffed penny loafers. Her hair fell from a neat navy bow at the back of her head and curled softly under at her nape. She looked, she thought ruefully, like an Ivy League college student. Her unintentional selection of clothing couldn't have more clearly illustrated the differences between her life-style and Rio's.

Maybe he wouldn't notice.

She found Rio scrubbing his hands in the large sink Tom had installed in the barn. "You're covered in paint," she said unnecessarily, surprised to see the splotches of red on his hands and splattered down one leg of the old, ripped jeans he'd been wearing the day he'd arrived.

He turned his head in response to her voice, his expression immediately shuttered. "Yeah." He squirted more industrial-strength soap onto his hands from the plastic bottle by the sink and turned back to his vigorous scrubbing.

Jill stepped closer to watch, her arms crossed at her waist to prevent them from reaching out to him. "What have you been doing?"

"Painting a barn."

She waited for the details. When none came, she sighed and demanded, "*Whose* barn?"

"Someone named McVey—old guy who lives a couple miles from here. I'd heard earlier in the week that he needed a barn painted, so that's what I've been doing the past couple of days. I finished this morning."

She felt like shaking him for so grudgingly giving her the information. She didn't remember it being so hard to communicate with him before she'd so foolishly blurted out her love for him. "So you've been working for Mr. McVey. I didn't really think you'd been sight-seeing."

Rio nodded curtly. "I'll keep part of what he paid me to get by on until I can find work on the road. The rest I'll leave as the first installment on my debt to Tom and Doc."

"That really isn't necessary, you know."

He dried his hands on a worn, once-white towel. "To me it is."

Jill let it pass. "Are you hungry? Tom and Gypsy are having lunch in town today with the minister who's marrying them, but I'd be happy to make something for you."

"Have you eaten?"

"No."

"Then I'll have whatever you have."

"I have cold chicken and potato salad left over from dinner Wednesday night."

"Sounds good. Thanks."

It hurt so badly to hear the man she loved talk to her as he would to a virtual stranger. She hated exchanging stilted formalities with him, hated being treated as though she were someone he hardly knew, someone he had to be polite to until he could get away from her. Biting her lower lip, she turned to leave.

His hand closed gently around her upper arm, detaining her. "Jill—"

She couldn't look at him. "Yes?"

"Are you okay?"

"I'm fine, Rio."

He paused for a moment, then sighed. "I'm sorry."

She closed her eyes. "Please don't start apologizing again. I really don't think I can handle that right now."

"I'm not apologizing," he explained gruffly. "I'm just sorry that things couldn't be different. I've spent the past few days trying to convince myself to stay here, to take that job with your father, to settle down and work at the relationship you've offered me."

Hope flared only briefly at his words, making her turn to look at him. It died stillborn when he shook his head, his dark eyes soft with regret. "It just wouldn't work. I don't know what it is I've been looking for, but I know it isn't a construction job in Arkansas. Can you understand that?"

She took pride in the evenness of her reply. "We've already discussed this, Rio. I told you then that I understood. I still do."

He sighed again, more heavily this time. "I wish to hell *I* did. Part of me thinks I'm an idiot for walking away from you, from this job, from the chance for a real home and a family. But an even stronger part of me knows I'd be making a mistake that would only hurt both of us in the end."

Jill held her chin high. "Then you should listen to your feelings."

He touched her cheek with the very tips of his fingertips, a butterfly touch that only left her aching for more. "I don't want to leave you. I only know I can't stay."

Her hands clenched convulsively—the only sign of the courage it took for her to meet his eyes then. "Has it ever occurred to you to ask me to go with you?"

A spasm of what might have been longing crossed his face. "Yes," he answered tightly. "It's occurred to me. But I won't ask."

In little more than a whisper, she asked, "Why not?"

"Because I can't—I won't—do that to you. I don't know where I'm going, where I'll sleep, where my next meals will come from. Winter's coming on. It gets cold on the back of a bike. That's no life for you."

She wouldn't cry. Her eyes remaining dry by nothing more than sheer willpower as she gazed up at him. "It doesn't sound like much of a life for you, either."

"It's the only one I've known for years."

"Don't you ever get lonely?"

"I haven't before," he answered honestly. "I think I will now."

The courage she'd needed to ask him to take her with him was nothing compared to the bravery she needed now. Clutching her pride in a shaky grip, she cleared her throat. "Rio? Could I ask you just one thing?"

He looked wary, studying the intensity in her face. "What?"

"Do you love me? Do you love me even a little?"

He flinched. "Don't ask me that," he ordered roughly.

"I have to know."

Turning his head, he groaned. "I've never wanted another woman the way I want you. I've never felt for anyone else the things I feel for you."

It wasn't a direct answer to her question. It was enough. Raising her hands to frame his face, to turn him back to her, she looked up at him with pleading, tender eyes. "Then would you please make love with me one last time? Would you leave me with that memory?"

His jaw clenched, the new scar on his forehead and the old one on his cheek standing out against his unnatural paleness. "I don't want to make our parting even harder for you. I thought it would be easier for you if I stayed away from you until I go."

"You were wrong." She slid her arms around his neck. "Do you really want me?"

His hands tightened convulsively at her waist. "So much I ache with it," he grated.

"We have the next hour alone. Let's not waste it."

Trying unsuccessfully to read his expression, she held her breath as he stared down at her. And then she released it in a long, unsteady sigh when his arms went around her. He captured the end of the sigh in his mouth as his lips covered hers.

Chapter Fifteen

Her arms tightening around his neck, Jill opened her mouth to Rio's kiss, sweetly inviting him inside. A low groan rumbled in his chest as he hungrily took her up on the offer, his tongue thrusting into the warm, wet depths he knew so intimately. Had he ever seen anything sexier than Jill's lush, pouty mouth?

His hands roamed her body, feverishly, reacquainting themselves with the slight, supple curves he'd memorized in such detail. Was any woman's body more perfect than Jill's?

His hands clutched her hips, pulling her more firmly against him. She trembled in his arms, and he bit back a raw moan. Had any woman ever responded so passionately, so excitingly to him?

No.

Tearing his mouth from hers, he gulped air before kissing her again from a new angle, his hands lifting to tangle in her hair, the bow that had held it back tumbling unnoticed to the dirt-and-straw floor. The days since he'd last made love to her stretched like months behind him, leaving him throbbing, impatient. The years he'd be without her lay like an eternity before him, leaving him aching, hollow, needing to fill himself with her.

He thought fleetingly of her bedroom, but it seemed so far away. He had her in his arms here, now. He couldn't bear to release her even long enough to walk to the house. She moved sinuously against him, her soft breasts brushing his chest, and he was lost to all rational thought.

Catching her by surprise, he grabbed the hem of her sweater and swept it over her head. She gasped, glanced quickly around, then looked back up at him with a shy, intrigued smile. "Here?"

The cool early-November air chilled her bare skin, puckering her rosy nipples. He covered them with his hands. "Here," he muttered, his fingers teasing those inviting peaks. "Now."

She reached up to unbutton his shirt. "Good."

He kissed her in quick approval. And then he dropped his hands to pull at her skirt, bunching it at her waist to seek out the slender curves beneath, the fire raging inside him making him impatient, almost clumsy in his hasty movements. He filled his hands with her softly rounded cheeks, the thin satin of her panties sliding against his palms. Ducking his head, he kissed her throat, grinding himself against her until she threw her head back with a strangled, pleading cry.

Releasing her only for a moment, he jerked off his shirt and threw it to the ground, as oblivious as she to the chill in the air, then bent to lift one small, perfect breast to his mouth. Jill quivered when he circled the tautly drawn peak with the tip of his tongue, then shuddered when he drew it deep into his mouth. Her fingers clenched his hair. "Oh, Rio."

He loved it when she said his name in that low, husky voice, loved feeling the pleasure running through her when he caressed her. He couldn't imagine ever touching another woman, ever wanting, needing anyone the way he wanted, needed Jill.

Leaving her breast moist and flushed, he turned his attention to its twin as his hand slid up her leg beneath the full skirt. He traced the lacy edge of her panties with one finger, then slipped inward to cup her feminine warmth in his palm. She moved instinctively against him, her breath catching in her throat as he stroked her through the rapidly dampening satin.

He raised his head to capture her lips at the same moment his finger edged beneath the fabric to caress her bare, swollen flesh. Jill cried out into his mouth, twisting in his arms, driving him half insane as her breasts rubbed against his bare chest.

And then it was he choking out a hoarse mutter of approval when her hand slid down to close over his aching arousal through the heavy denim binding him. Her fingers tightened and he gasped, shuddering heavily.

He couldn't wait any longer to be inside her. Glancing quickly around, he spotted a scarred wooden stool only a few feet behind him. Opening his jeans, he sat on the stool and reached under her skirt to remove her panties. And then he pulled her down to straddle his thighs, her skirt spreading around them.

His lips roamed her face, kissing her cheeks, her nose, her eyelids, her mouth. His hand stroked her beneath the skirt, readying her for his penetration. His pulse pounded through him, his breathing harsh in his own ears, drowning out her quiet, ragged whimpers. At the last moment, sanity returned briefly. He groaned. "Damn. I'm not wearing anything to protect you."

She cupped his face between trembling hands and kissed him, moving sinuously against him. "I don't care."

"I do," he muttered, lifting beneath her to shove his hand into the back pocket of his jeans for the foil package he'd carried for the past few weeks, just in case something like this happened. He couldn't prevent Jill from being hurt when he left, but he would protect her from being left alone to deal with any unforeseen consequences of their passion.

Moments later, he clasped her hips between his hands and guided her onto him, thrusting upward until he was buried as deeply within her as physically possible. Even then, he needed to be closer to her. He wrapped his arms around her and held her as tightly as he dared, his face buried in her throat.

Her legs wrapped securely around him, Jill held him with all her strength, crooning soft, loving endearments that made his throat and chest tighten almost painfully. He began to move—slow, rhythmic motions she picked up immediately. Their bodies rocked together in graceful synchronicity until madness swept through them, whipping them into an urgency that soon had them crying out in climax.

The roaring of Rio's pulse drowned out all sound for long moments afterward. The first thing he heard when reality began to return was Jill's voice, whispering over and over, "I love you, I love you..."

His arms tightening around her, he buried his face in her hair. He tasted blood, realizing only then that he was biting his lip, knowing he'd bitten back words he couldn't say to her.

This would be their farewell. It would only make it harder for both of them if he were to say the words echoing in his heart now.

* * *

The house was filled with people—men in their Sunday suits, women in their best dresses, children in ruffled frocks or crisply pressed slacks. Tom and Gypsy had planned a small wedding; this was as small as it could get, considering the size of the family who'd adopted them both.

Jill kept an eye on the clock, ready to signal everyone to find a seat when the appointed time for the ceremony arrived. The den was decorated with ribbons, flowers and candles, the regular furniture having been replaced with folding chairs to accommodate the guests. A huge wedding cake and two large bowls of sherbet-and-ginger-ale punch waited in the kitchen. The minister had arrived a few minutes before and was chatting in one corner with Jill's father.

And then it was time to begin.

As the family took their seats, Anita played the piano that had once belonged to Ellen. Tom and the minister stood before the fireplace along with Gordie, the proud best man.

At a prearranged signal from the piano, Sharon, the maid of honor, glided into the room in her long, dusty-rose gown, her hair curled and beribboned, her hated glasses left in her room. The bouquet of rosebuds and baby's breath in her hands trembled with her excitement. Jill's throat tightened at the blissfulness beaming from the child's eyes.

It hadn't been easy for Gypsy to talk Rio into walking her in, but she'd persisted until he'd reluctantly agreed. He wore one of his new flannel shirts and jeans, being too small to borrow anything from Tom or Jill's brothers and insisting that it would be a waste of money to buy a suit he would wear only once. Though everyone else looked at the bride as Gypsy and Rio entered the room, Jill's eyes lingered on Rio. She hoped the longing and regret she felt were hidden from anyone who might chance to look at her.

Rio's gaze caught hers and she knew that her feelings were painfully apparent to him. A muscle twitched in his hard jaw and then he glanced away, focusing on the fireplace where Tom awaited his bride.

Sighing, Jill finally looked at Gypsy. The bride was even more stunning than usual, her dark curls cascading down her back, her black eyes glowing as they swept the room to include everyone there in her happiness. She hadn't chosen a typical wedding gown, but then no one had expected her to. Gypsy's bright, vibrantly colored dress floated around her, emphasizing the bounce in her step, the vivaciousness that was so much a part of her. Jill glanced from Gypsy to Tom and then back again, reassured that this marriage would be a successful one.

Rio escorted his sister to Tom's side, then took a seat, draping himself into the uncomfortable metal chair as if he were perfectly at ease. For the next few minutes, Jill divided her attention between the man she loved and the ceremony, carefully suppressing any envy she may have felt of the happy bridal couple.

"I do," Tom said clearly, unhesitatingly, echoed moments later by Gypsy's fervent vows. And then the minister pronounced them husband and wife.

Hearing a faint sniff from beside her, Jill turned in concern to her mother, who was wiping her eyes on a lace-trimmed handkerchief. "Mother? Are you okay?" she whispered over the sound of applause from the other witnesses.

Determinedly holding back her tears, Ruth nodded and took Jill's hand. "I'm fine. I'm very happy for Tom and Gypsy. It's just—" She stopped and took a deep breath, her blue eyes expressing what she couldn't say.

Jill swallowed hard. "I know, Mama," she murmured, unconsciously falling back into the childhood appellation. She squeezed her mother's hand comfortingly.

Ruth sighed faintly, then looked toward the fireplace with a steady smile. "Let's go congratulate the bride and groom."

Jill stayed very busy for the next few hours, serving cake and punch, keeping a close eye on overly excited nieces and nephews, chatting with her family. She saw little of Rio, who remained on the fringe of the celebration, talking quietly with Jill's brothers, her father and Doc—one or two at a time. She watched him as closely as she discreetly could that afternoon, but he never met her gaze. She finally decided he was deliberately avoiding doing so.

She took what comfort she could in memories of the day before, of being locked so tightly in his arms she could hardly breathe, of knowing her every touch brought him pleasure, of being able to make him tremble. She knew she'd cling to those bittersweet memories for a very long time.

Rio was sitting alone on the porch swing when his sister found him later that evening.

"When did you start smoking again?" Gypsy demanded with marked disapproval.

Rio took the half-smoked cigarette from his mouth and looked at it as though he weren't quite sure how it had got there. "I haven't," he answered.

Her raised brow was just discernible in the shadows. Rio hadn't bothered to turn on the porch lights when he'd come out, nor did Gypsy now as she took a seat beside him on the swing. "What's that, then?"

"A lapse. Rusty offered me one before he left and I took it without thinking."

"Well, put it out. You know I don't like it."

Rio chuckled dryly, but did as she asked. "You sound like a married woman already," he accused her. "Nag, nag, nag."

She laughed and punched his arm with her fist. "Thanks a lot."

"Speaking of which, where's the groom?"

"The groom is putting his children to bed. They're exhausted, but still keyed up. He needed a little time to settle them down."

Rio idly twisted one of her long, black curls around the tip of his fingers. "Not exactly a romantic wedding night, is it?"

She smiled contentedly. "No complaints here."

He tugged lightly at the curl. "No regrets?" he asked, his tone casual, though his eyes searched her face gently.

She met the look without blinking. "No regrets."

"Good."

They sat in companionable silence for a few more minutes, Gypsy wrapped snugly in the sweater she'd pulled on over her colorful wedding ensemble, Rio ignoring the cold that crept through his flannel shirt. And then Gypsy spoke again, her voice hushed. "I felt her here today. Ellen, I mean."

Rio winced and squirmed on the seat. "Now, Gyps—"

She patted his arm, silencing him. "I know. You hate it when I get 'fanciful.' But I did, Rio. I felt her in the hearts of her children and her family. She was in their thoughts all day."

Rio cleared his throat, still uncomfortable with his sister's rather eccentric thought-processes. "Did it bother you?"

She shook her head. "No. Everyone was so sweet to me. I've never been hugged and kissed so much in my life. It makes me feel good to know that despite the love they had for her, they've still made room for me in their hearts. I think she'd approve."

"They're nice people."

"Yes. They are. I've made some very special friends here."

"I'm happy for you, sis," Rio said, somewhat awkwardly.

Her fingers squeezed his. "I know you are." She looked up at him imploringly. "Do you really have to go tomorrow?"

He nodded. "Yeah."

"I'll miss you."

"You won't be lonely this time."

"No. But I'll still miss you."

"I'll keep in touch. I'll know where to find you from now on."

"Yes. Will you come back soon to visit?"

Rio cut his eyes toward the house, thinking of Jill. "I'll call," he temporized, knowing he wouldn't be back. Not for a long time, anyway. And each time he called, he'd pray Jill wouldn't be the one to answer.

Gypsy turned to sit sideways on the swing, facing him, both hands clasping his. "Rio, I want you to know I understand why you have to go. I really do—probably better than anyone else could. But I think it's different for you this time. You're not running anymore. You're looking, now."

He stared at their hands, turning her words over in his mind. He tended to agree with her. Something had changed within him during his stay here. The old anger, the older bitterness was gone. In its place an emptiness waited to be filled with more productive emotions. A purpose. A place of his own. Goals he'd once thought unattainable.

Jill had done that for him, he thought numbly. Simply by finding something in him to love, she'd made him believe that he wasn't hopeless, that something better waited for him than the aimless, empty existence he'd known for the past nine years.

If only he'd found that destination before he'd met her, so that he had something—anything—to offer her now. He couldn't ask her to walk away from everyone she loved just to accompany him on his search. He couldn't ask her to wait for him until he'd found it.

He had to let her go in order to find himself.

Gypsy leaned forward and pressed a kiss on Rio's cheek. "Whatever it is you're looking for, I hope you find it soon. I love you, Rio. I want you to be as happy as I am now."

"Thanks, Gyps." His voice was gruff. "I love you, too."

"I know you do," she whispered. Her eyes were suspiciously bright when she released his hands and stood. "I think I'll go in now. My husband may be looking for me."

He smiled faintly at the pride in her voice. "He probably is. Good night, Gyps. See you in the morning."

"Good night, Rio. Sleep well."

He wouldn't, of course. He didn't expect to sleep a wink. Tomorrow he'd be leaving Jill. He couldn't even hold her in his arms again before he left.

He thought it might be a very long time before he slept easily again.

Sitting cross-legged on her bed, the only light coming from the small lamp on her bedside table, Jill slowly turned the pages of an old photo album, studying the yellowing prints arranged on the plastic-covered pages. She didn't know what impulse had made her drag out the album, why she'd felt the need to look at it at three in the morning, but at least it gave her something to do rather than lie staring at the ceiling, dreading daylight.

Moments of her past lay before her, frozen forever on little rectangles of paper. A thirteen-year-old Ellen carefully holding her tiny baby sister. Jill with her first Easter basket, lacy diaper-covering panties peeking from beneath an elaborately ruffled dress. Paul giving four-year-old Jill a piggyback ride, Jill squealing in delight as she tugged at his sandy hair.

A stiff studio portrait of the Hammond family, Ray and Ruth standing proudly behind their six uncomfortably posed children. Jill with her first boyfriend, both of them blushing as they'd submitted to having their pictures taken prior to attending a school dance. Tom and Ellen's wedding, Tom so much younger and more innocent than he'd looked today. Ellen holding her newborn son.

Swiping at an escaping tear, Jill raised her eyes from the book and stared blindly at one bedroom wall. So many changes, she thought, her fingertips tracing that old studio shot. Marriages, births, accomplishments. Death.

And now her life was changing again. It was time for her to move out of this house, to leave Tom and Gypsy to build their new life together with Tom's children. Perhaps more children before long. There was no place for Jill here now.

There was no place for her anywhere now, she thought with a pang of dejection. She'd have gone willingly with Rio, but he hadn't asked. And he'd turned her down when she'd tentatively invited herself along. Whether he truly thought he was acting in her best interests, or whether he couldn't make that commitment to her, he'd still made it quite clear that he intended to leave alone tomorrow.

She'd find an apartment, maybe move back to Little Rock and start her own tailoring business. Perhaps she'd go back to school, take the few courses remaining toward her degree in business. She'd make new friends, join a new church, perhaps a civic or business organization to give her something to do with her spare time. Maybe she'd even start to date again someday.

And she'd spend every night lying alone, wondering where Rio was, hoping he was happy, praying he was safe and well.

Loving him.

Biting her lip, she looked back down at the photo album. The last few pages were empty. She realized that she didn't even have a photograph of Rio to add to her mementos of the important events from her past. The most devastating occurrence in her life, her first—and probably last—love affair, and she didn't even have a snapshot to keep when it ended. Only a tiny, delicate wooden hummingbird he'd carved for her.

The tears began to fall in earnest then, as if that minor blow was simply one too many. Pushing the book aside, Jill buried her face in her hands and wept, afraid that nothing would ever be right again.

Chapter Sixteen

The family was rather subdued at breakfast the next morning, Rio's impending departure weighing heavily on everyone's mind, despite the lingering satisfaction of the wedding the day before. They'd agreed to skip church that morning and spend the day quietly, making plans, arranging new schedules. Watching Rio leave.

Jill picked unenthusiastically at her waffles, unable to swallow a bite. She drank three cups of coffee in near silence as the others talked quietly around her. Mike had shown up early, cheerfully inviting himself to breakfast with the newlyweds. Jill suspected his presence was really intended as moral support for her. She appreciated the gesture, though nothing could ease the pain of saying goodbye to Rio.

"By the way, Rio, I brought you a going-away present," Mike announced when the family moved into the den after breakfast.

Rio looked startled. "You didn't have to do that."

Mike shrugged. "I wanted to. Hang on, I'll get it." He left the room, whistling an unrecognizable tune.

Making a face in response to Mike's off-key whistling, Tom looked at his new brother-in-law. "I have something I want to give you, too, Rio." He opened the cabinet beside him and pulled out the expensive carving set. "You'll get more use out of this than I ever will. I'd like you to have it."

Rio shifted uncomfortably on his booted feet, his hands at his sides as he stared at the offered gift with reluctant longing. "I can't accept that."

"Yes, you can. I insist." Tom pushed the box firmly into Rio's hand. "Take good care of it."

Rio stared at the wooden case for a moment, then looked up with what, to Jill, looked suspiciously like uncharacteristic shyness. She smiled mistily as he muttered, "I will. Thanks, Tom."

Having left the room for a few minutes, Gypsy reappeared with a lined leather jacket in her hands. "This is from me, Rio. You'll need a warm coat now that winter is setting in."

"You didn't have to do that."

"Call it a Christmas present."

He gave her a weak, one-sided smile. "Christmas is nearly two months away."

"You planning to be here then?" she asked blandly.

He glanced at Jill, then quickly away. "No, probably not."

"All right, then. Merry Christmas, little brother."

He sighed his surrender and accepted the jacket. "Thanks, Gyps."

"We have something for you, too, Uncle Rio," Sharon announced shyly, extending a rather creatively wrapped package. "It's from me and Gordie. Gypsy said you'd like it. We wrapped it ourselves."

"I cut the paper and Sharon put on the tape," Gordie added, hovering nearby as Rio slowly took the gift. "Hope you like it." He didn't look as though he actually expected Rio to like the gift, Jill thought with a hidden smile, knowing what the children had purchased, knowing exactly how well Rio would like it.

Setting aside the jacket and carving set, Rio carefully unwrapped the gift. *"Walden,"* he murmured, reading the title on the slim, leather-bound book.

"You like it, Rio?" Gordie asked anxiously. "I didn't think so, but Gypsy said you would."

"It's my favorite book," Rio assured the boy gently. "My copy was lost when my things were stolen. This one's even nicer than the book I had before. Thank you. You, too, Sharon."

Mike returned from his car with his gift, a heavy army-surplus duffel bag. "Heard you lost one like this. Can't carry your stuff in a paper bag," he said offhandedly, tossing the bag to Rio.

Rio shuffled his feet in almost boyish embarrassment and shoved a hand through his hair. "I don't know what to say," he murmured finally, glancing around the room. "I appreciate the gifts."

Jill took a deep breath and reached down for the large shopping bag beside her chair. Standing, she offered it to him. "I have something for you, too."

Rio stiffened just perceptibly, his jaw tightening. "Uh— thanks." He didn't quite meet her eyes.

"You haven't opened it yet," she told him lightly, placing the bag in his hands.

He met her gaze for a moment, and she thought she saw her own quiet anguish reflected there. And then the expression was gone and he looked away, turning his attention to her gift. She'd bought him a motorcycle helmet, the most expensive one she could find, hoping its price reflected its effectiveness. It would be well worth the drain on her savings account if it kept Rio safe.

Rio stared at the helmet for a long time, then looked up at her. The room was very quiet, the adults watching with sympathetic awareness, the children sensing undercurrents they didn't quite understand. Rio cleared his throat, the sound harsh in the sudden silence. "Thanks, Jill," he said softly.

Forcing her voice through her painfully stiff smile, she answered him. "You're welcome. Wear it, okay?"

"I will." He tore his gaze from hers and turned to gather his gifts. "Guess I'll go pack my stuff in my new duffel bag. Thanks again, everyone."

Mike waited until Rio had left the room and Gypsy had distracted the children before putting an arm around his sister. "You okay, Jill?"

She turned to rest her forehead on his comfortingly massive chest. "No," she whispered candidly. "I'm not."

He sighed and hugged her closer. "I know, babe. I know. Dammit."

She wouldn't cry, she told herself bleakly, drawing warmth from her brother's loving embrace. She'd shed her tears during the night. But she hurt so badly she wasn't sure she'd survive the rest of the day.

Gypsy had tried to talk Rio into staying until after lunch, but he refused, claiming he needed to get on the road to put some distance behind him before dark. The children cried as they watched him strap his belongings to the motorcycle, Sharon copiously, Gordie wiping surreptitiously at his eyes with the sleeve of his jacket. Jill's eyes remained dry, her arms locked tightly at her waist as she stood to one side with Mike, watching the man she loved preparing to leave her.

Visibly ill at ease with the emotional farewells, Rio tried awkwardly to comfort Sharon. "Don't cry, Sharon. I'll see you again sometime."

"But what if you hurt yourself again?" the child sobbed, clutching his leather jacket. "Who'll take care of you?"

"I'll be careful," he promised. "I'll wear the helmet your aunt Jill gave me. All the time."

Sharon sniffed and nodded. "Will you talk to me sometime when you call Gypsy?"

"Bet on it." He turned to Gordie. "Take care of my sister for me, will you, Gord-o?"

Gordie tried to be brave. "Don't worry about Gypsy, Rio. My dad'll take care of her."

Rio ruffled the boy's hair. "Then you just take care of yourself. I'll be seeing you, kid."

Gordie nodded, unable to answer without bursting into tears.

Jill watched miserably from within the loose circle of Mike's arm as Rio turned to Gypsy. She watched him kiss his sister's cheek, murmuring something Jill couldn't hear. And then Rio shook Tom's hand. "Thanks for everything, Tom. I'll be sending that money soon as I get a job."

Knowing by now how useless argument was with this stubborn, proud young man, Tom only nodded. "Just keep in touch with us so we'll know you're okay."

"Yeah, I will." Reluctance evident in the set of his shoulders, Rio turned to Jill and Mike. Evading Jill's eyes for another moment, he extended a hand to her brother. "See you, Mike."

Mike looked from the proffered hand to his unhappy sister, then back at Rio. "I don't know whether to wish you luck or break your damned leg again," he growled disgruntedly, then exhaled loudly and gripped Rio's hand. "Good luck, Rio."

Grimacing, Rio nodded, carefully flexing his fingers when Mike released them from the near-crushing grip. "Yeah. Thanks."

And then he turned to Jill.

They stood there, staring at each other, both aware of the eyes watching them, the minutes ticking away. She wouldn't cry, Jill told herself again, keeping her eyes dry with every ounce of her willpower. She wouldn't see him off in tears.

"Be careful, Rio," she whispered, holding out her hand as he had done with Mike.

Rio looked at that small, extended hand, his jaw working, then muttered a curse and tugged her into his arms. "Dammit," he muttered, his cheek against her hair as she clung to him with her eyes tightly closed. "This has to be the hardest thing I've ever done. Probably the dumbest thing."

She couldn't argue with that. She could only hold him tighter.

He pulled back, his hands on her shoulders. "You'll be okay?"

She shrugged beneath his palms. "I'll try," she answered honestly.

His thumb traced her lower lip in a painfully familiar gesture. She swallowed hard. Heedless of their audience, Rio lowered his head to kiss her lingeringly. "Goodbye, Jill."

She couldn't answer. She could only touch his beautiful, scarred cheek as he drew slowly away.

Shoving a hand through his hair, Rio turned and slung a leg over his bike. "Bye, everyone," he said gruffly, then kicked the motorcycle into roaring life. He grasped the new helmet between both hands, but paused for one more look at Jill before putting it on.

Their eyes met and held. Jill's widened as she read his for-once unshuttered expression, the love he'd never been able to express verbally. Her knees weakened, making her cling to Mike's arm for support. Rio loved her. She knew it as surely as if he'd shouted the words.

Rio abruptly pulled on the helmet, snapping the smoked visor in place to hide his face. His knuckles white on the handlegrips, he gunned the engine, waved briefly and pulled away.

Jill stared at his back until sheer, mindless panic exploded inside her, hurtling her out of Mike's arms and down the drive behind Rio, screaming his name. She thought Mike tried to detain her, but she broke easily away from him, all her energy focused on stopping Rio. "Rio, stop! Please, stop! *Rio!*"

Somehow, over the roar of the motorcycle, through the muffling helmet, he heard her. The bike slowed to a stop, Rio's booted foot bracing it as he waited, head bowed. Breathing hard, Jill skidded to a stop beside him, her hands over her pounding heart. "Rio," she whispered, beseechingly.

He tugged off the helmet, the November breeze catching his disheveled black hair and tumbling it around his set face. "Don't do this, Jill. I can't stay. You're only making it harder for both of us."

Fortifying her courage with the memory of the look he'd given her, the love they shared, she clutched his rigid, rock-solid arm, her fingers digging into the soft new leather. "Take me with you. Please, Rio. Take me with you."

His eyes closed in a brief spasm. "Jill, don't. I can't. You know I can't."

Her fingers tightened, her voice reedy with desperation. "I know what you said before. I know you think you're doing the best thing for me. But you're wrong. We belong together. There's nothing here for me now. My place is with you.''

Hanging the helmet from the handlebars, he groaned and slid his hands into her hair, her face between his palms. ''I won't be responsible for taking you away from your home and your family when I don't even know where I'm going to sleep tonight.''

''Don't you see?'' she whispered, the hot tears she'd tried to hold back burning her eyes. ''I don't care where we sleep as long as we sleep together. I don't care where our next meal comes from as long as we share it. I love you, Rio. I don't want to live without you. Whatever you're looking for, we'll find it together. I know we will.''

He rested his forehead against hers, his breath warm on her face. ''You don't know what you're saying, babe. You'd be miserable living on the road. You'd miss your family, your home. You're not meant for that life.''

''I'll have you,'' she answered flatly, covering his hands with hers. ''And I know you won't stay away from Gypsy for long. You'll want to see her again, just as I'll want to see my family. But in the meantime, we'll have each other.''

She spoke more quickly when he started to argue, knowing she had to make him listen to her now or lose him forever. ''Rio, can't you understand? I've been looking for something, too, taking care of Tom's family while I tried to decide what to do with my own life. And then you came along and I knew what I wanted. I want you.''

''And a home? Marriage? Children? What about those things, Jill?'' he asked harshly.

''What about them?'' she returned steadily. ''I've spent the past two years raising children, Rio. I'd like to wait a few years before starting over with my own. Maybe by that time, you'll find you're ready for a family, yourself.''

''And maybe I won't.''

"No. Maybe you won't. Maybe by then you'll be tired of me, ready to send me back."

His hands flexed convulsively. "I don't think you'd have to worry about that," he answered honestly. "You're the one who's more likely to change her mind."

"No," she whispered, drawing back to look at him, trembling at the heat burning in his eyes. Hope ballooned inside her, making it hard to breathe. "Please, Rio. Give us a chance. Don't leave me here alone."

His throat worked with his hard swallow. "Jill, I—"

She quickly covered his mouth with emotion-chilled fingers. "I warn you, the only way I'll accept no for an answer is if you can look at me and tell me you don't love me. That you don't want me with you," she told him unsteadily, fervently praying her ultimatum proved successful.

He started to speak, stopped, then sighed deeply and shook his head. "I can't lie to you."

She caught her breath, her hands clutching the lapels of his jacket. "You love me?"

He cupped her cheek tenderly in one callused palm. "I love you, Jill. I have from the day I met you, I think."

She closed her eyes, knees weakening. "Oh, Rio."

"Ah, hell." Pulling her into his arms, he held her tightly, both of them oblivious to the awkwardness of the motorcycle between them. "I love you, Jill. I don't need to leave—it's you I've been looking for all my life. I'll take the job your father has offered, we'll find a house, build a life together. We'll make it work."

She shook her head against his shoulder, her smile tremulous, cheeks wet with tears of relief and joy. "You'd be miserable," she told him firmly. "I refuse to let you do that when we both know it's not right for you. We're young, Rio. We have our whole lives ahead of us."

"Oh, God, Jill," he muttered, his own eyes unnaturally bright. "I can't believe you'd walk away from everything to take a gamble like that on me."

She nestled closer, touched by the near awe in his voice. "I love you, Rio. I want to share your search with you. If you want me, of course."

"I want you," he said deeply. Pulling back, he held her hands. "I thought maybe I'd try making a living with the carving, as you once suggested. I could try getting a job with a craft shop—Silver Dollar City in Missouri, maybe, or one of the craft colonies I've read about in New England. Maybe something will come of it—or maybe I'll end up building houses, after all," he added warningly.

"I think it sounds wonderful," she assured him. "I can work, too, you know. I can make dolls, quilts, clothing. Maybe there will be a place for me at that craft colony. We'll get by. I know we will."

He stared at her thoughtfully, making her tense in hopeful anticipation. "Your family's going to think you lost your mind," he grumbled at last.

She smiled. "Maybe I have. I don't care." And then her smile faded. "Take me with you, Rio."

He slipped the helmet off the handlebars and held it out to her. "Wear this and get on behind me."

She glanced from the helmet to the motorcycle, thinking fleetingly of clothing, toiletries, her purse. Her family. Rio's eyes remained on her face, steadily.

She smiled again and took the helmet, pulling it on and then swinging one leg behind him to settle tentatively on the motorcycle, her arms linked trustingly around his waist.

Rio looked over his shoulder with a crooked grin of approval. "Just like that?" he asked, gruffly.

"Just like that," she answered.

He nodded, snapped the visor down over her face, then gunned the engine.

Jill tightened her arms around him, sending a silent goodbye to her family. But instead of heading the bike for the main road, Rio turned and drove back toward the house, where Jill's curious family waited with visible impatience.

"The departure's been delayed," Rio called out when the others stepped forward in question.

Jill tugged off the helmet. "For how long?" she demanded, tapping on Rio's shoulder.

He turned to grin at her. "How do you feel about a honeymoon on the back of a motorcycle?"

She gaped at him. "A—uh—honeymoon?" she repeated weakly. "Rio, are you sure?"

Killing the engine, he got off the motorcycle, then steadied her when she followed. "I wouldn't have made it five miles before I'd have turned around and come back for you," he admitted with a rueful smile. "This partnership is forever. I want to make it a legal one."

Switching so quickly from abject misery to intense happiness made her a bit dizzy. She clutched his arm for support. "When?"

"As soon as we can get a license and round up the family for another wedding. Any objections?"

Ignoring their delighted audience, Jill threw her arms around his neck. "Not a one."

He kissed her quickly. "Good."

She pulled his head back down to hers for a longer, more satisfying kiss, blissfully content with the knowledge that in this man she'd found her destiny, regardless of where life would lead them.

* * * * *

Silhouette Special Edition

presents

SONNY'S GIRLS

by Emilie Richards, Celeste Hamilton and Erica Spindler

They had been Sonny's girls, irresistibly drawn to the charismatic high school football hero. Ten years later, none could forget the night that changed their lives forever.

In July—
ALL THOSE YEARS AGO by Emilie Richards (SSE #684)
Meredith Robbins had left town in shame. Could she ever banish the past and reach for love again?

In August—
DON'T LOOK BACK by Celeste Hamilton (SSE #690)
Cyndi Saint was Sonny's steady. Ten years later, she remembered only his hurtful parting words....

In September—
LONGER THAN... by Erica Spindler (SSE #696)
Bubbly Jennifer Joyce was everybody's friend. But nobody knew the secret longings she felt for bad boy Ryder Hayes....

Take 4 bestselling love stories FREE

Plus get a FREE surprise gift!

Silhouette Special Edition

proudly hails

WOMEN OF GLORY

from Lindsay McKenna

Soar with Dana Coulter, Molly Rutledge and Maggie Donovan—Lindsay McKenna's WOMEN OF GLORY. On land, sea or air, these three Annapolis grads challenge danger head-on, risking life and limb for the glory of their country—and for the men they love!

May: NO QUARTER GIVEN (SE #667) Dana Coulter is on the brink of achieving her lifelong dream of flying—and of meeting the man who would love to take her to new heights!

June: THE GAUNTLET (SE #673) Molly Rutledge is determined to excel on her own merit, but Captain Cameron Sinclair is equally determined to take gentle Molly under his wing....

July: UNDER FIRE (SE #679) Indomitable Maggie never thought her career—or her heart—would come under fire. But all that changes when she teams up with Lieutenant Wes Bishop!